STARS
IN YOUR
EYES

STARS
IN YOUR
EYES

KACEN
CALLENDER

FOREVER
New York Boston

Copyright © 2023 by Kacen Callender

Cover design and art by Daniela Medina
Cover copyright © 2023 by Hachette Book Group, Inc.

Forever
Hachette Book Group
1290 Avenue of the Americas, New York, NY 10104
read-forever.com
twitter.com/readforeverpub

First Edition: October 2023

Forever is an imprint of Grand Central Publishing. The Forever name and logo are trademarks of Hachette Book Group, Inc.

The publisher is not responsible for websites (or their content) that are not owned by the publisher.

The Hachette Speakers Bureau provides a wide range of authors for speaking events. To find out more, go to hachettespeakersbureau.com or email HachetteSpeakers@hbgusa.com.

Forever books may be purchased in bulk for business, educational, or promotional use. For information, please contact your local bookseller or the Hachette Book Group Special Markets Department at special.markets@hbgusa.com.

Library of Congress Cataloging-in-Publication Data

Names: Callender, Kacen, author.
Title: Stars in your eyes / Kacen Callender. Description: First edition. | New York : Forever, 2023.
Identifiers: LCCN 2023020946 | ISBN 9781538726037 (hardcover) | ISBN 9781538726051 (ebook)
Subjects: LCSH: Actors—Fiction. | LCGFT: Romance fiction. | Gay fiction. | Novels.
Classification: LCC PS3603.A44624226 C35 2023 | DDC 813/.6—dc23/eng /20230502
LC record available at https://lccn.loc.gov/2023020946

ISBN: 9781538726037 (hardcover), 9781538726051 (ebook)

Printed in the United States of America

LSC

Printing 1, 2023

Dear Reader,

Stars in Your Eyes *is a deeply personal story that explores trauma's effects on relationships. While there is ultimately healing, hope, joy, and love, there is also content that might trigger some readers, including: mentions of past childhood sexual abuse, sexual assault, bullying and harassment online, suicidal thoughts, homophobia and biphobia, parental rejection and verbal abuse, and mentions of potential overdose.*

Especially when exploring painful topics, I understand that it can sometimes feel invalidating when a portrayal of trauma does not reflect our own. While many of these experiences are personal, I want to acknowledge that not everyone's response to trauma is the same. Please, take care of yourself while reading.

With love,
Kacen

Deadline Exclusive:

[Two photos, side by side: twenty-three-year-old Matthew Cole with freckled brown skin, curly brown hair, and dark brown eyes, wearing a pink graphic t-shirt and a cheerful grin; twenty-four-year-old Logan Gray with lighter brown skin, straight-wavy black hair, and dark brown eyes lined by long eyelashes, wearing all black and a bored scowl.]

Matthew Cole has joined the cast of the much-anticipated film *Write Anything* (a pun on the 1989 film *Say Anything*), based on the *New York Times* bestselling romance novel by Cordelia Cameron about two male authors who are forced to work together and inevitably fall in love. Logan Gray has already been cast in the lead as Quinn Evans; Matthew Cole will play opposite as Riley Mason. The film is slated to be released early next year.

Video begins:

YouTube personality star Shaina Lively sits in front of bright yellow lights; in the background is an office, wall plastered with posters for various rom-com films. Shaina leans into the camera and begins to speak with a Southern accent:

"Hey, y'all! I know you're just as excited as I am to hear the news that *Matthew Cole* will be joining the cast of *Write Anything*!"

She screams and jumps up and down in her seat.

"Oh, my God, I'm sorry, I'm just beside myself. I *love* this book, and I *love* Mattie, so I know this is going to be a match made in heaven. Ah!

"Now, I've already started to hear some grumbling complaints that Matthew is *too young* and that he isn't a *serious* actor—but if anything, it's really *Logan Gray* that we need to be worried about. Yeah, I know he's won Oscars or whatever, but I'm willing to bet each and every one of you that Logan is going to mess up this film someway, somehow, and our poor Matthew is gonna pay the price. And if that happens, I might just have to shank a bitch."

She gives a warm smile. "Well, that's all for now! Until next time."

She blows a kiss at the camera.

Video ends.

MATTIE

I'M LED DOWN halls with fresh white paint and tiled floors that smell like bleach. I'm wheezing and sweating, trying to take a deep breath and cool down before I enter the room, desert heat still sticking to my skin. I'm very late. I know I'll get some points knocked off on first impressions for that alone, and I don't think anyone will take an "I'm sorry, I'm not used to LA traffic" as an excuse anymore. It might've worked for my first role, but I've been in and out of the city going on a year now.

Samantha, the assistant who leads me down the halls, seems as nervous as me, and that's saying something. "Are you sure you don't want a water? Coffee?" she asks for the third time.

"I'm okay," I say, still breathless. I catch her looking at me, gaze flitting away quickly, and I realize—oh, yeah, I'm supposed to be famous. I'm still not used to it. *Love Me Dearly* was released about six months ago, and after the promo tour ended, I wasn't prepared for this kind of everyday attention. I feel self-conscious and try not to pull at my shirt, a nervous habit my manager, Paola, said I should work on.

Samantha opens the door for me at the end of the hall. I thank her as I hurry inside, trying not to flat-out run but also not wanting to stroll like I've got all the time in the world. The room has one huge conference table with a dozen or so people seated around it in a circle, and there's a smaller table pushed up against the farthest wall with coffee and fruit. As soon as I step inside, everyone's heads turn to me. My heart thuds. You'd think an actor would be all right with so many eyes on him, but my big secret is that I still have stage fright.

"Matthew!"

The director, Dave Miller, stands up. He's white and has gray sideburns with a patchy beard. His button-up has a dot of a coffee stain on the collar. He pats my shoulder as he gestures to the room. "Everyone, Mattie. Mattie, everyone."

There's a mix of friendly smiles and handwaves and exhausted nods. I'm nervous not only because I'm standing in a room full of strangers staring at me but because of *who* the strangers are. I've watched most of these actors in my favorite shows and movies since I was a kid. And now I'm going to be in a movie with *them*. That's the actual dream, and I'm still amazed each and every day that I've managed to make it this far. Now I just have to make sure I don't screw it up.

One person at the table hasn't bothered to look in my direction. Logan Gray. For a moment, I think that he might be asleep. He has shades on even though we're inside and the room isn't very bright, and he wears a hoodie that admittedly looks extremely comfortable as he leans back in one of the conference room chairs, his boots up on the chair next to him. He emits a small snore. Yep, definitely asleep.

I'd auditioned for the lead in *Write Anything*. Riley Mason is a great character, but he feels similar to the roles I've had before: upbeat, optimistic, the character audiences automatically love. I'm worried about being typecast so early in my career, and I wanted to push myself with Quinn Evans. Quinn is…more complicated. He messes up, hurts himself and others in his own attempts to grow. He's the sort of character that's more challenging for an actor. If I'd gotten the role, it would've been hard work to stay true to Quinn and the source material. It would've been difficult to find glimmers of sympathy for his character while delving into the pits of his self-loathing, all while trying to make him sympathetic to the viewer, too.

I was beside myself to get cast in a movie like this at all. Crying and jumping up and down with my mom and my sister is one of my happiest memories. I have to admit that I was also disappointed to lose the role out to Gray, though I can't say I'm surprised. Gray's been typecast as well. He's the kind of actor who screams drugs and sex in a way I probably never will, no matter how much I try. "He has that *edge*," my publicist said.

Gray is among the actors I admire. He's got raw talent. I've studied him. I've watched interviews with him, trying to figure out a kernel of his magic. I'm amazed at how easily he scoffs at technique and process. He rolls his eyes at interviewers whenever he's asked about craft, saying that it's just a fancy word assholes made up as an excuse to say who is allowed to be nominated for awards and who is not.

And there was the other, more recent interview I'd seen with Gray, too, just two weeks before, right after I was cast. A bolt of anger flashes through me, but I remember what I'd decided: I'll pretend I never saw the interview at all. That's what I'll have to do, if I'm going to be able to work with him.

Dave either doesn't notice that Logan is fast asleep, or he's used to this behavior. He invites me to grab a seat, and I sit down awkwardly in between Scott Anders (five-time Oscar award winner, one of the greatest actors of all time, I could watch and rewatch his brilliant performance in *Duchess Down* a thousand times, and I'm pretty sure I have) and Monica Meyers (nominated for Best Supporting Actress five times, though she has not yet won, clearly a coup, especially for her heart-wrenching performance in *The Sky Cries*). Scott grins and shakes my hand and says he's a big fan of my performance in *Love Me Dearly*. I have to force the inner fanboy to calm down, while Monica purses her lips, probably miffed that I'm late.

Copies of the script with each actor's name on the covers have already been passed around. This is technically the second table read, but since I was brought on so late in the process, it's my first. Writers and assistants and a ton of other people sit in chairs along the wall of the conference room with copies of the script, pens ready and laptops open. More people to perform for.

Dave sits at the head of the table and adjusts his ball cap. "Someone wake up Sleeping Beauty," he says, opening his script.

Samantha rushes forward. She clears her throat and taps Gray's shoulder. He doesn't stir. She tries again. "Mr. Gray...?"

He grunts something, sits up—looks around the room like he's forgotten where he is, and maybe he has.

Dave opens his script. "Gray, if you don't mind removing your sunglasses so that we can see those beautiful brown eyes of yours."

Gray doesn't move for one long second as he stares at Dave

silently. I shift uncomfortably. Heat begins to radiate in the room. Dave, again, doesn't seem to notice as he licks a finger and turns the page of the script, but it's clear to everyone that we won't begin until Gray does what he was asked.

Logan removes the shades. There are a few (okay, maybe a little melodramatic, we *are* actors after all) gasps around the room. I swallow thickly. A purple bruise flourishes over Gray's swollen right eye.

Dave glances up. "Oh, Jesus Christ."

"Same old shit, right?" Gray says, voice hoarse.

"This isn't a joke. God, fucking…" He twists in his seat to look at an assistant. "There isn't any footage in the tabloids, is there?"

⌐ ⌐

Video begins:

A crowd in a nightclub has formed. Streaks of light blur across the screen, but Logan Gray's face is clear for one moment. Another man shouts unintelligibly. Derogatory slurs based on sexual identity are used. He is notably much larger than Logan. Logan only smiles, before he spits in the stranger's face. There are gasps, the camera shakes. There is the distinct sound of a fist impacting skin.

Video ends.

⌐ ⌐

From the awkward glances, it's clear that there *is* footage in the tabloids. I haven't seen it myself because I try to stay away from papers and gossip sites. That's a one-way ticket into a weekend of self-pity and depression. Even the word *tabloids* makes certain phrases echo in my mind: "wannabe Tom Holland," "Leonardo DiCaprio in his prime if Leo wasn't as talented or cute." Ouch.

Dave rubs his temples. "Damn it. Sam, set up a meeting with me and Logan's manager. What's her name again? Louise?"

"Audrey."

"Let's see if we can stop this man-child from ruining the film before it's even begun." Sam nods and excuses herself.

If Logan has any feelings on being called a man-child, he doesn't show them. "Getting punched in the face hasn't impacted my ability to read," he says.

Dave's eyes narrow dangerously for one moment, before he straightens. "Then let's begin."

The morning's drama firmly put aside, the professionals around me open their scripts, and the table read starts. Richard, the AD, speeds through the narration and directions so that the actors can focus on their roles, the writers on edits and Dave announcing his own thoughts every now and then. Even though I play opposite the lead, I don't appear until a few scenes in, so I get to sit back in my chair and watch the magic of my idols.

Gray is amazing, of course, even half-asleep, with a black eye, and possibly a hangover. He transforms into Quinn Evans: charismatic, smug, an asshole you can't help but love. Monica already brings tears to my eyes with her reading as his mother, widowed and worried that Quinn will never open his heart to finding true love. Scott, Quinn's boss, has too understated a role to really take advantage of his enormous talent, but I assume there are publicity reasons he's been brought on, along with a ton of money. Keith Mackey, playing Quinn's best friend and comic relief sidekick, lands all the laughs, even when Dave murmurs something to one of the head writers, who nods in agreement and starts to scribble red all over the script.

My heart begins to speed up. I'd started acting in junior high, but this fear—the jump before the performance—has never gone away. If anything, it's only gotten worse. But once I've done it—once I've managed to leap from the cliff and fly through the air—the exhilaration soars through me, and every time I seem to forget how much I hate the feeling of nervousness that comes right before I open my mouth.

Keith leans back in his chair with a grin, swiping bleached hair out of his face. "Hey—pretty boy," he says, glancing up at me.

I swallow. My words begin to blur on my script. "Sorry, do you mean me?"

I can hear the hollowness in my voice. It doesn't ring true. There isn't enough authenticity. I clear my throat. Scott glances up from beside me.

Keith goes on like he hasn't noticed. "Is there anyone else around that you'd describe as *pretty*?" he says. He barks a laugh, then seems to crack himself up and keeps laughing. Smiles widen at the table.

My hands are hidden beneath the table in my lap. I tug on the end of my shirt. "No—uh, no, maybe not."

The smiles around the table are a little tighter now. Gray watches me from across the room, eyes focused, calculating, dissecting my entire performance even though it's only been a few lines. I try to block out the memory of the interview I'd seen, against my better judgment—but it was everywhere, all over social media and popping up in Google alerts every three seconds. A reporter shoves a mic in Logan Gray's face on the red carpet and asks him, "What do you think about Matthew

Cole joining the cast of *Write Anything*?" Logan didn't hide his annoyance. He rolled his eyes. "He's a shitty actor," he said. "I hate people who get by on looks and charm and absolutely zero talent."

I try to block out the memory of the interview, but Gray's voice rises in my head with every vacant word I speak. "Wait, hold on," I say, turning the page with sweaty fingers. "Aren't you Quinn Evans? The author?"

The next line belongs to Logan. He doesn't look away from me as he leans in his chair, rocking back and forth slightly with a squeak, squeak, squeak.

"Gray," Dave says, annoyance a little more obvious now. "That's you."

Gray's eyes don't leave me. "So are we all just going to pretend this isn't happening?"

My heart plummets. Everyone looks up before heads turn and gazes rest on me for a brief second. We all know what he means. Dave clenches his jaw. "Just read your line, Gray."

"It's a waste of time," he says. "I'm not going to do a table read with someone who can't even figure out his character. That impacts how I end up playing my role. Don't punish me because you decided to choose Hollywood's flavor of the week."

Julie, who plays the main antagonist as Quinn's girlfriend, whispers loudly enough for us all to hear. "Don't be a fucking asshole, Gray."

"Am I an asshole for saying the truth?" He shrugs. "Fine. Okay."

Heat grows in my throat. I cry easily. That's always been my biggest problem, my dad used to say. I cry whenever I see cute toddlers hugging puppies. I cry whenever someone is cruel to another person and I'm too angry to speak. I cry whenever I hear a beautiful song. I sure as hell cry whenever my feelings are hurt—when I've been humiliated in a room filled with people I look up to and admire. Easily crying has its uses, especially on the stage and in front of the camera, but the tears only add to the humiliation now.

Dave's mouth hangs open. "Okay," he says loudly. "Let's take five."

Chairs roll back, people begin to chat about their weekends, recent industry announcements, LA traffic, anything but what just happened. I rub my eye as I get up to find a bathroom, walking away from the table before anyone can stop me. I just need a second to look at myself in the mirror, splash some water on my face, and get myself together.

Someone follows me out of the swinging doors of the conference room. I expect it to be Dave, but when a hand touches my elbow, I turn around to see Julie.

"Hey," she says, "are you okay? Gray can be such a dick sometimes."

It takes me a second to process the fact that *Julie Rodriguez* is talking to me. She played the lead role in one of my favorite Disney Channel shows growing up. She's stunning in person, even with her hair pulled up in a messy bun and bags under her eyes.

Even though I feel humiliated, I still struggle to not be starstruck. "Yeah, I'm fine," I say. "He's—you know, he's right. That was an awful read."

"We've all been there. And this is your first lead role, right?" When I nod, she pats my arm. "You'll be fine. Don't let him get into your head. Everyone's really excited that you're a part of the cast, Matt."

I thank her—and I mean really, truly thank her—and she gives me a reassuring smile before she walks back into the room. Logan Gray might not be happy to share this film with me, but I can't let him scare me away. Not when a role like this has been my dream—everything I've worked toward for so many years. I take a deep breath, and I force myself to walk into the room again.

Inside Hollywood Blog

There have been reports that the stars of the upcoming film 'Write Anything,' Matthew Cole and Logan Gray, have been at odds before principal photography has even begun. This would be understandable, after the disastrous and awkward interview Gray gave on the red carpet of the premiere of 'Hawkseye Down,' claiming that his then-recently cast costar has "zero talent." If the two romantic leads to one of Hollywood's biggest summer blockbusters hate each other as much as the rumors suggest, we're willing to bet that 'Write Anything' is likely to fail before it's even begun.

LOGAN

I SIT IN the second-floor lounge with a massive headache. Nothing's helped. Not pills, not sleep, not sex. I'm just starting to wonder if getting punched in the face gave me permanent brain damage when Willow appears beside me. She sits down on the old-fashioned red velvet seat, crosses her legs, and stirs a straw in her favorite martini I'd ordered so that it would be here by the time she arrived.

"Did you call me here to break up?" she asks, picking up the glass and taking a sip.

"Yeah," I say, leaning back. "Three months. That's what we agreed, right?"

She sighs. "It was fun while it lasted." She'd been the one to come up with the idea, a few months ago after we met in some club and she followed me back to mine. This kind of shit is usually set up by PR and involves a fuck ton of NDAs, but I guess she wanted to go around the bureaucratic rope. Easier to just deal with me.

Something else is clearly on her mind. She glances up. "We could release a publicity statement, as usual, saying things didn't work out as planned, thank you for the support, blah, blah, blah."

"Or...?"

"Or we could try something new. Something fresh. Ariana Grande released an entire song and album once."

"You're a musician now?"

She ignores me. "I was on your phone the other night."

She pauses, maybe expecting annoyance. I *am* annoyed, but I don't see the point in saying anything about it. We're about to break up this publicity stunt of a relationship anyway.

"I noticed you had some photos," she says. "A video."

I know which one she means. Willow and I agreed to treat this like a monogamous relationship. Polyamory and open relationships aren't widely accepted by the public yet. I wasn't supposed to date anyone else, wasn't supposed to have sex with anyone else, but about a month in an old friend, an actor named Briggs, visited from Sydney and stayed in town for a weekend, and, well, one thing led to another. Briggs took a quick video for the memory and texted it to me, and I forgot it was still on my phone.

Willow isn't as angry as someone might be to find out their boyfriend was cheating on them, but then again, I wasn't her real boyfriend. She continues. "I wondered if it might be interesting to...I don't know, release the video. One last publicity stunt."

"You want me to post my homemade porno?"

She must sense my agitation. "It's not a big deal, right?"

"It's a little dramatic, isn't it? A little into *attention whore* territory, even for you?"

Now she's pissed. "You're as much a part of this as I am."

Willow's right, I know. I didn't really want to go along with this bullshit at first, but she was fun and I was bored. Besides, the act did its job. Sure, she just wanted to use me, but this boosted my profile, too. Now, I'm the bad boy boyfriend of innocent Willow Grace—not just the drugged-up asshole no one wants to work with in Hollywood.

"We agreed to do this fake shit," I say, "but going through my phone…asking me to post my private video…"

She at least has the decency to look a little ashamed, though in a city like this, it's hard to know what to believe. She raises her chin. "I'm sorry if it was a bit much, but we need a believable reason to break up, and this would be a way to go out in style. The headlines, the gossip sites—they'd go absolutely *mad*, Gray. And everyone would get a good reminder of how fucking hot you are." She pauses when I don't answer. She must feel how upset I am, even if I'm not showing it. "I didn't think it'd be such a big deal. This isn't your first—you know, film." She takes another sip.

It's not even my second. The first video I took was on my eighteenth birthday, officially marking the end of my innocent child actor career. It was purposeful. A big *fuck you* to the industry and my father. The second film was difficult to see. It was just my back and my ass 90 percent of the time, hands tied to the bedframe, but enough people recognized my side profile when I twisted around, strip of cloth wrapped around my eyes. It was taken without my knowledge or permission. Pretty sure it's still up on Pornhub, no matter how many times my team's tried to get it taken down. And now this.

Willow says she doesn't think it'd be a big deal to release it, but I know it's a calculated move on her part. Her career had been waning, and this drama of dating me, one of the most hated people in Hollywood, has thrust her back into the spotlight. Now this video will only earn her sympathy points from around the world. Fans will flock to her, saying that I didn't deserve her, that she's too much of an angel for a devil like me. I've already quit social media. The number of trolls was impossible for my social media manager and her assistants to control. I decided to fold them into my manager's team so they wouldn't lose their jobs just because people can't fucking stand me, but there's nothing for them to do. It doesn't matter.

If the video is released, my manager, Audrey, and the others will need to go into overdrive (and probably overtime) trying to contain the story and control my image. I have to be a persona. A character I play off-screen, too. I entertain people in movies, sure, but I learned early on that my entire life is a source of entertainment also. I'm the villain. People enjoy picking me apart and berating me. I give them someone to hate. I'm used to this. I even look forward to it, sometimes. It's all that I know. It feels like a comfort. People screaming "You're an asshole, Gray!" is like a lullaby after a while. Besides, maybe this will give my social media team something to do.

"Fine," I tell her. "Post the video."

Twitter.com

Trending for You
#WeLoveYouWillow
#LoganGrayIsOverParty
Fuck You Gray
#WillowGraceDeservesBetter

@willowgracefanforlife
I can't believe he would break her heart like that.
Willow is the kindest woman in this industry. People,
listen up. You can't change or save anyone. They will
only hurt you in the end.
💬 708   🔁 6.1K   ♥ 10.3K

@everydayhustlin
This is why I don't date bisexual men lol they're all
sluts
💬 506   🔁 2.1K   ♥ 5.2K

@robertklingon
why is Logan Gray still around? he should just overdose on drugs and kill himself already tbqh
💬 301   🔁 1.1K.   ♥ 3K

RED ALERT: BREAKING NEWS

Hello, my little Cherubs. I'm sure most of you have already seen the latest film of our favorite love-to-hate asshole Logan Gray, but I thought it might be nice to repost the video here for your viewing pleasure.

[Video begins: A dark, grainy film. It's difficult to see what is on the screen. There's a moan. The video pivots down. Logan Gray looks up, mouth—well—full. He seems surprised to be filmed, then grins and makes a performance of it. The screen shakes. Video ends.]

Don't you just love the way our garbage fire of a man completely shreds the last of his dignity? I know I'd claimed that Gray's lowest point was being caught in an, ahem, certain *steamy* film, but I think we might have a new reigning moment of secondhand embarrassment.

Seriously, why does anyone let Gray go outside at all? There've already been enough rumors that he's about to be fired from the film *Write Anything* for being a total and complete trashcan of a human being. Oh, well! With this new incident, I'm happily expecting the official announcement any minute now.

Signing off,

Angel

MATTIE

MY MANAGER PAOLA was frantic when she told me Dave had called for a meeting. "Just play it cool. But not too cool. You don't want to look like you don't care. Tell them you've been rehearsing a lot more. But, you know. Don't act like you're desperate."

Word got back to her about my not-so-great table read, and she thinks I'm going to be fired. She might be right. My heart sinks at the thought.

"It would be fucked up, absolutely fucked up, if they fired you after watching you perform for five minutes," she said under her breath.

"Do you really think they'll fire me?"

I could practically hear her catch herself over the phone. "No—no, of course not," she told me, but I know she only wants me to be in a good headspace.

I hired her when my career was just starting to explode, right when I got cast for *Love Me Dearly*. I liked that she was also from Atlanta, and that she would meet my eye with raised brows at Hollywood parties, like when a weed sommelier walked up to us and asked in a fake British accent,

"What sort of high would you like?" We both think that LA is a little ridiculous. We both want to succeed here anyway. We've made a good pair. I'd be devastated if I got fired, but I'd feel even more guilty if I took Paola down with me.

The meeting is at a restaurant, the kind I'll never feel fully comfortable in. It's not just the *know which fork to use* kind of place, but it screams—I don't know—fame. Like even if you're rich, you've still got to prove you belong there with your aura alone, with your presence, with other people deciding you are worthy. Not sure I'd pass that test, though I've passed the first requirement of wealth. That's a weird thought. I never had more than twenty dollars in my bank account at one time, and now I have five hundred thousand, after giving my mom most of my money to help pay off her debts and mortgage, and after I paid for my little sister's college tuition.

They tried to fight me on it. "There's no way in hell I actually need one million dollars," I told them. Five hundred thousand is nowhere near a lot in LA, but it definitely is for me. I feel a little like I don't know what to do with myself. Do I start saving up to buy a house? (I'm trying to ignore that a home here would probably be a quarter of the price in Decatur.) Or do I rent out one of those lavish condos for a few months? Pretend to be a part of this lifestyle for as long as possible? I hate money. I hate that I need so much of it just to have this dream of acting.

The restaurant is shiny with golden reflective walls and a bar that glows soft colors and large light bulbs that hang from the ceiling, plants everywhere. Paola walks closely beside me, heels clacking on the concrete floor. She's got dark brown hair that tumbles over her shoulders, paler skin that might have a touch too much blush on her cheeks. She's taller than me by a few inches. Most people don't expect me to be this short in real life. I'm an average five foot, six inches, unlike the six-to seven-foot Adonis actors. Pretty sure Logan Gray is about six feet, three inches. I wonder how our height difference will look on-screen. If I don't get fired, anyway.

"Breathe," she says. "Just breathe." I'm not sure if she's talking to herself or to me.

"Even if I'm fired, there'll be other roles to audition for, right?"

"You're not going to be fired."

"But if I am..."

She hesitates. "Sure. Yeah. Of course."

I think I know what she's afraid to say. Stars rise and fall quickly in LA. Everyone's screaming my name right now, so it's better to capitalize on the moment and get a role like this one so that my profile will continue to skyrocket. Losing this chance could just as easily mean that my profile will plummet, and within a month, no one will care about who I am.

I feel like I usually do right before I step in front of a camera. I have pre-performance nerves, because that's what is about to happen: I need to perform. I have to show fake confidence and apologize for yesterday. "I wasn't feeling too well," I could explain.

The restaurant is almost empty. People are still setting up some tables. I think only high-profile guests might be allowed inside early. I see someone who might be Keanu Reeves eating lunch in the corner, reading a newspaper. Paola visibly stiffens when we see the table we're supposed to reach. But I think it might be a flinch of surprise more than anything. That's why I get stiff, anyway. Dave Miller is there. So is Reynolds Bachmann, one of the executive producers. Not surprising, for a *sorry, we have to let you go* sort of meeting.

Not as expected, though? Logan Gray and his manager,

Audrey. Why would they be here if I'm going to be fired? Are we both about to be let go from the film? Is production about to be stopped altogether?

Audrey has white-blonde hair and blue eyes that I think might be color contacts. She reached out to me and Paola when I was hired a couple of weeks back. She suggested a friendly meeting with Logan, and I'd accepted, but Gray cancelled at the last second, and then that not-so-friendly interview on the red carpet...

Logan's leaning back in his seat, shades back on. He doesn't look up when Dave stands, arms wide in welcome. His collared shirt has some sweat stains today, not that I mind. The fact that Dave doesn't care about appearances has made me feel more comfortable with him.

"Great. You're here. Please, sit."

Paola and I take the last two empty chairs. Audrey gives a friendly hello. Reynolds checks his phone. He's much more a suit-and-tie guy, not something I see a lot in LA. His silver-gray jacket might just be over a couple thousand dollars. I've never understood spending so much money on clothes, especially in a place where so many people are struggling to find a place to live and food to eat. But maybe I'm not so different. I live here, too, and have more money than I really need.

Reynolds nods at me and Paola. "Appointment coming up," he says to Dave.

"Something to drink?" Dave asks us, ignoring him.

"Just water," Paola answers for both of us. She knows I'm sober.

Dave waves down a woman passing by in uniform, who nods.

"Sorry we're a bit late," Paola says.

"Five minutes?" Dave shrugs.

"Ten," Reynolds corrects.

Gray's sigh is loud. Audrey kicks him under the table, a little more obviously than she probably expected. Her face turns red as she sips her own glass of water.

The woman comes back and puts the two glasses on the table. Her eyes linger on Gray for a long second. Gray meets her gaze with a smirk.

"Business, then," Dave says. "Let's get to it. We've—well, we've got a problem. Take off your shades, Gray."

Gray takes his time slipping the shades off. The bruise has started to turn green. Paola sits straight, almost quivering with tension. I try to relax into my role, but my voice cracks a little. "Yeah? Is everything okay?"

"Not really. No." Dave scratches his beard under his chin. "Publicity for the film is—it's not great. This is supposed to be the number one rom-com of the season. Got word from PR. The negative attention is already affecting buzz for the film." His eyes land heavily on Gray.

"Look, Dave," Gray says, "if you're going to fire me, then fucking fire me."

I exchange looks with Paola. "Sorry," I say, "why would Gray be fired?" The only thing I can think is that fight he'd gotten into, but Gray had gotten into fights before he was hired, too.

Everyone stares blankly at me, except for Paola, who is also frowning in confusion. She does her best, but I know she isn't as much a part of this LA scene yet, either, and has clearly missed something.

"You didn't see?" Reynolds asks. "Really?" He snorts.

Audrey leans in and whispers, though I don't know why, since everyone can still hear her. "Gray was found—er—unfortunately—um—"

"A video of me sucking my friend's dick was released, and now everyone hates me for cheating on Willow Grace," Gray says, staring up at the ceiling.

Paola's mouth falls open. Mine does, too.

"Who the hell even has a name like that?" Audrey mutters. "*Willow Grace.*"

Dave rubs the back of his neck. "Like I said. The negative press is turning potential viewers away."

Gray shrugs. "Wasn't thinking about the film's publicity when it was leaked."

"Bullshit," Reynolds says, but he's still looking at his phone and doesn't seem mad. I wonder how many meetings like this he deals with daily. "Video like that? Had to be released on purpose."

"It doesn't matter either way," Dave says, tapping the table. "The consequences are the same. *Write Anything* is becoming a joke. Online, in the news."

"That's what we get for hiring him, I suppose," Reynolds mutters. I have the sense that he was never really on board with Logan Gray being the film's star. "Can't hire the bad boy archetype and not expect him to act like the bad boy archetype. Would've been better with Phillip Desmond." Phillip Desmond: another up-and-coming actor, but he's always felt a little expected to me, with his blonde hair and blue eyes and empty smile. My biggest insecurity is that I'm not much different from Phillip. If he'd been hired instead of Gray, the film would've been boring. Phillip and I wouldn't have had any sort of chemistry.

Not that Gray and I have any sort of chemistry.

But, well—I have to admit, he is attractive. And feeling attraction isn't always the sort of thing that's easy to act out on-screen.

"Sorry," Paola says, hands gripped in her lap so tightly I can see her biceps clenching. "I'm not sure what the purpose of this meeting is, exactly."

We—the four of us—look at Dave and Reynolds. Dave looks at Reynolds. Reynolds finally slips his phone into his jacket's inner pocket.

"We need to get the publicity of this film back on track. After that interview Gray did, calling golden boy here a shitty actor, everyone's decided that Gray hates Matthew. Not great, when they're supposed to be in love on-screen."

"Get to the point," Gray says under his breath.

Reynolds glares at him. "We need you two to start up a public relationship."

The silence that follows might just last a full minute.

It takes me a second to process what he's saying. As an actor, I've been trained to figure out emotions quickly—to pinpoint them, figure out where I feel them in my body, make sure they're being expressed organically. But now? My mouth opens and closes silently.

Gray's snort interrupts the quiet. "Seriously?"

"We've been having meetings with publicity to figure this out. We agreed you'd help each other," Dave says. His tone is more delicate. "Matthew has a softness to him. He's got that Southern charm thing going on. All manners, politeness. If you start to date each other, that could affect your image, too," he tells Gray. "People will likely start to feel you're being—er—*saved*. Evangelized in a way. That you're starting to change, and that Matt's helping you."

Audrey is thoughtful. "That might not be a bad idea."

Paola might be nervous, coming into a big meeting like this, but I hired her for a reason. "But why should Mattie—sorry, Matthew—agree to something like that?" she asks. Her voice only quivers a little. "I mean, the opposite is possible too, isn't it? His image might…" She hesitates, probably not wanting to offend Gray.

"We thought about that, too," Dave says. He shrugs a little. "No offense, kid, but some early response to you has suggested you might be a little boring. You're just…*too* good, you know what I mean?"

I know exactly what he means. I've seen that response also—and I can't blame anyone for thinking it. I am boring in comparison to someone like Gray. I've wished I could figure out how to break out of my shell more. Be more spontaneous, not care so much about what people think of me. If I could be more exciting, then I might be able to break out into different roles also. I'm honestly a little jealous of people like Gray, who give zero fucks—just a little. "No offense taken," I say.

Gray rolls his eyes. "So, what? I'm supposed to make him edgy? Interesting, exciting? One of us has the harder job here."

"Fucking hell, Gray," Dave snaps. "Just stop being an asshole for one minute and listen. This is the only compromise we could come to, all right?"

His meaning is clear.

Audrey's face is pinched. She leans into Gray and whispers—actually whispers this time. I only hear a word here and there. "One shot…last chance…your father."

Gray's expression doesn't change. He looks more like a sullen teenager than he ever has. I've read articles about the lives of former child stars—how most of them never actually got much of a chance to grow up. "Fine," he says.

Dave's satisfied. He looks at me, waiting for my response now.

I wish I had more of a chance to think it over and talk about

27

it with Paola. I've heard about celebrities who do this, some-times: engage in these fake relationships, tricking the public for mutual benefits in fame or success. I heard a rumor that Pete Davidson was a favorite fake boyfriend for a few years. I just never thought I would be someone to consider this. It'd be the role of a century, pretending to be in love with a jack-ass like Gray. We'd probably have our own publicity for this particular off-screen film: going on dates, talking about how we fell for each other in interviews . . .

"Can I think about it?"

"No," Reynolds says. "Here and now. I need to give Vanessa an answer." Vanessa Stone, the boss of the EPs and owner of the production company. I've met her once, from across the room. She's terrifying.

"What if I say no?"

"Then this fucker is out," Reynolds says, not bothering to look at Gray. "We'll find a replacement before the week is done."

Gray doesn't meet my eye. I have the power to get him fired, and after the way he's treated me? I'm tempted. But . . . there's another part of me. The part that, despite it all, still admires Logan Gray the actor, even if I can't stand him as a person. I know I'm not at the skill level I want to be. There's so much I could learn from him, being his co-star. And, honestly, without Logan as one of the leads, this film might just be lost. They could hire a Phillip Desmond–type, someone who acts just as well as me. Even with the best writing and directing in the world, the film could fall flat. That'd ultimately affect me, too, and my own dream.

I've got to put my feelings aside for this one. "All right," I say with a nod. "I agree. Gray and I will . . . go out."

"More than go out," Reynolds says gruffly, grabbing his

phone again. He stands up, pushing out his chair, and leaves without another word. Wow. LA, huh?

I can see the relief in Audrey's gaze. She's trying to radiate gratitude to me silently. *Thank you*, she mouths. Gray still won't look at me. I don't think he likes that I had so much power over his role and his future.

Paola watches me closely. "Are you sure?" she whispers.

I nod. "Yeah. I'm sure."

Dave claps his hands together. "It's decided, then. It'll need to look organic, of course. Natural. We can't have the PR team too tied up in this—too many hands and eyes, too many potential leaks—so everything stays between us. I'll moonlight as a publicity manager on this." Gray snorts, but Dave ignores him. "You'll need to convince your co-stars and everyone else on set, too. Don't worry about it. We'll plan it all out."

I don't know if he means to look as excited as he does,

LOGAN

LA TRAFFIC ISN'T so bad when you're high as fuck. AC and IC3PEAK blasts, shades saving my eyeballs from melting. This city is too fucking sunny. I read some article that the traffic is actually due to racism, shitty highways created specifically to cut off certain neighborhoods. Everything in this country eventually returns to racism, huh?

My apartment is on the edge of WeHo, what should be about fifteen minutes away from the studios' headquarters in North Hollywood turning into a forty-five-minute jam of stop, start, stop, start. I park in the apartment building's garage and head to the elevator and up to my apartment on the top floor. It's still trashed from when Briggs came over. That was, what, three weeks ago? The housecleaner my dad hired, Sandra, has been calling, asking if she should come by, but I'm ashamed to let her see my place like this. Used condoms stuck to the bedroom floor, rotting food in the sinks, piles of clothes every-where with no clue what's clean, a baggie of cocaine forgotten on the living room's central table. Fuck.

This is my dad's apartment. He bought it for me. It was only a few months in that I noticed the security camera. It's small as hell, in the corner of the living room, with full view of everything that happens. I have no idea if my dad watches me, or if he just has it there for control. But I checked the camera out, got access to the website where I can see the footage, and decided that this will be a separate film that I act in for my dad privately. I do the most fucked up shit imaginable to piss him off. To prove to him, and me, that he can't control me anymore.

My buzz is wearing off, and my head is starting to throb, so I pour some vodka to help ease me out of the hangover and fall onto my sofa, turning Spotify onto the FEVER 333 station. Just loud enough to almost drown out my thoughts. I can't remember the last time I watched TV or a movie for pleasure. It's hard to watch actors play roles when you know them personally. It gets in the way of suspending the disbelief and makes it hard to get into the story when you know the main character's a pain in the ass in real life, or when you know what the love interest's dick looks like.

My phone rings over the speakers. I hit answer. My father's voice wipes away my smirk.

"Logan," he says. "You're a fucking disgrace." I lean my head back and close my eyes, swirling the vodka around in a circle. "Are you fucking kidding me, Logan, with that fucking tape? You're twenty-four. You're not a child. Stop acting like a piece of shit. Get yourself the fuck together."

He hangs up. I sigh and drain the glass. This might be my last chance to relax before filming begins. Filming's from August to November, according to the schedule I was sent. Twelve-hour workdays. At least it's here in LA, but I'm going to stay at a hotel in Studio City so I don't have to bother driving back and forth. I've been stressing about this character. Quinn Evans. He's me, basically. A fuckup. Arrogant. I read the book. It was fucking awful, but that doesn't matter. Studying his character for the last few months has forced me to look in the mirror a lot more than I usually would. I don't think about it very much, how much I hate myself, but it's been a good fact to focus on and pull me deeper into my role.

I haven't been in a film for the past couple of years, after my last time at rehab. It'll take me a second to get back into the flow, remember what life is like on set. I feel an extra pressure to prove I haven't lost it. I'm still fucking talented. The stress of all that, plus this bullshit relationship with Matthew Cole. Fuck. At least Willow had enough of a personality to keep things interesting.

I pull out my phone and head to messages. I text Willow. A simple *hey*. We used to text all the time, when we were pretending to date. Nothing serious. Sarcastic banter at how social media was reacting to our relationship. I see the bubbles appear and disappear. Left on read.

I scroll through messages until I find Briggs. I try again. Hey. Bubbles appear. His response is quick. You all right? Kinda in the middle of something. I spin the phone around and around. Yeah. If only the blogs could see me now. Even worse, I think, that I actually fit the overprivileged asshole stereotype, feeling sorry for myself.

Willow's response buzzes. No point in continuing to text, right? We're not pretending to be together anymore.

I take another sip.

Fuck it. I'm bored.

I look up Matthew Cole on my phone and begin to scroll.

Happily Ever After: A Memoir

by Matthew Cole

By the time I was twelve years old, I had some inkling that I was interested in other boys, though I was afraid to acknowledge this fact even to myself.

One memory that stays with me to this day is the moment I sat with my father and we watched a queer film together for the first time. I'd scoured the LGBTQ+ section in Netflix, but I had never watched a film with queer characters with another person before. My father and I weren't close. We struggled to communicate, to find ways to hold conversations. If I said something, he would only be silent. "I had fun at school today." Silence. "I joined the drama club." Silence. I didn't know how to talk to him about anything that really mattered. I couldn't tell him about my fears, my dreams. And if *he* ever said something, it was only an instruction. "Don't walk like that, Matthew. Don't talk to adults unless they speak to you first. Stop laughing so loudly. You're embarrassing yourself."

Movies were the one way we connected, because we didn't have to speak. We would sit together to watch a film once a week. Now that I look back on those days, I suspect my mother was the one who pushed my father to spend more time with me.

This particular memory, though—well, I can't even remember which film it was. It wasn't a movie with overtly queer characters. It was an action, something my dad usually enjoyed. There were two men who were close throughout the film. They didn't do anything, not in the way queerness is much more openly accepted now, with kisses and long, romantic embraces, and sexually graphic scenes that don't fade to black. The men only touched each other's hands, just barely, just enough for the audience to understand who they were to one another as they fought off the end of the world. It was still a time when even this was groundbreaking, but this touch made me explode with embarrassment and curiosity and just a touch of pre-teen longing, a wondering of whether I could ever touch another boy with that sort of tenderness. My father scowled. He spoke more than he usually would. "Disgusting," he said. That was all he said, but it was enough.

I would go to church on Sundays with my family. I called myself a Christian, then, in the sense that I believe there is a force that we humans can't comprehend, a force that has different names across languages and cultures—but I'd always believed, even as a young child, that this force didn't understand our human definitions of sin. This force would not understand why one man could not love another. This force only knew love and compassion. It was painful that my father couldn't understand the same.

MATTIE

PAOLA DID AN amazing job, negotiating for me to be put up in the Winchester, a small luxury hotel near Studio City. One bedroom, kitchenette, pristine white walls and marble countertops. Still, it can be lonely in a city like Los Angeles, even when I have little ways of distracting myself. I bought a little pothos at a garden shop that I water when the leaves look wilted. I play *Stardew Valley* on my laptop (I'm trying to marry Elliott), and I've been slowly making my way through the Louise Penny series to keep my thoughts from spiraling. I've even recently started listening to podcasts on my phone, just so that the other voices make me feel like I'm not in an otherwise empty room. It started with me typing into the search bar *how to not feel so alone* and, over the past few days, the podcasts have ended up in *attachment style theory* and *healing queer trauma*. These kinds of topics would've made me cringe, once, but that doesn't stop me from playing a new episode every night.

The only people who have visited me in my hotel room are from the wardrobe department, to fit me for the costumes they're preparing, and the makeup and hair folks, to let me know what they're planning. I stand on the balcony, watching the pale blue sky turn pink and gold as I dial my sister's number on FaceTime.

Emma picks up on the first ring. "Mattie!"

"God, I miss you, Em." So much that I might just start to cry. Every time I feel tears well up, I hear my father yelling at me to be a man. He never believed that men should have emotions.

"I miss you, too. Mom's stalking you in the news. She tells me every time her Google alert for your name goes off. Which is, like, every five minutes."

Emma and I look a lot alike in facial features, but that's about it. We had a white person somewhere in our lineage, like most Black families, so my skin tone turned out different. She has medium brown skin with thicker black hair and dark brown eyes. I have golden-brown skin that's covered with freckles and the sort of curly-wavy texture of hair that makes most people assume that I'm white with a strong tan, like Ariana Grande or a Kardashian when they were still in their appropriate-Black-culture phases. Either that, or they're not sure of my race at all. The "look" of *ethnically ambiguous* has been trendy in LA for a while now.

I know it's because of colorism and racism that I've even made it this far. The characters in the novel *Write Anything* were both white, but the studio decided to take a risk and let me and other people of color audition instead. I lost out to Gray for the lead, and I thought that was the end of it—until they rang me up two months later and asked if I wanted to be the love interest.

I was surprised that they were willing to give two Black men the lead roles, even if colorism was a big part of our acceptance. Logan is mixed—Black and white—with lighter brown skin and wavy black hair. He could easily be mistaken as white.

My agent, Jacqueline, is all business in comparison to Paola. I barely interact with her except when she's offering me roles or information. "There's been an uptick in financial success for movies featuring Black leads. *Write Anything* on its own isn't enough to stand out, with the growing popularity of queer films. They're hoping you and Logan Gray will bring more success to the film with your diversity."

I wasn't exactly sold on her pitch—it sounded like an invitation to microaggression hell—but Paola spoke to me after the phone call. Yeah, it sucks to be *the diverse inclusion*, but this is also one of the few chances I might have to propel my career forward. And, if I'm successful, I can really start to make change from within the industry. I'm disappointed I didn't get the main role, but I have to admit: it's pretty cool to be the love interest of a blockbuster romantic film, and not being the white, blonde-haired, blue-eyed prince that I had to grow up with. Seeing only one kind of person as the one who is worthy of love messed with my head when I was younger. It made me think that I wasn't good enough for that role, too.

Emma is seventeen, about to start her first year at Sarah Lawrence. I've always been overprotective of my little sister. I have memories of being ten years old and clutching her hand when she was four, making sure she wouldn't fall down. I'm afraid for her to go off to a new place by herself, but I'm excited for her, too. I can't help but grin. "Are you finished packing?"

She groans. "Not you, too. Mom won't leave me alone about it."

It's like she's summoned our mother. She sticks her head into the frame. She looks more like Emma with her darker brown skin and thick hair. "You finally found a moment in your busy life?"

"I'm sorry, I should've called sooner."

Emma rolls her eyes. "Mom needs to realize you can't speak every single day anymore. You're famous now."

Maybe it's ridiculous that I'm twenty-three and I still talk to my mom all the time, but I love her too much not to call. She's always supported me—always, no matter what. She'd drive me into Atlanta to enroll me in acting lessons when I was young. A lot of mothers would probably insist that I go to college, I think, and find a reliable source of income, but she understood and supported me when I decided to defer my acceptance to Boston College to focus on auditions. She flew with me to LA when I turned eighteen, always there as a shoulder to cry on when I wasn't offered roles. *Love Me Dearly* was a miracle, and maybe the opportunity came because my mom prayed so hard. It's like she demanded my dream work out for me. I'm here because of her.

"Have you been looking at the blogs?"

"No, not really."

"They love you," she tells me. "They say you're a sweetheart. But of course they do. I raised you right."

People think that I'm polite and that I have Southern charm. They think that I'm *too* good, and that I'm boring. I wonder what my mom would think of this whole scheme with Logan Gray. She's definitely not going to be happy when she sees in the tabloids that I'm dating him. "I get a little worried," I say, "that I might start to lose myself out here."

"You've always been so grounded," my mom says. "You never let things like *money* or *fame* go to your head. You'd never let anyone change you."

I hesitate, mouth opening to tell her and Emma the truth.

But, well—I already know what they'd say, don't I? They wouldn't be happy with me or the idea. My mom would be shocked that I'd even consider it. I already made my decision to move forward with this. I might try to admit the truth to them eventually, but not right now. There isn't any point.

"So," I say, "where's Dad?"

The brightness in their faces fades a little. "Sitting over here."

He's been feet away from them, but he hasn't bothered to come over to say hello. That's not surprising. I nod. "Tell him I say hi," I say, even though he can probably hear me just fine.

My mom's nod is clipped. "Okay, I will. I have to get back to grading papers, but Mattie—just know we're all so proud of you."

"Thanks, Mom. I love you."

"I love you, too."

She leaves the frame, and from the movement behind my sister and the sly grin on her face, I know she's leaving the living room for her bedroom for a little more privacy. "So what's it like acting with *Logan Gray*?" she asks, voice lowered.

I shrug with a flinch of annoyance—not at her, but at even the mention of the name. That's the effect he has on me, I guess. "He's kind of an asshole."

She grins. "As to be expected. God, have you looked at Twitter recently? Everyone's eating him alive for what he did to Willow Grace."

I think Emma feels like I'm a portal into a reality TV episode. Not that I should judge. *Real Housewives* is a guilty pleasure of mine, too. "You know I try to stay away from all of that. If they're eating Logan Gray alive, then that means they might eat me alive one day, too."

"No way. You're not a jerk like him." She pauses. "So does that mean you haven't looked him up?"

"I know who he is, Em."

"You can't know everything that's on his Wiki page."

"You read his Wiki page?"

"Did you know he's been to rehab *twice*? Jesus. I'm amazed they even gave him the role."

"It feels a little like what they did with Robert Downey Jr."

"Huh? Who is that?"

Ouch. "I'm not that much older than you. Come on. You know, the guy that plays Iron Man?"

"Oh, him?"

"Yeah. He was basically the resident bad boy of Hollywood, too, and then he was hired on for Marvel, and—anyway, I don't know. I can't pretend I know what the studio's thinking by hiring him."

"I mean, he is really, really famous. Well, more like in-famous." Emma quirks a single eyebrow, smirk growing. I already know where she's going with this. "Have you checked out the video?"

"Em. First of all, you're too young to be looking at stuff like that."

"I didn't *look* at it," she protests, "and besides, I'm seven-teen!"

"And second of all—hell no. That'd feel weird. He's my coworker. And—I don't know, it'd feel like a violation."

"You two are going to get to know each other *pretty well* before the filming is over. I read the book."

I roll my eyes to hide my embarrassment. Emma always knows how to go in for the kill, even when she's teasing. I'd read *Write Anything* a few times, too. "Yeah, well, it's just my job. We're professionals."

The book only described heavy make-out scenes that eventually faded to black, thankfully, but that still means I'll be kissing Logan Gray shirtless. That was all a part of the casting, too. Paola getting in touch with the intimacy coordinator, making sure we all agreed on our personal levels of comfort. The movie is PG-13, but this particular scene will push the film closer to the edge of R-rated territory.

"I mean, you can't complain *too* much," Emma says, still teasing. "He might be an asshole, but he's really, really hot."

I unfortunately agree. Not that I'm going to admit that, mostly because I don't really want to talk to Emma about this sort of thing. (Why are teenagers so much more flippant about sex these days?)

But the other reason lingers in the air. I told my family I was gay almost five years ago. It's old news. My sister didn't care. My mom had a few months of saying offensive, hurtful things before she understood that, no, I will never be interested in marrying a woman. That was the only rift in our relationship, but we've had enough conversations that we're in a better place now. But my dad...We never talked much to begin with, but he stopped talking to me altogether. He never yelled at me or told me I was going to hell or anything I expected. It was like that was enough for him to decide that he didn't love me anymore.

I don't want to admit it to anyone—I barely want to admit it to myself—but that shame is still there. It's a seed in my chest, growing whenever I find a man attractive. I understand consciously that I have nothing to be ashamed about—but it's like my body still hasn't caught up. My heart races, my skin flushes, and I feel like I'm already burning in hell. Nothing has helped—not the podcasts, not the books or articles I've read. I haven't gone out with anyone since the tour for *Love Me*

Dearly ended, though I've gotten many interested messages. And now this: making out with another man in a blockbuster film. Everyone will expect me to be the sort of actor who will be out and proud about my sexuality to help publicize the movie. That was one of the reasons they reached out to me, another tick on their checklist for *diversity*.

Riley Mason struggles with shame in the book and film also, before he accepts himself with Quinn's help. Maybe that's partly why I took the job, in the end. I hope that I'll work through the shame, too. I'm not the first actor to use my job as therapy.

Emma picked up our mom's kindness, even more than I did. "You doing okay, Mattie? Really. Tell me the truth."

I take a breath. "I'm scared. But I think I'll be all right, you know?"

Los Angeles Times Feature

In Conversation:

The Rise of Matthew Cole

The young actor's road to fame was seemingly an over-night success, but Matthew Cole details the dedicated years of work he put into becoming the phenomenon currently sweeping the nation.

By Louise Renner
August 2, 2023
(excerpt)

Matthew Coles's hotel room is not what I would have expected of a young twentysomething celebrity grow-ing in fame. Most stars would live in private penthouses or manors in the Hills, but Matthew—or Mattie, as his friends, family, and fans adoringly know him as—explains that he hasn't had the chance to settle in yet. The inside of Matthew's hotel room is bare. He hasn't yet put up any decorations. "It'd feel weird to, since I don't actually live here."

When I ask him if he plans on permanently moving to Los Angeles for his budding career as a well-loved actor, he seems hesitant. "I might eventually," he tells me, "but—well, it's hard to take the jump right now. I feel like I'm in between two worlds still."

Originally from the humble town of Decatur, Georgia,

Mattie is more familiar with the slower pace of the South. I'm not fully convinced that Matthew wants to move to a city such as this one, but if he wants to continue his future in acting, he might not have much of a choice. With an expected politeness, Mattie asks if I'd like any water, and when I decline, he eyes my phone and its recording app I've placed on the side table between our chairs.

Mattie is visibly nervous, which is curious for an actor of his caliber. He fidgets with the end of his wrinkled graphic t-shirt and bounces his knee, which peeks through a hole in his jeans. He seems to realize that he moves his hands too much as he talks, so he sits on them instead. This shy, earnest twenty-three-year-old feels like a person one might want to protect from the world of Hollywood.

Matthew Cole has been dubbed the new golden boy of the film industry. His rise to fame began with his discovery in the role "Love Me Dearly" (2022). Though Mattie only played Angela Simmons's younger brother, Nick, his optimistic performance as a younger boy exploring his sexuality in a conservative town gained the attention of viewers.

Matthew's momentum didn't stop there. Months after the publicity tour of "Love Me Dearly," Mattie was cast in the much-anticipated film for the bestselling novel "Write Anything," this time in a leading role as Riley Mason, the love interest to Quinn Evans. Many have compared the young Matthew Coles's growing popularity to that of Timothée Chalamet and Tom Holland when they first hit the scene. Matthew, however, has not been as well-received by the critics, with many claiming he is simply Hollywood's newest obsession, and will likely be forgotten as someone who does not have the necessary skill, talent, or presence to truly stand out in a hungry sea of actors. Most notably among Matthew's critics is his own co-star for the newest film, Logan Gray, who infamously criticized Mattie on the red-carpet premiere of "Hawkseye Down."

One thing is certain, however: for as many critics Mattie finds, he will be followed by fans, rooting for this underdog's success. When I ask Matthew what his secret is, he seems uncomfortable and fumbles with a response. I ask instead if he's nervous with his success, and he responds without hesitation. "Yes," he says. "I never really wanted to be famous."

"What *do* you want, then?"

"I just want to act. I've always loved acting, ever since I was a kid. I'm not sure I want everything else that comes with it."

Perhaps it's Mattie's humility and vulnerability that tug at the heartstrings of so many, allowing us to connect to his performances. If Matthew Cole is at fault for anything, it's that he is almost too sweet, to the point of innocence. I would hate to witness his inevitable disillusion.

LOGAN

DRINKING ALONE IN a hotel bar? Sounds about right. A few years ago, I'd be falling over drunk by now. It's an improvement, believe me, that I'm only on my third bourbon. Still. I told myself I'd keep it together this time around. If I'm going to get away from my father, I need to do better. I wonder, just for a second, if I'm sabotaging myself by drinking, but that shit's a little too deep for me right now.

There's a stack of papers for sale, face out on the other end of the counter, alongside cigars. Front page says there's a feature on Matthew Cole on page twenty-two. It's like I can't escape the fucking guy. And, like I've materialized him out of thin air, just as I glance out of the bar and into the lobby of the hotel, Matthew Cole himself strolls through. Before I can pretend I didn't see him, he turns like he can feel someone's eyes on him and looks right at me, tensing up with surprise and a glimmer of dislike that I've come to recognize on most people and—god fucking damn it, of course he feels the need to come over and talk to me.

"Hey," he says, slowing down and looking at the glass in front of me. "Waiting for someone?" His tone is hopeful, like he thinks this could be a good excuse to leave immediately. Newsflash, Matt: you could've avoided this situation altogether if you pretended you hadn't seen me, too.

"Nope," I say. "No. I'm staying here."

"At the Winchester?" Matt says, surprised.

I stare at him blankly. "Yeah." Obviously.

He wipes his expression clean, though he can't hide the flicker of annoyance, as if he'd actually decided to give me a chance. "I thought you live in LA," he says.

"I do." I sigh at his confused expression. I don't want to explain that I want to take the chance to escape the apartment my father owns, so I tell him the second reason. "I thought it'd be easier to just stay in a hotel that's close to the studio so I don't have to drive back and forth."

I hadn't realized it would sound so bad, but now saying it aloud, I hear how much I sound like a rich piece of shit.

Matt's face is strained. "Oh. Okay."

He looks miserable, like he can't believe I'm the person he's going to have to pretend to be in love with both on- and off-screen, and—fine, all right, I'm in a crappy mood because I was sitting in a bar, thinking about my father and feeling sorry for myself. Besides. I need Matt, too. I need this movie to work, and if pretending he's my boyfriend is the only way, then yeah—I'll do it.

I drain the rest of my drink. No one's sitting anywhere near me. I have that effect on people. "Dave's task list is bullshit, right?"

Matt looks relieved at my attempt of a civil conversation. "Yeah. The schedule's really fast. I don't know if it's believable."

"Why? Because we hate each other so much?"

Matt frowns. "I don't hate you, Logan."

I meet his eye, and he's watching me carefully, and—yeah, I don't know. Things don't need to get that intense. "Thanks, I guess," I say. "For agreeing to do this." I don't want to admit it, but he saved my ass.

"I needed this also."

"Why?"

He looks surprised that I even asked. I am, too. I didn't think about the question before it came out of my mouth. But I'm curious. It would've been the perfect moment, the perfect chance for him to say fuck you, Gray, and watch me get fired in revenge for the way I've treated him. His mercy was shocking as hell. It's not something people often show me.

"Well," Matthew starts, slowly. He won't meet my eye. He seems embarrassed.

"You didn't agree to do this because you *wanted* to pretend to be in a relationship with me, right?" That'd be fucking weird.

He glares. "No. Christ. I just thought the movie would be lost without—well, without someone of your caliber. That'd mess with my future, too."

I understand the embarrassment now. I wasn't expecting a compliment from him. I raise a brow. "Someone of my caliber?"

He's very embarrassed now, which is cute. It's not ground-breaking news that Matthew Cole is attractive. It's why he was hired in the first place. But I've also had a few too many drinks.

"Anyway," he says, "I hope that we can move past the awkwardness and agree on a truce."

"A truce? What are we, five?"

He ignores me and sticks out his hand. "We need to work together, right?"

I roll my eyes and take his hand. It's obnoxiously soft. His shake is surprisingly firm. He lets go first, like he's dying to wipe his hand off but doesn't want to offend me. "See you tomorrow, Logan."

"Right. See you."

He leaves without another glance. I debate ordering another bourbon. I get the bartender's attention. "One more," I say. I pause. "And a paper, please."

I can see why *Write Anything* was greenlit with a quickness and cut the line to production. It's much more about character, less about fancy locations. The budget couldn't have been much with the few sets we have around LA: a coffee shop, the park, a random sidewalk. Everything else is built at the studio location. People walk and run back and forth on set. Studio execs talk at the side, assistants following like shadows. There's the cinematographer, production designer, assistant on the camera, the key grip and best boy electric, extras who stand around excitedly, publicists and the producer's assistant, a cast assistant who walks up to me and asks if I need anything...Good thing I'm not an introvert and don't become exhausted just by being around a shit ton of people. Ha.

First scene that I have to film is the most complicated one I've got. Probably to get it out of the way. We're outside in the hot sun with a giant fan, water blowing. The big scene where I sprint through the rain so that Quinn can confess his-my-our love to Riley. Quinn's been guarded, afraid to commit, so this is his big moment of breaking free. The water as a symbol of freedom has shown up in movies since the beginning of time. It's a little cliché, but I'm not here to judge the writers. At least the water will feel good after almost dying of heatstroke.

It'll need a few takes. Wardrobe is spread throughout the holding tent, ready with identical outfits and an overkill of dozens of towels so I can change in and out after being soaked. I nurse a headache from a slight hangover as I sit on the metal steps leading up to my trailer's door and read the *LA Times* feature on Matthew. *Mattie*, apparently. I've always taken my roles seriously, and if I have to act like I'm in love with this guy, then I need to do my homework on him.

Scott sighs and leans against the trailer beside me. "Hot as hell today, huh?"

It's always fucking hot. It's fucking LA. I barely glance up. Scott's the only other actor on set who'll bother to talk to me outside of shared scenes. Keith's got a hard job, acting as my best friend, since he's always hated me. I'm not sure why. We barely interact. Maybe he follows the tabloids. Monica thinks everyone is beneath her, but especially a drug addict porn star like me. And Julie? She just thinks I'm a dick. I mean. She's right.

But Scott's been on different sets with me for a while. He tends to give me fatherly disapproving looks, but that's about it.

He nods his head at the article. "Reading up on your co-star?"

"Color me curious." I pause and glance up at him. "Do you think this whole golden boy thing is an act?"

"What do you mean?"

"It's hard to believe anyone would be in this city and actually be that innocent."

"Matthew's not from here, right?"

"Yeah, but if you want to survive, you've got to learn pretty quickly."

"Maybe you can help him with that."

I snort and drop the paper to the side. The article was boring. A lot like Matthew Cole himself. "I guess not everyone can be a drugged-out alcoholic mentally ill asshole with unprocessed trauma."

Scott raises his eyebrows at me with a blank stare.

"Joking," I say.

Once I'm put through hair and makeup (I don't know why they bother, it's going to get messed up with every take), I'm dressed and mic'd up and positioned on one end of the block, ready to run to Mattie's stand-in waiting at the doorway of the townhouse on the other side, camera on a giant dolly that starts out close to my face before it pulls away for a wide shot. This feels like my big moment, the first time in years that I have the chance to get my life back on track.

"Quiet on set. Take one . . . Action!"

I don't ever let my guard down. Why would I? Letting down walls means getting hurt. There's no way around that one. I would never be like Quinn. Deciding that love was worth taking a risk, sprinting through the rain just so that he could possibly, maybe get his heart broken. Sure. Yeah. This movie has a happy ending. We all know life is very different.

I've never been in love, either, but I still have to get myself into that frame of mind. The fear. The hope. The excitement. That's what I'd planned for in this scene, but a new emotion begins to bubble. The realization that I'll probably never feel the way Quinn does. I'll never be in love. I'll never take my walls down, and because of that, I'll always be alone. I've never been so alone in my life as I am now. I don't know how to connect with people, and fuck—fuck, it's painful to look at others falling in love, even fake characters like Quinn and Riley. It's hard to see other people building friendships and relationships and families that I want, too, even if I'd never admit it out loud. I've given up. I don't think I'm meant to have anyone in my life sometimes. I'm too fucked up for anyone to really love.

The scene starts with me sprinting, but the emotion leaves me gasping. I stop halfway and lean over, hands on my knees, face twisted in more pain than I'm expecting to release. Dave doesn't call cut, so I keep going. Stand up straight, chest and shoulders heaving. Fuck. I'm actually crying. The realization makes me laugh. I shake my head, wipe my eyes. Have to finish the scene. I keep running.

I hit the end of the block. Dave calls *cut*, and I'm immediately swarmed by wardrobe. Dave comes up behind a woman who's jabbing a soft towel at my face.

"Wasn't expecting that direction, Gray," he says. He doesn't seem upset.

"Yeah. I don't know. It just came out."

Dave shrugs. "It works. More interesting than only running down the block like the script says. An extra beat of emotion." He eyes me carefully. I don't know what he's thinking. Probably that it's a good thing that I can act, because otherwise, I'd be nothing but an annoying piece of shit. "All right. Let's do another take. Just try running down the block this time, okay? To give some options."

"Sure. Okay."

When I get back to the starting point, I notice Matt standing under the shade of the holding tent. He's watching me. When I meet his gaze he looks away quickly. Huh. Maybe he's studying up on me, too. It'd be good if he was. We're going to need to be serious about our other roles if we want to fool anyone.

MATTIE

LOVE ME DEARLY had long days, and I wasn't even a lead actor, but for whatever reason the schedule for *Write Anything* is much gentler. My scenes start shooting around noon. But... I'm curious. I stand beneath the holding tent. There's a monitor where I can watch Logan from the camera's perspective, but I want to see *him* in action, study his skill and see what I can learn. It's embarrassing when he looks up and catches me staring.

I've got the script in hand. I've spent basically every free second going over my lines again and again, even though they're so memorized I'm pretty sure they're burned into my brain for the rest of my life. I took up Dave's offer to get an assistant to rehearse with me, too. I was grateful that he made it sound like it was up to me, and not a firm request. That table read was pretty abysmal, after all, I have to admit. When I apologized to him for it, he shrugged. "Don't worry about it. You came in a lot later than everyone else. You haven't had a chance to figure out your character yet." His smile became just a little more forced in that second. "Just. You know. Try to figure it out before you get onto set."

Riley is similar to me in some ways, like when it comes to shame about his sexuality—but personality-wise? He's the opposite of me. He's everything I wish I could be. He laughs loudly, freely, dances when he wants to dance and sings when he wants to sing. He could happily run through the middle of a field butt naked. I've always been the kind of guy who would rather suppress myself so that I won't be judged. I think that's why it hurts, more than anything, when someone says I'm *boring*. There's nothing wrong with being an introvert, but I wouldn't say that I am one. I actually love speaking to people—feel energized when I get to know others. But I can also be so shy and awkward and like I'm trapped in a shell, and...I'll never be the life of the party, like Logan Gray and his celebrity friends, but I wish I could feel comfortable enough in my skin to just be myself.

Gray's scenes wrap quickly. He's talented as hell, no one can deny that, and he nails each take. There's no point in wasting money and time by doing more than necessary. He has his mic taken off, and he's given the green light to take a break. I'm surprised when I see him walking off set—and right toward me. He's still wet, his hair dripping. He pats it dry with a towel, and some black strands cutely stick up straight. It's funny that his hair's texture also changes when it's wet, like mine. Maybe it's because he's mixed. His father, Jameson Gray, is white. He seems like an intimidating man, from what I've seen in photos and interviews. Jameson's production company tends to release Michael Bay–like films. It's almost funny, how unalike Jameson and Logan Gray seem to be.

Logan's smirk inches onto his face as he gets closer to me. "Staring at me longingly from across set? Isn't it a little too early for that?"

My face heats up. "No. I was just watching. I was curious."

He leans against the table where I'd set up camp. "Relax. I figured I'd come over. Check off our assignment for the day."

Dave had created a literal schedule and even printed it out for us. "Your emails might be hacked," he said, but I think he was just excited to hand us the papers like they were for an official production. Right now, Logan and I are supposed to be seen speaking and laughing, as if we're starting to like each other. Dave is talking to his assistant, but he meets my eye from across set with a grin. He looks like he's seconds from giving a thumbs-up. He isn't as subtle as he could be.

"Right. This is going to be kind of weird, huh?"

Gray shrugs, grabs a cup, and presses down on a nozzle for some coffee. Isn't it too hot for that? "Not really. Just got out of one of these—ah—*arrangements*."

It takes me a second before it clicks. "Wait, really? *Willow Grace* was—?"

"Keep it down."

I clear my throat and turn my back to the rest of set, also facing the table. God. Emma would flip if I told her about this one. "So, all of that with the breakup...?"

"Planned. She wanted to release the video. I went along with it."

I wasn't going to mention the video. I rub my cheek awkwardly.

Logan notices. "You're not shy about my porno, are you?" He practically laughs at my silent non-reaction. "You'll have to get over that shyness pretty quickly."

"I don't have a problem with sexuality while acting," I say, though I wouldn't really know for sure. In *Love Me Dearly*, I kissed my crush, the boy next door, and that was it. Other smaller productions before my breakout role never had any sex. "I'm a professional."

He does laugh at that one. "God, you're so fucking uptight."

That rattles me more than I'd like to admit. An assistant passes by, and I force a blushing smile. "Yeah. Well," I say under my breath, "not everyone has the luxury of fucking up all of the time."

Harsh. I didn't mean for it to come out so—well—*mean*. There's an awkward silence where Gray looks up at me, holding my gaze. I blink, open my mouth to apologize, but he interrupts.

"Look at that. Golden boy has some bite to him after all."

"I'm sorry. That was unnecessary."

He shrugs a shoulder, still eyeing me. "Let's get to the point of this."

There was one main goal Dave had for us today. A conversation where it seems we're liking each other more than we thought—and by the end, some easy flirtation. Nothing much. Just enough for anyone watching closely to notice. And someone always is. There are reporters on the edge of set speaking to a publicist, craning their necks to get a look at us. It's not like it'd be new, for two actors to hook up outside of their roles. Long work days usually mean even longer partying hours for cast and crew, and sets can start to resemble sororities and frat houses with all the drama of who slept with who.

Gray takes a sip of his coffee. "It's going to take a lot for us to pull this off."

He's waiting. I didn't expect he'd leave the first move up to me. I laugh as if he's said something funny. "Why?"

"Because not many people are going to believe I'm actually attracted to you outside of filming."

I falter. Maybe I brought that one on myself. I insulted him first, after all.

"I'm not that bad looking, am I?" These words are a little *too* close to actually sounding flirtatious. It was a real question. But pair that with the softer smile, leaning in, hand on his arm...

Logan Gray laughs, and I don't think it's a part of the act. "That's what you call flirting?"

I force myself not to yank my arm back. I pull away smoothly, confidently. "Yes."

"How many relationships have you been in?"

Zero. "That's none of your business." I pause. "Why?"

He shrugs. "Your lack of experience shows."

My face is hot. I haven't been in any official relationships, but I've dated several guys, and I've experimented a lot in bed, even if I would have shame spirals afterward. I'm offended that Gray would assume I don't have any experience—and that, apparently, I'm not very good at flirting.

He reaches across me, suddenly much closer than necessary, as he grabs his coffee cup from the table. His hand grazes my abdomen, his arm against me. His eyes are hooded, and his face is just a couple of inches away, as if he's thinking about closing the gap for a kiss. I feel like I'm being pulled closer by gravity. His voice is low. "This is how you flirt."

I freeze, eyes widening. I realize how I look: exactly like the startled, inexperienced guy he's assuming I am.

Gray whispers in my ear. "You're really going to need to work on your intimacy scenes before we start filming."

He grabs his coffee and leaves without another word. I lean against the table for support. He managed to insult me and piss me off while also making my heart race. Damn, he's good.

Gray isn't on set anymore, so I don't have any reason to keep watching him, but after that trick, I'm having a hard time keeping my eyes off him. I feel the lingering shame that finds me whenever I feel attraction for another man.

A cast assistant, Andrew, followed him to his trailer, where Logan will probably wait for a couple of hours before shooting the next scene. Andrew is small and pale and looks like he's gotten less sleep than anyone else around him. He's talking to Gray as if he might've taken some Adderall before he drops his clipboard, and in his attempt to catch it, knocks the coffee cup out of Gray's hand. Brown liquid spills on Gray on the way down. I immediately tense up. I haven't been in Hollywood long, but I've seen a number of actors act like the divas so many people stereotype us to be, screaming at assistants for mistakes, and especially one like this? I don't want to watch Gray make a scene and humiliate this poor guy.

Andrew is apologizing profusely, and I see a few people glance over, too, but I don't think Gray has noticed that others are watching. He waves a hand back and forth. I can practically see what he's saying from here. "Don't worry about it. Seriously. It's fine."

Gray bends over and picks up the empty coffee cup and the clipboard, gathering the papers that scattered. He takes the towel from around his shoulders, and instead of using it to wipe himself off, he offers it to Andrew, pointing out the coffee that'd gotten on him, too. I frown as I watch, crossing my arms. Andrew still looks like he's about to cry, but Gray's just acting like it's a joke. He pats the guy on the shoulder, walks up the steps and into his trailer.

That's not the Gray I would've expected to see. The Gray I know would have yelled and called the guy an idiot, would have cursed and been annoyed and rolled his eyes as he stormed away and slammed his trailer's door shut behind him. It's funny that this is what I would expect—almost like Gray himself is just a character, playing a role in a film. I'm starting to get the feeling that Gray's a little better at putting on acts than he would want anyone to know.

RED ALERT: BREAKING NEWS

Cherubs! I'm back with the latest breaking news, and praise the Lord Almighty, you are in for a *doozy* with this one.

As we're all well aware, Logan Gray and Matthew Cole have been cast as co-stars in the upcoming romantic film *Write Anything* and Garbage Gray actually had the nerve to insult his colleague.

Well! Apparently, the infamous trash fire of a human being has changed his mind about Matthew Cole. The two were seen cozying up to each other on set in a scene that wasn't scripted.

Don't believe me? HERE'S A WHOLE ASS PHOTO TO PROVE IT.

[Photo taken by paparazzi from across the street: a blurred image, but it's obvious that Logan is stand ing beside Matt at a table with coffee. Logan has a towel over his shoulders as Mattie puts a hand on his arm. They're both smiling at each other with some attraction in their gazes.]

I can't believe that someone like Mattie Cole would sink low enough to consider Gray—but, well, the immaculate Willow

Grace made a similar mistake and had to live with the consequences. Seems like not many people can resist the charm of the devil.

Signing off,

Angel

Project X Schedule

August 3: Flirtatious conversation—you need people to think you're starting to like each other, make sure you sell it!

August 7: Dinner date at Alli Mai, have a visibly good time

August 13: Interview with Pop! Movie Magazine; LG to apologize for insulting MC and say he's enjoyed MC as a costar with heavy emphasis on *enjoy*

August 20: Rumor to be leaked by unknown source (i.e.: me) that you both have started a relationship

September 1: Announcement that you are, in fact, official

LOGAN

ALLI MAI—A restaurant popular with celebrities, often the backdrop of many photos taken by the paparazzi. Dave's hoping we'll get seen again. It's six by the time Matt and I are finishing up on set, and the reservation's for seven. Matt says he's just going to head over to the Winchester to change. We obviously don't want to share a car to the hotel. It's enough that we spent the entire day in character and that we'll have to eat dinner together for our second act of the day. He says he'll walk. "It's only thirty minutes from here."

"Only?"

"Walking is good for you."

Yeah. I don't care. Last time I walked anywhere in public, I was chased down by people with cameras, flash going off in my face every three seconds. I ask one of the drivers on site to take me to the hotel. We pass Mattie as we pull out from the studio. He's talking to someone on the phone, laughing. I'm jealous of people like him. Doesn't seem like he has a care in the world.

It pisses me off.

Only a little.

After I've freshened up, I wait for Matt in the lobby, with its old-school leather Chesterfield chairs. Days of nonstop filming are starting to get to me. My neck is sore with stress. Shit. I used to be able to handle shooting without much of an issue. Being high probably helped. I can't afford to lose it. This movie's my only shot to make a comeback. Enough of a splash to be welcomed into the industry so that I can start getting jobs again. I blew all my money years ago. Been depending on my dad. (I really hope that particular detail never leaks to the tabloids.) If I can get my life back in order, I can tell him to fuck off. Feel free for once.

The scene Matt and I worked on today was in a constructed apartment for a house party. Keith's character, Paul, had just introduced us. A problem, because Quinn had just spent the last five minutes unknowingly trash-talking the romance author Riley Mason right to his face. Now, even the joyful Riley can't fucking stand Quinn. Maybe Matt had an easy time with that scene because it's not far off from how he feels about me anyway. Ha.

Matt's better to work with than I expected. Yeah, there're a few lines here or there that are hollow as hell, and Dave has to call cut and walk onto set to talk him through it, but— well, he isn't as bad as the table read, anyway. His acting skills have improved since *Love Me Dearly*, too. I shouldn't have said he has zero talent in that interview. I feel bad about it now, but it might be awkward to bring it up and apologize out of nowhere.

Like I've summoned him with my thought alone, Matt— *Mattie*—pops up behind me with a bright as fuck smile. I turn away before he can speak. Save it for the tabloids. I drive him to Alli Mai in my Porsche, which I'd left in the hotel's garage. I hadn't planned on driving much when I'll be on set almost every day, but I brought it anyway. I'm wearing my regular attire. Black t-shirt, ripped black jeans, black boots. Mattie, meanwhile, is wearing a pink graphic t-shirt and faded light blue jeans and yellow sneakers. Maybe we should've tried to coordinate, to make it look a little more convincing that a goth would be going on a date with a rainbow-colored golden retriever.

Our seats are center stage, right next to a huge plate-glass window that looks out on Santa Monica Boulevard in the heart of Hollywood. Could Dave have been any more obvious? The waitress is stammering with nerves as she asks us if we'd like anything to drink. But she's blushing at Matt, not me. That's new.

I lean back in my seat, staring openly at Matthew, while he fiddles with his hands, looking around at his surroundings like a nervous kid. I snort.

He frowns. "What?"

"Nothing."

"Well, it's not nothing if you're laughing at me."

I lean forward. "Careful. We're supposed to like each other, remember?"

He bites his lip. Something he does a lot, I've realized. "Sorry. I'm a little more snappy than usual. Just...tired."

"Yeah. Well. Filming every day for twelve hours can do that." The waitress brings the water and takes our orders. Mattie asks for sweet potato fries while I'm fine with my bourbon. She nods and whisks away. I take a sip of my water. "This is your first major role," I say. "How does it feel?"

He squints his eyes at me. "What're you doing?"

"What do you mean?" I raise a hand at him, gesturing at I don't know what. "I'm trying to get to know you. Have an actual conversation. Is that okay?"

He's still skeptical. Suspicious. "Yeah. Sure." He plays with his napkin. "It's exciting, but it's—you know, it's also really stressful. There's a lot of pressure. Like this is the role that can define my entire career, and if I don't do well, or the movie bombs, then I'll fail."

I understand that feeling of pressure. But even if the movie doesn't do well, Mattie will be fine. Hollywood would give a golden boy like him a second chance. "You can only focus on yourself, right? Concentrate on your skill. Everything else tends to follow."

His expression is thoughtful. "That's good advice."

The waitress returns with shaking hands. She puts the bourbon in front of me and leaves quickly.

"If you don't mind me asking," he says, "I saw in interviews that you didn't like the idea of craft."

"I don't."

I know what he's said in interviews, but... "Why?"

"Craft is a set of rules made up by people who want to gatekeep what is technically good and what is not. If they get to have the power to decide what's good, then they have the power of who makes it in this industry. Not a shocker that we're surrounded by a bunch of white men, right?"

"I've always thought craft was more like guidelines," Matt says. "Take it or leave it. Do what works for us individually."

"What works for you?"

He gives a self-conscious smile. "Personalization. I know, it's a little expected."

"Yeah, well." I eye him for a second. "You need to have lived experiences to pull from, for personalization to work."

He meets my gaze. "Why would you assume I don't have any experiences?"

Because he's so *innocent*. He's a fucking cinnamon roll. "Tell me. What've you experienced?" I add, before he can speak, "Start with romance."

"Why there?"

"I need to know what you're like as a boyfriend to be more convincing." Also, I'm nosy as fuck.

He shrugs, but seems embarrassed. "I've never actually had a partner."

I squint at him. I have the feeling that there's more to the story. "But you've been on dates, right?"

"Here and there." He seems nervous.

"Have you had sex?"

His eyes glint. He's pissed off. "Is that any of your business?"

I watch him. Funny enough, I get the feeling that he's had sex before. A lot. I recognize the typical way he won't meet my eye, like he's flustered and ashamed and trying to hide the fact that he's had a shit ton of casual sex and one-night stands. Interesting. He isn't the innocent golden boy everyone thinks he is. That just makes me more curious.

Matt looks away, arms crossed. "There was this one guy that I was casually seeing for a while, but it never really went anywhere. I've just been too busy, you know? With the filming and everything."

"Bullshit." I take a sip of bourbon.

"What?"

"That's bull. That's what everyone says when they're scared to date. *I'm busy.*" I snort.

His expression is tight. "Tell me more about you, then. Why were you in a fake relationship with Willow Grace?"

"She needed the publicity, and I wasn't working yet. We

both got some spotlight out of it, and then I was cast in this film, so I guess it worked."

"Any real relationships?"

"Nope." I smile. "Unlike you, I have the time. People just can't fucking stand me."

Matt sits straighter in his seat. The waitress returns with his fries. "Thanks," he says with a smile at her that makes her turn even redder. When she's left again, he plays with a fry like he doesn't plan on eating. The food here sucks. "I want to challenge you a little, if you don't mind."

Okay. Also interesting. "Fine."

"You say people can't stand you, with this tone like—I don't know, you can't do anything about it. But you can. You could change your behavior, if you wanted to."

"You know that Riley *saving* Quinn is just supposed to stay in the film, right?" That trope has always annoyed the hell out of me. No one can save another person.

"I don't think you're as much of a jerk as you pretend to be. I think it's another role that you choose to perform."

"Oh, really?" Another sip.

"I saw you helping out that assistant," he says. "Andrew."

"I didn't realize you really were a stalker, Mattie."

"You're a lot kinder than anyone would think, when you want to be."

"Emphasis on *when I want to be*," I say. "I don't want to be kind very often."

"Why not?"

"What's with the twenty-one questions?"

"I think it's so that you don't have to worry about anyone getting close to you. It's your defense. That's what I think."

I spin my bourbon around in my glass. He's right. I've already discovered all of this on my own. It's the mask that I choose. It's a little annoying that he would judge that choice with a steady, holier-than-thou gaze.

"You've got a guard, too, right?" I say. "Too busy to date. Focus on your work. Try so hard to be perfect. Maybe you're not in a position to judge."

Matt's voice is lower. "I'm not judging you."

"Sure."

I drain my bourbon and think of ordering another one. Matt eats a fry. He gives me a quick smile. "We're supposed to be having a good time. Sorry. I got a little too serious."

"That's all right. We're actors. We analyze other people."

"True." His smile widens. "I know that we haven't gotten off on the right foot, but—well, I wanted to say I'm grateful to be working with you." He looks away awkwardly. "I—uh—admire you a lot. As an actor, I mean."

I raise an eyebrow. "Yeah?"

"You're amazing."

He still won't look at me. It's a little hard to figure him out right now. Is he *actually* starting to flirt with me?

I rub an impatient hand through my hair. "You're not as bad as I thought."

He looks up, surprised.

"I misspoke. At that interview, I mean. I shouldn't have said you have zero talent without giving you a chance."

"My table read was pretty bad," he admits.

"Yeah, it was. But you came on a full two months after I did. I had a chance to get to know Quinn more. You've still got some areas to work on, sure," I say, "but I wanted to say that I'm sorry."

He looks pleasantly surprised. "Thanks, Gray."

We're quiet. I can see outside that there're a few guys with cameras, snapping away. Mission complete.

"Can I ask you something?" Mattie says. He's even more nervous, playing with the napkin on the table.

"Sure."

"Do you have—um—any advice for me?"

"Advice?"

"Tips," he says. "To become better."

To be a better actor? "Well, the one thing that's struck me is that you hide what you're really feeling."

"What do you mean?"

"You always have on this smile. If you got in touch with your true emotions more often, instead of trying to be positive all the time, you might get realer with yourself. Authentic. That'll let you express more emotion at the end of the day."

He doesn't say anything to this. I can't tell if he's peeved that I basically called him fake, or if he's taking it in. "Yeah," he finally says. "I think I know what you mean." He nods, meeting my eye. "Thank you."

Huh. Wasn't expecting that reaction. There's more, I can tell—something he's thinking, maybe on the edge of saying, but he changes his mind and picks up his glass of water. There's no point in staying here much longer. Dave's revised schedule will have us announcing that we're officially boyfriends in a few weeks. This was the easy part. That's when the real work will begin.

More cameras click. Some heads are turning. So much attention, so many whispers. Mattie squirms.

I smirk. "You're an actor, you know," I tell him. "You might want to get a little more comfortable with the spotlight."

He scratches an ear. "I've always hated being the center of attention."

I almost laugh, before I realize he isn't joking. I want to say something sarcastic. Maybe this isn't the best industry for him. But I don't know. I feel a little bad for golden boy. I'm not bad with the spotlight. I'm used to it. But I've had my days, too, when I can't stand being around so many people, watching my every move.

"Wanna get out of here?"

"And end the date? Dave said we should be together for at least two hours. Make it look like we're having a good time."

"Yeah, well. We're not having a good time. Might as well hang out somewhere else."

He looks like the brainiac A+ student who was just offered pot by the bad boy behind the bleachers. "I don't know."

I roll my eyes. "Come on, Matt. Fuck it. Let's go."

MATTIE

I THINK GRAY might be taking me on his idea of a good date—not that we're actually on a date. It's not hard to remember that. Gray barely talks to me in the car, except to grumble that the food at the restaurant is shit. He drives me to a taco truck about fifteen minutes away, across empty avenues and boulevards, beneath underpasses and past the glimmering glass of shops and restaurants, the expected avenues lined with palm trees.

It's chillier now that it's night, open windows letting in a cool breeze. I have no idea where we are when we reach a parking lot that's empty except for a couple sitting at a bench. After placing an order for sweet potato and plantain tacos, we sit on the edge of the sidewalk and—

"Holy God."

He smirks. He can be so smug. "Yup."

"How is it so juicy?"

"I know."

We finish eating in silence. Gray dusts his hands off. "You have tacos in—Georgia, right? That's where you're from?"

I stare at him, not sure if he's joking. "*What*? Gray—yes, of course we have tacos in Georgia."

He shrugs. "I wouldn't know. It's the South. All I ever hear about the South is that there's a shit ton of racism and anti-gay churches and shit like that."

"How does that translate into *no tacos?*"

"Fuck, Matt. I was just messing around, okay?"

I squint at him, not sure if he was really kidding or not. "Besides—I mean, yeah, there's racism and homophobia, but just like anywhere, right?"

"Sure. It's not as bad here, though."

I'm not so sure about that. I haven't dealt with anti-gay slurs since I arrived in LA, but maybe it's because I'm working on a set every day for a gay romance film. Besides that, there's *definitely* racism here. It's just the kind that's hidden behind smiles.

"Don't you ever deal with racism?" I ask.

"Yeah, I used to get the obvious racist shit on socials. But some people look at me and assume I'm white. They don't realize that my mom's Roxane Taylor."

She was a huge actress in the '90s, but she hasn't starred in a film in a while. She just kind of . . . disappeared. I lean forward to listen, knees to my chest, interested to hear more.

"White people think I'm safe for them to be racist to," he says. "Like they'll say fucked up shit, and then I'll be like—you know I'm Black, right? And then they scramble. Sometimes the looks on their faces are worth it." Gray leans back on his hands, staring blankly at nothing. "I think about it a lot. How fucked up it is that I probably only got as far as I did because my skin isn't as dark as my mom's."

I nod. "I know what you mean. I'm Black, but—I don't know, I think some people would rather think I'm an *ambiguous race* or a white person with a strong tan. I feel guilty, sometimes, knowing I got this role because of colorism."

"Colorism, and the fact that you're a good actor."

"Oh, so I'm a good actor, now? Earlier you only said I was better than you thought I would be."

He rolls his eyes at me. He pulls out his phone and checks the time. I feel a pinch of disappointment. I'm actually enjoying being with Gray right now—seeing this side of him that isn't his usual forced role. I'm a little relieved when he puts the phone away and doesn't suggest that we leave.

"What was it like, growing up in LA as a child star?" I ask him. "Having a movie star for a mom and a famous director and producer for a dad?"

He clenches his jaw, and I suddenly feel like I've overstepped. It felt like a safer question to ask to get to know him—safer than asking about his later years, anyway.

"Not as glamorous as you'd think," he says. "There were a lot of rules. Ways I was expected to act. Sometimes I envied kids who didn't have to deal with that bullshit. Could just have a normal life and go to school and have friends and hang out at the movies, instead of being the kid on the movie screen."

"That's funny. I'd look at someone like you and dream about having your life instead."

"We should've met when we were kids and switched."

"Someone probably would've figured it out eventually."

"The thing I envied the most was this idea I got in my head," he says, "that if I wasn't famous, I could've been out as bisexual if I wanted to."

"You couldn't be out?"

"Not really. Not before I said fuck it and started to do whatever the hell I wanted to."

I feel a small rush, a jolt of excitement, at the idea of doing whatever the hell I want to.

"By the time I turned twelve, I knew I was bi," he says, "but the industry only pretends to be progressive. They refuse to show our stories. Still ruled by white straight guys who think only one kind of story sells, so those are the ones that get greenlit, over and over again. I was told it wasn't a good image, being out as bi, because I was supposed to be this heartthrob for teen girls." He sighs. "Plus there's the usual biphobic bullshit. People saying I'm just confused. I need to make up my mind. I'm bi because I'm a slut. It's a stereotype to be a bi person who enjoys sex. I think I hated that I couldn't be myself because of a stereotype, so I had as much sex as I fucking wanted."

My face heats up when he meets my eye. I look away quickly. "I wasn't really able to be out, either," I tell him, speaking fast to cover up my embarrassment. "My dad thinks it's wrong that I'm gay. He was raised as a conservative Christian, so he had me going to church every Sunday. The Bible didn't even originally say that homosexuality is a sin. It mentioned pedophilia. The church edited the Bible, changing pedophilia to homosexuality. Isn't that crazy?"

When I look up at Gray, I lean back. His eyes—I don't know, they've gotten hollow, shadow falling over his face as he frowns and turns his head away from me. "Yeah. Crazy."

I frown. There was a sudden shift just now, and I want to ask if he's okay, but I'm not sure he would tell me the truth anyway. We become quiet for a moment. Questions are rising. I want to ask so much about Logan's life. I'm feeling more and more curious about him. I think it was easier to say he was an asshole and leave it at that, but he's been showing me his more human layers, and—I don't know, it's surprising to see that they aren't all that bad.

Gray and I ride back to the hotel in an unexpectedly comfortable silence. Well, I don't know if he's ever really uncomfortable when he simply doesn't care, but I definitely don't feel as awkward with him as I would've yesterday. Maybe we have a chance of pulling off this publicity stunt. We might even become friends by the end of it all. Well, I shouldn't hope for *too* much.

It's almost nine by the time we say good night in the elevator. I open my hotel door and sigh as I lean against it, closing it behind me. I want to take a nap, but first I call up Emma on FaceTime—she's a night owl and goes to bed at three in the morning, so I know she's awake. She answers before the first ring has a chance to finish.

"Um, *excuse* me?" she says immediately, face so close to the camera that I can only see her nostril and cheek.

I laugh. She can be so dramatic sometimes. "What?"

She turns the phone. There's a blur of light, and then I see she's zoomed in on her laptop screen. A tabloid site has a photo of me and Gray sitting together at the table from earlier, looking comfortable and friendly. The screen is too bright to read what the blog says, but I catch a few words: *speculation, budding romance on set*. Wow. That was fast.

Emma turns the phone back around to face her. "*What* is *happening?* You're not dating Logan Gray, are you?"

I hesitate. I really, really hate lying to Emma like this. But I know I can't risk telling her the truth. As much as I love my little sister, chances are she'll spill the secret accidentally in a conversation with one of her friends. It'd be damaging if the press found out that this was just a publicity stunt—not only to me, but to Logan and the rest of the cast and everyone involved in this movie.

I try to change the subject. "Got your first week of school outfits picked out yet?"

"Nuh-uh—nope, you're not avoiding my question."

"We work together. We're just getting to know each other. Logan and I barely met a week ago," I add for good measure.

"Oh, so it's *Logan* now?"

"Emma. Come on."

"Okay, but you *have* to like him like that, right? If you're getting dinner, and you're sneaking flirty smiles with each other?"

I groan and rub a hand over my face. This isn't the first time Em's stuck her nose into my love life. I think she wants me to know that she's a supportive sister and that she doesn't care if I'm gay. She just takes it a little far sometimes.

But her questioning makes me pause, too. It's true that Logan hasn't turned out to be nearly as bad as I thought he would be. He's more fearful and cautious than I expected, afraid to let anyone in, and a part of me—the part that loves getting to know other people—wants to be given permission to access those hidden sides of him. But we're only in a fake relationship. He isn't my real boyfriend. I don't know why he would ever tell me his secrets if he doesn't tell anyone else.

"We're just getting to know each other right now," I tell her again. "That's it. Don't get excited over nothing, okay?"

She's visibly disappointed. She must think *I* am a part of the newest reality show that lets her see into the lives of the famous actors in Hollywood.

"I have to go. Tell Mom good night for me." I pause. "And Dad, too."

She nods. "Love you, Mattie."

"Love you, Em."

I change out of my clothes and pull on jogging shorts before I flop into the bed that has no business being this comfortable. I'm tired, but so grateful to be here. This is the dream, right?

I try to close my eyes and get some sleep, but I hear Gray's words echoing in my ears. Sure, I character analyzed him tonight, but he analyzed me, too. Is he right? Do I protect myself by saying I'm too busy for a relationship?

He said that I would become a better actor if I figured out how to get in touch with my real emotions—if I was more authentic with myself. It was a shock to realize he'd seen through me. It's true that I try to be perfect. If I'm not perfect and I'm not loved, then I'd have no choice but to think I might be right about myself—that I deserve this shame inside of me. Sometimes I'm worried that everyone else is right about me, too: my dad and the people at the church I used to attend and the bullies in high school who figured out I was gay. I'm worried that I'm not actually worthy of love, in the end.

This fear is getting in the way of letting my guard down—of me becoming a better actor. And, apparently, I only want to be a better actor because I need to be perfect, so that I can use my career as a wall for protection.

If that isn't a mindfuck, then I don't know what is.

I sigh and roll over, closing my eyes. It's a while before my thoughts start to quiet down and I feel sleep coming.

I wake up to the hotel phone ringing. I look around, confused for a second. Pale light filters in through a crack in the heavy curtains. I still expect to be in my bedroom back in Decatur. Then I remember, and I realize what the sound is, and—

"Shit!" I scramble out of bed, almost falling, and grab the phone. "Hello?"

"Mattie?" Dave's voice grumbles. "You okay?"

I check the time on my cell. It's nine in the morning. I have a shit ton of missed calls from the second assistant director, but my phone was on silent. I was supposed to be on set thirty minutes ago.

"I'm so sorry, Dave," I say. "I overslept, and I forgot to turn on my alarm—"

"It's all right. Breathe."

How did this even happen? It's not like I was out all night partying, which I would never do, anyway. The hours on set must've caught up with me.

"You think you're the first actor to be late?" Dave asks. I can still hear the twinge of annoyance in his voice, but it helps that he isn't yelling at me. "Just get here as quickly as possible. There're a few shots we can work on without you."

Click. I hang up the phone and try not to sink to the floor. I'm a perfectionist because I feel like I need to prove to other people that I'm worthy of love. I have to earn their love by being the best. Where did that even come from? My mom has always loved me, unconditionally, and so has Emma...but my dad, when I was younger, always shouted at me to work harder, to be the best in sports and bring home the best grades. I failed his idea of what it meant to be a man. Maybe that's affected me more than I've realized.

I can already feel the overwhelming shame of this massive mistake coming on. People are going to realize that I'm not perfect. That I'm not the golden boy of Hollywood that I've worked so hard to be. These are the moments that I wish I could be more like Gray and say fuck it—I don't care what anyone thinks. I've got a while before I can reach that place, I think.

Love in the Club

uwuhearts99

Summary:
Mattie Cole and Logan Gray can't keep their hands to themselves.

Notes:
Okay, so I KNOW this is weird, but...the idea of Mattie Cole and Logan Gray together is DOING THINGS TO ME!!! I hope y'all like this.

Chapter 1: The Club

Gray pressed a hand to Mattie's bare chest. His heart was beating rapidly in sync to the music that flowed around him. The club's lights strobed and pulsed, just like the bulge in Gray's pants, which was painfully hard to ignore.

"I never thought I would ever feel anything like this," Gray said. "You've thawed my cold heart, Mattie."

Mattie couldn't wait any longer. He wanted Gray, here and now—on the dance floor. He sank to his knees. "I'm always happy to be of service, Gray."

Gray began to unzip his jeans. Mattie slid down Gray's boxers, releasing the painful bulge. Mattie gasped. Gray was HUGE!

People began to notice, but Mattie and Gray were used to performing. They were famous actors, after all. Mattie opened his mouth wide and Gray groaned. Neither of them cared that everyone in the club was staring. This was something they had both wanted for so long, and no one was going to stop them now.

LOGAN

THE SCHEDULE FOR the day gets switched around. I've got a few scenes with Keith and a reshoot with Monica. I was supposed to focus on working with Matt. More than a few people around set are peeved. I feel bad. I'd considered sending him a text this morning to see if he wanted to ride over together. But I figured it would be better to keep some space between us. If we're not performing our characters or our fake relationship, no need to spend extra time together like we did last night. Eating tacos and talking about personal shit. Why? It'll just get too complicated after a while. I don't know. I had a good time, but when I got back to my room, I started to feel an old tension filling my chest. I'd rather not deal with it.

Matt rushes in almost an hour after call time, apologizing over and over as he's ushered to wardrobe and makeup, Dave's assistant following close behind. I snort. There've been days when I wandered onto set five hours late, cocaine still on my nose. I didn't need to work to live back then.

I've already eaten breakfast and waited for another hour in my trailer before hair and makeup came. That's the one thing I'll probably never get used to, no matter how long I'm in this industry. How many fucking hours I have to sit around doing nothing. The stand-ins help the crew make sure the lighting and blocking is as planned, and when they're done, it's like we're all waiting for someone else to say it's time to begin.

We're about to start a new scene. Monica and I sit at a kitchen table. Her black hair is pulled into a messy bun, shadows painted under her eyes. Mrs. Evans is the overworked, exhausted mother. She always has time for her son, who has been too afraid to really open himself up and risk falling in love. Figuring out any of my characters' relationships with their mothers is probably the hardest part of the job, since I'm not sure about my own relationship with my mom. We barely interact. If I ever disappointed her, she didn't show it. Just left the discipline to my dad.

She wasn't always so cold. I have memories of her smiling as I opened presents, of sitting with me by the pool of my dad's mansion. Looking back now, I understand why I'd find her crying in the bathroom sometimes. Whenever I visit her in Florida and open the cabinet over the bathroom sink, it's filled with prescription pills. Sometimes I think she hated my father as much as I do. At least she figured out how to escape him. I'm mad that she didn't take me with her.

Monica's character isn't anything like my mom, even if Monica herself tends to be cold and distant. Mrs. Evans is loving and comforting. The mother I wish I had, I guess.

"Quiet on set. Take one. Action!"

She puts a hand on my arm. "Quinn, the one thing I wish I did when I was young was follow my heart. No matter what."

God, these fucking lines. I ignore the corniness and focus. I have trouble meeting her eye. It hurts, that her character is so supportive of mine. It always hurts, just a little, whenever I see parents who love their kids, on-screen or in real life. I never had that. Why not?

"You really don't care that Riley's a guy?"

"Why would I?" Her smile is warm. "Do you love him?"

"Yes."

"Does he love you?"

"I think he might."

"Then that's all that matters." She even has tears in her eyes. My mom half stands and wraps her arms around me. I let myself think that she really is my mom, saying the words I've always needed to hear. I swallow. It's hard to keep the tears from coming. I roll my eyes. It pisses me off, it really does, that I feel so sorry for myself. But it doesn't stop the dramatic, lone tear from rolling down my face.

Dave's voice echoes. "Cut!"

I wipe my face with a palm impatiently. Monica purses her lips as she sits back into her chair. "You wet my shirt, Gray."

"Sorry. I'll try to aim my tears better next time."

She glares at me. Monica doesn't like many people. Bitter, I think, that she never got her due as an actress with so much talent. I try not to take it personally.

Dave ambles over. "That was pretty good. Possibly a little melodramatic, though."

"I agree."

"Let's try another take."

I nod. Monica and I run our lines again, and though I feel emotion well up, I try to feel more comfortable with her. Trust that she really means what she says. Envision that maybe, one day, I could have someone like her in my life. Someone who cares about me, even when I mess up. The smile I give is genuine this time. Dave says that was the better take. Rare to see a smile on my face, I guess.

Monica and I are finished for the day, so I've got my next scenes with Matt. When I'm leaving set, I see him with the stylist, who is giving instructions to the assistants. But Matt's gaze is on me. He realizes I've caught him staring. Again. He practically jumps and turns away, blushing. Interesting. Okay.

Same set, different scene, much earlier in the timeline of the story: I've invited Riley over to discuss the project we're being forced to work on together. I don't love him yet, but by this point, Riley and Quinn have a good amount of sexual tension. We constantly fight about the book's direction. Riley considers himself to be commercial, popular, more of a *guilty pleasure* sort of romance writer, whereas Quinn is a snob about his craft and writes literary books that win a shit ton of awards but almost no one reads or buys. When we're both done with hair and makeup, cameras in position and sound ready, I lean against the counter while Matt awkwardly stands in the middle of the kitchen, looking out of place and uncertain. Not sure if he's just acting that one.

This is the first scene we're shooting alone, just the two of us together. It made sense production-wise, but it's taking a second to adjust to what I'm supposed to be feeling about him. Condescension. Frustration. Attraction, and anger that I'm attracted to him.

Matt isn't exactly my type. He's shorter than me, with a smaller frame. I usually go for guys like Briggs: taller, bigger and stronger, a jerk in and out of bed. Mattie is unbearably wholesome. Like a live-action version of some cartoon

character that's filled with an overwhelming amount of innocent joy. Some people just don't have any childhood trauma,
and it shows. I'd feel like I'm dirty, somehow, if I even
considered fucking him.

Mattie takes a deep breath and gathers this look of determination. Something tells me he's struggling, too. Trying to
find even an inch of attraction for me. Organic chemistry can
be hard to get on-screen, but I've always been good at setting
aside my own feelings. Just pretend it's Briggs, standing in the
kitchen with his arms crossed, smirking down at me.

"Take one. Action!"

"Commercial is always better," Riley says. He gestures in
frustration. Unnecessary hand movement. I haven't seen Riley
gesture in many of the scenes I observed before this one.
"What's the point in writing a book if no one is even going
to read it?"

I sneer. "So you're willing to forgo your dignity for a few
extra reads?"

Riley glares. "Try a few extra thousand. I'm a bestselling
romance author for a reason."

This hits a nerve. Quinn works hard and is particular about
his craft, but he hasn't hit any bestseller lists before, something
that he's wanted for some time now. "I'm not going to become
a sellout and write the sort of book everyone will like just to
hit the bestseller list. I have my craft to think about."

"There's nothing wrong with writing a book that people
will enjoy."

There we go. Mattie's getting into it now. Leaning forward
with some softness. I glance at his mouth. I hadn't planned it,
but he's biting the corner of his lip again, waiting for my response. No, Matt isn't anything like Briggs or anyone else I've
invited into my bed before. But I wonder how fun that could

be. Figure out how to make golden boy squirm. I smirk. He stands straighter, clenching his jaw. That's one thing you learn when you've acted for most of your life. Energy is real. Feeling what another person is feeling. Matt's looking at me like he straight up saw the image that flashed through my head.

"Sure," I tell him. "Because no one enjoys reading my books."

He swallows. "I didn't say that." Pause. "I didn't mean to say that. I'm sorry. But, well, there's a reason Jake Powers asked us to work together on this one."

"Right. So I can finally get a few sales," I say. "But let's not forget he paired you with me for a reason, too. People might love your books, but they're trashed in the reviews."

Riley struggles with the truth, but only for a second. "Fine. Let's figure out a book we'd both be genuinely happy to write. Together."

"Cut!"

Dave is happy enough. "Let's go again. Pay attention to your hand movements in the beginning, all right?"

Makeup assistants come on and brush more foundation onto our faces. The lights burning on us feel hotter than usual. Or maybe the heat's coming from the certain thoughts I started to have. Matt meets my eye for a second before he looks away. Yeah. Maybe I'm starting to feel a little more attraction than I thought.

MATTIE

WHEN SHOOTING'S DONE for the day, I get undressed in my trailer and have my makeup wiped off with the help of the stylist Angela. There's a knock on the door. My shirt's off, but Angela doesn't see the problem. "Come in!"

Logan opens the door and hesitates. He probably didn't expect to see me half-naked. I didn't expect him to see me half-naked, either. My face and neck get hot. Is it just me, or does he look like he's about to laugh? "I can come back later."

"Oh, I'm sorry," Angela says. "I thought it'd be Rick or Shelly." I notice her hesitation and her careful stare, wondering if Logan Gray is visiting me because we really are falling for each other. Gossip must be on fire around set.

"That's okay," I tell her. I need to remember my second role when we're in front of other people, too. "Hey, Logan," I say, leaning into the blushing act.

Angela pats my shoulder to say she's done. I yank on the t-shirt that's been hanging off the back of my chair since this morning. I don't know why I'm so embarrassed. Gray is going to see a lot more of me over the next few months.

"Was that planned?" I ask him once Angela is gone, door shut behind her.

"I figured it might be a good moment. Let everyone see me walking into your trailer, wonder what we're doing."

I have a harder time looking at him than usual. The lingering stares he gave me on set today are burned into my memory. I didn't think the chemistry would be a problem, but I also didn't consider how much my attraction to him would distract me. I was surprised by his take on the scene. I didn't read it as having romantic or sexual tension, just anger between the two characters. If Gray keeps looking at me like that—like he's imagining a hundred and one different ways to fuck me...

He walks farther inside, picking up a magazine that belongs to one of the stylists before he tosses it back down again. "Good job today."

Does he really mean that? I can't tell. He's usually so sarcastic. "It was good working with you in a scene. Just the two of us, I mean."

He nods slowly. "You must've been looking forward to it. A change from stalking me." He pauses. "Sorry. That didn't come out the way I meant it."

I know he's caught me observing him more than a few times. My chest is on fire with embarrassment. I was starting to think we might be able to pull off this publicity stunt, but maybe that was me being too optimistic again.

"How did you mean it, then?"

"I was just trying to tease you, and...I sounded like a piece of shit. As usual." He shrugs.

"You're right. I do watch you a lot."

He quirks a brow with interest. "Why is that?"

"I already told you, didn't I?" I can't meet his eyes. "I think you're an amazing actor. I have a lot to learn from you, and...I don't know, watching you in action helps me think more about my craft."

He's quiet for long enough that I feel like I might die of humiliation. I could spontaneously combust. That's a real thing, isn't it? People randomly burst into flames with no scientific explanation.

"That's kind of you," he finally says. His voice sounds mechanical, like he's doing his best to be nice for a change, but he's a robot that's struggling with new programming.

"I'm sorry if I made you uncomfortable," I tell him. "I can stop watching, if you—"

He cuts me off. "Do you want to run lines together?"

"What?"

"Rehearse our lines." He shrugs again. He does that a lot. I think it's because he wants the world to think that he doesn't care, maybe to distract us from the question of whether he really does or not. "If you want to learn from me so badly, it'd be even better if we got together and went over the scenes."

We had the official group rehearsals, though they were rushed. I know most actors rehearse together on their own, and a part of me has wanted to ask him to read with me. My perfectionism is soothed when I practice and take the unexpected out of the equation. If I know what Logan will say and do in scene, then there isn't as much room for error. Still, I didn't want to ask him only to be shot down. And even on the small chance that he did accept, I also didn't want to be around him more than necessary.

But—well, he hasn't been so awful lately. "Really? You want to?"

He looks like he could care less what my answer will be. "Over-rehearsing takes away from the unpredictability that can make a scene more organic, but sometimes it's okay to try something new for a change, right?" His eyes become hooded, just a little, and I wonder if he has a different meaning, or if that particular moment is all in my head, too.

Logan suggests we go back to one of our hotel rooms, and I agree. We can be ourselves without having to worry about this act of pretending to like each other more than we really do. Logan says we might want to go to mine, and I wonder if he's living the typical rock star life with a trashed room and ten naked people strewn across on his bed and floor. But it isn't really any of my business, and I don't mind. My room is clean enough, and there's a separate living area space with couches where we can sit beside the balcony.

When we get to my room after riding together off set, Logan walks in and looks around curiously. I awkwardly hover in the kitchenette area. "Do you want something to drink?"

He sits on the couch, making himself comfortable. "Got any bourbon?"

"No. I'm sober."

I don't know why I told him that. People usually judge me the second I say it. They get tense, as if they think that I'm an alcoholic, which makes them uncomfortable, or they think that I'm boring, or—even worse—they think I'm judging them for drinking alcohol, when the truth is, I don't care. I'm sober because I've never liked the taste of alcohol, and because, while I want to find freedom, I don't like the idea of it happening because of something outside of myself. I don't want to feel free because I have a drink. I want to feel free because of who I am: uninhibited and unafraid.

As expected, Gray raises a judgmental brow at me, but he doesn't say anything. "Let's just get started."

Gray says he doesn't need his copy of the script, but I grab mine just in case. "Which—ah—scene should we run?" I ask, unable to look up as I sit opposite him. We're inevitably going to have to make out with each other, in front of Dave and the entire crew. Maybe it *would* be better to get that fear over with now, before I have to perform it in front of a camera.

But Logan seems oblivious to my thoughts. He leans back in the couch. "Tomorrow's scenes are in the office."

Scott's character introduces us. We—Riley and Quinn, I mean—agreed to work together on a book without meeting each other or even knowing we would be partners, and, well, the first impression really wasn't the best at the house party.

I take a moment to sink into character. I glance at Gray. His eyes are closed. Probably doing the same. Or maybe not. Maybe he's going to run through the lines half-asleep.

"It's really nice to meet you, Quinn." A sarcastic line, since the first moment I actually met him was when he was telling me my books are complete shit.

He peeks an eye open at me and says, voice dripping with derision. "Charmed."

I remember with a flinch the interview Gray had given. It wasn't my first impression of him, but it colored a lot of our first moments together. He apologized, but some of that anger and hurt is still there.

"I'm sorry," I say. "Did I do something to offend you?"

He sits up now with a smirk. "No. But your books did."

We both leave a breath for Scott's voice: Quinn!

Quinn is supposed to be drunk. His words slur. "What? I told him the same thing last night."

"How, exactly, have my books offended you?"

"By being total garbage."

"I didn't realize I would be asked to work with someone homophobic, Mr. Powers."

"Oh, no," Quinn laughs. "I'm gay, too. Why do you think they paired me with you?"

"Then what's your problem?"

"There's no soul to your work. It's painful to read. Even more painful to realize I actually have to write a book with you."

These lines hit a little harder than I was expecting them to. It feels like Logan is talking to me about my craft as an actor, and why he went out of his way to show that he didn't respect me in that interview.

"It isn't too late, you know," I tell him. "You could always back out of the contract."

Gray doesn't snap back with Quinn's response. His gaze reminds me of the way he watched me at the table read: calculating and judgmental.

I squirm under his stare. "What?"

"You sound like you're giving your best friend financial advice."

Ouch. "I was trying to sound sarcastic and upset."

"I know. You failed."

"Thanks for the honesty."

He tilts his head as he scrutinizes me. "Do you ever let yourself feel angry?"

The truth? "Not really. No."

He frowns. "Why not? Do you think it's wrong to be angry?"

I hesitate. Do I? It's true that I feel shame at the thought of being upset. These aren't very positive emotions. They're unprofessional and messy and imperfect. I'd rather pretend I don't feel anything at all than give in to anger. "I think I have a hard time feeling all emotions, not just anger."

"Why?"

Gray watches me like I'm a puzzle he wants to figure out, with that same dissecting stare. I feel awkward, but I know getting to the root of this issue will ultimately help my acting—and help the film. "My dad. I had a lot of feelings as a kid, and he always shamed me for that."

"Daddy issues, huh?" Gray says. "Who in this city doesn't have that?"

I look up at him and wonder if he includes himself in that category, but I don't have the courage to ask.

"Can't use that as an excuse for the rest of your life. Come on, Mattie," he says. "Get mad."

"I'm not sure I know how."

"Who pisses you off the most?"

"Right now? You."

"That's fair," he says without flinching. There's something about the way he's watching me now—carefully, curiously. "What pisses you off about me?"

I bite my lip. "I don't know. I guess I'm jealous."

"Jealous?"

"Not just of your acting, though I envy that, too. I'm jealous that you do whatever you want, whenever you want, not caring about what other people will think or say—even if people will hate you for it. It doesn't seem fair," I tell him, a small laugh escaping, though it sounds bitter even to my ear. "I follow all of the rules, exactly the way I'm supposed to, and you…"

He's still staring at me with that look. He doesn't answer for a while. And then he says, "Maybe you just need someone to help you break the rules."

I'm not completely sure what he means by that, but I think I have enough of an idea. My skin gets hot. He meets my eye like it's a challenge, not blinking or looking away—and then he smirks, like it was just a joke. Right. Why would Logan Gray be interested in someone like me?

"At Alli Mai," I start, then pause, struggling to gather my thoughts. "I've been thinking about what you said. About authenticity, I mean."

"Yeah?"

"Well, to be authentic," I say before taking a deep breath, trying to push the words out, "I have shame about a lot of things."

He squints at me. "Like what?"

God, this is so embarrassing to admit. "I'm ashamed that I'm gay."

He raises his eyebrows, and I wait for the barrage of judgment. How can I be ashamed of my sexuality? I'm the queer lead of a queer movie, one of the most beloved openly gay celebrities.

Logan still doesn't say anything, and I feel the need to cover up the silence. "I know," I say, forcing a laugh. "I'm a total fraud."

He frowns. "That isn't what I was going to say."

That's surprising. "What were you going to say, then?"

Logan looks away. "Just that I'm sorry, I guess. That sounds hard."

I blink and look away, too. "Oh."

"Why do you think you're ashamed?"

"My dad never accepted me the way that I needed him to."

"Right. Conservative Christian and thinks it's a sin."

I'm surprised he remembers our conversation over tacos. "Yeah. Exactly." I'm not comfortable with the spotlight on me, so I shift it to him. "What about you? Did your parents accept that you're bisexual?" He'd told me how the industry rejected him, but he never spoke about his parents.

"I don't know if my mom accepted me. We never spoke about it. She has to know by now, right? My dad—not as

97

much," Logan says. "But not because he thinks it's wrong. He was more concerned about the money. If I was going to lose out on work because I'm bi, if people wouldn't want to support his productions because of me, that kind of shit."

"Your dad didn't accept you, too, but you're not ashamed of being bi."

"No, I'm not," Logan says. "I spent too much energy not giving a fuck to care about something like that."

And that—yes, that's what I'm jealous of, what I wish I could figure out for myself.

"What're you going to do?" he asks me.

"About what?"

"The scenes with you and me."

My entire body burns. My throat closes up. "I think I was kind of hoping that those scenes would help me, actually," I say. "Help me work through the shame, I mean."

"It's funny that Riley's struggling with the same shit," he says.

"That's another reason why I was excited for the role. I hoped that Riley figuring out how to let go of his shame would help me figure out how to get rid of mine, too."

"Acting as therapy. Wouldn't be the first time."

He eyes me, as if he's started to imagine the scene, specifically, that he'd mentioned—as if maybe he's considering suggesting that we practice that scene after all, to help me shake the shame and the obvious nerves beforehand. I hope I don't regret telling him the truth. I hope he won't use this against me.

"I should try to get some sleep," he says.

"Oh." I'm surprised—rehearsing with another actor can last hours sometimes—but I don't want to push and ask him to stay. "Okay. Thanks for coming over to help." My smile is genuine this time. "You really can be kind when you want to be, you know? You're not as much of a jerk as you want people to believe." It's just another role he's playing. I shouldn't be judgmental. We're all playing roles, aren't we?

"You should post that up on socials. Get people to think you're actually in love with me."

"Why *do* you put on this act so much?" I ask him as I walk him to the door.

"How do you know it's an act? Maybe this is who I really am."

"You don't show this kinder side of you to the public. It's like you don't want people to know you can be nice sometimes."

He gives a flippant smirk that doesn't reach his eyes. "Daddy issues, I guess." He walks out, door closing behind him.

Notes of Amy Tanner (Confidential)
Patient: Logan Gray
Age: 25
Diagnosis: CPTSD

Logan told me about a memory of his father in today's session.

Jameson Gray held an industry event at his home for the celebration of the release of a film. Logan was ten years old at the time. Logan has mentioned several times now that he had no peers his own age unless he worked with them on set. He never learned how to create genuine, meaningful friendships from a young age, or learned how to feel trust in others, perhaps due to a lack of healthy familial foundation.

At this event, Logan made the mistake of dropping a glass. It shattered and grabbed the attention of several partygoers. Logan was embarrassed and afraid of his father's reaction. Jameson Gray showed an appropriate amount of affection and assurance to Logan in that moment, which was rare for his father. Logan recounted that this was one of his happiest moments in his childhood, to see his father laugh at a mistake he had made, and put a loving, assuring hand on his son's shoulder. Logan remembered that he was rarely hugged or kissed by his parents. Logan had not yet learned to expect his father's consistent cruelty as Jameson steered him away from the mess and to the privacy of Logan's bedroom. Jameson verbally abused Logan for, quote, humiliating his father. Logan remembers many of the words used: piece of shit, idiot, ungrateful. Logan tells me blithely that he believed he was lucky, then, because his father never physically abused him.

Logan still holds to a thought process that his father's abuse was "not as bad as it could be."

Perfection was expected of Logan from an early age. He rebelled against this need for perfection as he grew older and realized that nothing he did could earn his father's love or approval. Logan has since come to expect a certain level of hostility which, unfortunately, so much of the world has often obliged.

Logan's growing self-awareness for the connections of these traumatic events to his current behaviors is promising, and I have already begun to observe a great deal of improvement in the level of distrust he shows me, the staff, and the other clients. He still struggles with emotional distance, which is unusual after having been a patient here for a little over a year now.

Love in the Club

uwuhearts99

Summary:
Mattie Cole and Logan Gray can't keep their hands to themselves.

Notes:
Hear me out. Phillip Desmond is SO EFFING HOT. And Matthew Cole and Logan Gray are of course the secret hottie couple of the century. So please, enjoy this blessing that the creativity gods have bestowed upon me.

Chapter 2: The Posh Englishwolf

Phillip Desmond did not often go to the club. He was too posh for something so low class. However, the throbbing between his legs took over like an animalistic desire he could not control. He could practically smell the scent of Matthew Cole. The pheromones called to him like sweet nectar. It was a secret he had to hide, that he was an actor by day and an Alpha werewolf by night.

He walked into the club of pulsing lights. He saw Mattie at once. Mattie was dancing in the center of the floor, hands in the air and shirt off. The wretched Logan Gray was with him. Phillip knew that he needed to have Mattie to himself, whatever it would take.

Phillip pushed his way past the crowds until he finally stopped beside Mattie. He breathed in the intoxicating scent that overtook him, rushing through his blood and making his groin harden. He knew only one thing that would help.

"Matthew Cole," Phillip said. "I've been looking forward to meeting you."

Logan Gray was always jealous and protective of his boy-friend, since the first moment they'd had sex on this very dance floor. He cleared his throat. "Excuse me," he said loudly, "but who are you?"

Phillip sneered. "I am the man who is going to take your mate away from you."

LOGAN

THE BEST PART of having a coffee shop as one of the sets is getting unlimited coffee for the entire day. I've just finished up a few takes with Matt. A scene where we sit and try to work on our novel. Instead, we end up having a real conversation for the first time. The typical *getting to know you* scene, with flirtatious glances and building chemistry. I never would've thought, not for a second, that Mattie struggles with shame for being gay. He's a better actor than I gave him credit for.

We're waiting for Dave to finish an impromptu business meeting with Reynolds. If Reynolds has come and not one of the other lower ranking studio execs, something's up. I can see them outside, through the coffee shop's glass wall. They're arguing. No idea about what. Could be the fact that I'm still attached to the film, could be that the publicity is waning again, could be the lighting. Sound said something about an issue with our mics and sent someone over to take them off, so it feels like a real break without having to worry about someone listening in.

Matt isn't as awkward with me today. He doesn't look like a scared puppy, anyway. Maybe he's getting used to me. He feels my stare from across the small table we share and looks up from his phone. He offers a smile.

"My sister's sending me links on Twitter," he says. "Looks like we're trending."

He turns the screen around as proof. Yep. Dave's let the rumor drop to BuzzFeed as an "unknown source" on set, and from the top few posts, I can see that people are arguing over whether we're really dating or not. Some people are mad at the insinuation that two queer guys can't breathe the same air without wanting to fuck. Others are mad at the people who are mad for suggesting there'd be something wrong with us falling in love.

I take a sip of my coffee. "Instant headache."

He laughs. "Yeah. I usually don't pay attention to this kind of thing, but a part of me wants to see if"—he lowers his voice and glances around—"you know, it's working."

The coffee shop door opens and Dave walks in. He drags over a chair and drops into his seat beside us.

"Lay it on us," I say. "Who's getting fired?"

Matt's startled expression is funny.

Dave rolls his eyes. He isn't in the mood today. "We've got competition. Phillip Desmond is starring in a gay romance. Some shit about dogwalkers, I don't know. It was just announced last night. Inside sources tell us that the production schedule is tight." *Inside sources.* We always manage to make filmmaking sound like some sort of FBI operation. "They're trying to beat us to opening. Profit off our buzz and excitement. Reynolds wants us to move up the production schedule."

"Longer days?" I ask.

"No. Fewer takes."

It's risky, quality-wise, but I understand. Longer days and

going into overtime with this cast could mean another hundred million.

"We need you—everyone—to be more on top of things." Dave glances at Matt, who swallows with a nod. Dave taps the table as he stands back up, then hesitates. "Oh," he says, "you two should probably announce that you're official today."

He leaves. Matt's eyebrows are comically high when he meets my gaze.

"Just moving the schedule up by a few days," I say with a shrug. It's a smart move. The announcement will steal the thunder from this other movie, whatever it's called, and make people focus on us again. It might be a little obvious to anyone paying enough attention. But that doesn't really matter in the end. As long as they don't have any proof that this relationship is total bullshit.

Dave immediately shifts into the new frame of mind of moving scenes along more quickly, and after we have our replacement mics, we're finished after a few takes. The rest of the day will be for the scene with Scott's and Keith's characters as they stand in line for coffee, talking about Quinn behind his back—he takes himself too seriously, maybe someone like Riley will get him to loosen up, etc. One of the coffee shop's real baristas is there, incredibly excited to be an extra. They grab me another cup without having to ask for my order, and I blink at Matt when he ends up beside me.

"All black?" he says.

"Do you even drink coffee?"

"Sure. Caramel cappuccinos are my favorite."

I stare at him blankly, not sure if he's joking. He has that same cheerful expression on his face. Is he trying to give me the impression that he's happy to be around me now? Or is he seriously always this fucking happy?

I turn away from him, waiting for the order, and lower my voice. "Maybe we should make ourselves official in an unexpected way. Grab more attention for the spotlight." I've had practice at this.

"How so?"

"You'll end up posting to social inevitably, but we could have some fun with the paparazzi first."

I thank the barista when they hand me my coffee, and Matt and I head out of the shop. We're still in wardrobe, but at least it's more comfortable than the other outfits I've had to wear. I'm in sweatpants and a white t-shirt, giving off the vibes that I don't give a fuck. Which is, you know, accurate. Mattie's in jeans and a pink t-shirt, sneakers. The street's closed off, but there are plenty of curious onlookers from beyond the barricades. Most of them are probably tourists. Not many people in LA blink twice when they see filming for yet another movie. I notice some paparazzi and reporters chatting with publicity assistants. I give a half shrug at Mattie and offer my hand. He hesitates, but only for a second, before he takes it. I even go the extra mile and intertwine fingers.

"What the fuck do you use on your hands?" I ask. "Baby powder?"

"It's called lotion, Gray."

It's surprisingly comfortable, holding hands with him. Usually, I get itchy when any part of me feels trapped, but his hand is loose in mine, swinging a little, casual—like we really are boyfriends who wouldn't think about it twice. We walk past the line of trailers. I'm not sure if I'm just imagining the hush that falls on set, or the excited whispers from the people watching behind the barricades. He bumps my shoulder with his own and looks up at me with this smile. My heart stutters.

Just a little. He really is good at letting that *happiness joy love* thing radiate from his eyes.

No one's ever looked at me like that before. I freeze for a second, my head as empty as my expression. I forget, for that split second, that it's only an act.

His smile fades with the tilt of his head. "You all right?"

"Yeah. Sure." I take a sip of my coffee. "We probably got the shot."

He squeezes my hand and lets go, pretending that he needed his hand to pull out his phone. By the time we make it to the edge of set, to the driver waiting to take us back to the hotel, photos of us holding hands are already making the rounds on social. On the elevator, Matt asks me if I want to come over to his room. Dave already gave us the joint statement he wants us to make, but Matt suggests we take it a step further.

"My little sister is obsessed with celebrities who end up together," he says, "and she always shows me these selfies they take with their official announcements. Maybe it could be a good idea if we do one."

Usually shit like this is planned by PR—all the "natural" social media posts and selfies are scheduled, photos edited in advance and posted to Insta by some assistant. If we weren't so worried about a leak, we probably would've scheduled a photoshoot and invited TMZ. But Mattie's too fucking innocent to know the way this industry really works, and I'm not in the mood to taint him. "Yeah. Sure."

Nothing's changed in his hotel room since the last time I came over. No piles of clothes and forgotten candy wrappers and empty plates from in-room dining. He's self-conscious as he grabs his phone. "I don't think we need to be kissing or anything cheesy like that." He fiddles with his phone a little longer than necessary at the suggestion. I decide to let that one slide.

We snap a picture. I have my typical expression: intense gaze, touch of a smirk, like this is all a big fucking joke, which it is. Matt's grin brightens the entire picture. When people see it, they'll probably worry for Mattie. He looks too pure, too naïve, to be dating someone like me. He sets up his laptop, sending the photo to himself, and types out the statement from Dave, printed out on a paper along with the old schedule. I get Dave and Reynolds's fear about a leak if we trust this kind of thing to the publicity team—more mouths usually mean more gossip—but the amount of work that falls on us is a pain in the ass. Not that I'm actually doing anything. Since I don't have any socials, it's Matt's responsibility now.

As some of you have already figured out, Logan and I have started seeing each other, and we are excited to announce that we are officially partners. I'll be the first to admit that it was a pretty rough start between us, but spending time together on and off set has given me a chance to meet a different version of Logan that he rarely shows anyone else. I'm excited and honored that he's chosen to give me a chance, and I can't wait to see where our new relationship takes us.

God, Dave, can you be any cornier? But that's the point of all of this. Give the people what they want. When Matt posts the message, his socials explode. His phone starts to ring. He groans and rubs a hand through his hair.

"It's my sister," he tells me.

"I can leave, if you want to answer it."

"No, it's all right. I'll call her back later." He sends her to voicemail and closes the laptop.

"Don't you want to see what everyone's saying?"

"Not really. It doesn't matter anyway, right? It doesn't change what we've got to do." He leans back in his seat, but I think he's putting on a show of looking comfortable more than anything. "Do you ever feel...I don't know, guilty?"

"About lying to people?" I snort. "No, I don't. Half of the industry is lying. People only care if they're making money."

"I don't know if I want to be that way, too."

"Then you should find a different industry." He frowns. Maybe I'm being a little short with him. I try again. "This is innocent in comparison to half of the shit people pull, you know? Don't worry about it. You haven't sold your soul just yet."

Matt seems to consider this for a second, before he says, "Sorry, I should've asked. Do you want something to drink?"

"Still only have water?"

"Yep."

Unsurprising. I sigh. "Sure."

He fiddles around in the kitchenette area before he comes back over, offering me a glass. He sips from his own and pulls at the end of his shirt.

"I'm glad we've gotten to a better place," he says. "It's never a lot of fun, working with someone you don't get along with."

Are we in a better place? I glance up at him. The smile he offers me. It reminds me of the way he looked at me outside the coffee shop, when we were holding hands. The way he started looking at me as we sat together over tacos. That's the kind of smile that's reserved for people you care about. For friends and family and people you love. Matt and I aren't any of the above. He shouldn't be smiling at me like that.

He's probably mixing up reality with this act. That happens

a lot. It's the reason so many actors fall in love on set and then break up the second filming is done. He's becoming too comfortable. Deciding that he cares about me when he doesn't even know me. So, what? He figured out I like to be an asshole on purpose, and suddenly he's my friend now? If he knew the real me, he'd leave me in a heartbeat.

"We're not friends," I tell him.

He sucks in a quick breath, smile falling instantly.

"I don't want you to think that we are. We're working together on a film. We're in this fake relationship. But that's it."

He still doesn't answer. He blinks. Gives that *well, fuck* expression.

"Anyway. I don't want you to get the wrong idea, you know? This—these feelings we're pretending to have for each other. Don't forget it's all fake. It's just a role."

"Okay."

"I think you're starting to forget. Or mix things up, you know?"

He nods slowly. I think he's embarrassed. Not my problem.

I shouldn't have come over. That just confuses shit even more. I stand up and put the glass down on the counter. "Thanks for the water."

"Yeah. No problem."

Neither of us says anything else when I leave, slamming the door.

Video begins:

YouTube personality star Shaina Lively sits in front of bright yellow lights in her usual office space. Her eyes are wide and panicked.

"Y'all! I don't know *what* to do with the news that—oh, my God, I think I'm going to be sick! *Matthew Cole* and *Logan Gray* are in a relationship?! Please, God. Please, say it ain't so."

She seems near tears as she looks off camera, face scrunching up and eyes shining.

"Mattie is an *angel*. He's the sweetest soul to ever walk this earth, and he's Logan Gray's boyfriend?! Gray is the literal *worst*. He cheats on *everyone, probably* because he's bi! No offense to my bisexual viewers."

Shaina reaches out of frame and grabs a glass of water and drinks all of it in a few gulps. She lets out a sharp breath.

"And now it's like watching a car wreck in slow motion. Obviously Gray is going to break Mattie's heart, and Mattie—poor Mattie doesn't deserve any of this!"

She lets out a gasp and a sniffle, wiping her eyes.

"I'm sorry. It's just so sad. I can't do this...Excuse me."

Video ends.

Happily Ever After: A Memoir

by Matthew Cole

My first boyfriend wasn't really a boyfriend, only because we never used that label with each other. We were both sixteen, and he was a friend of a friend, the sort who would sit with your group at the cafeteria table and whose name you knew, even if you barely spoke to each other. My school was small enough that it was impossible to not run into classmates several times a day in the halls and by our lockers. I'd caught him looking at me a few times as I switched textbooks in between periods, and I'd caught myself looking at him a few times, too.

I wasn't out yet, and neither was he, but there was an energy that drew us together, long, silent conversations with our feelings and thoughts alone. We sat beside each other during lunch without speaking out loud and read beside each other in the library without saying hello and walked home together for several blocks while only mentioning homework or the pop quiz we'd had that day and mainly staying quiet as we sweated together in that Georgian heat.

There were openly gay people at our school, but they dealt with enough bullying that it made me even more certain I didn't want to tell anyone, not yet. But this boy—he made me wonder if it might be worth it all, the world finding out about these feelings I'd had for so long. Our first kiss wasn't very romantic. It'd happened because of another silent conversation. He only spoke to ask if I wanted to hang out. I ended up at his house after school to drink in the woods behind his backyard. It was my first time drinking beer, too, and close to being my last, before I decided I just didn't like the taste or feeling of alcohol.

But the alcohol was needed that day for the liquid courage—for both of us, I think. We didn't say anything as we drank one beer and then another. He leaned in to kiss me first, and I wasn't surprised, even though I pretended I was. We kissed and kissed and kissed for what felt like hours in the woods, though it was probably only a few minutes. I went back many more times after that. We still didn't speak at school, but I would go to his house, and eventually, he would come to mine on the days my parents had late hours at work and when my sister had to stay after school for one of her many clubs.

Our relationship ended when one day, he came over and we sat together in my bedroom. We'd already kissed that afternoon before my dad came back home from work. Maybe we should've been more careful. I should've realized that if we could speak with energy, then others could pick up on our energy, too. My dad walked by in the hall. He stopped, turned around, and looked into my open door, where I sat with my boyfriend on the floor, doing homework. My dad didn't say anything. He only eyed us before he walked away again. After my boyfriend left, my dad said at the dinner table that he didn't want "that kid" to come back over here again.

It was enough. Somehow, my boyfriend picked up on this energy, too, and he never invited me back to his house, and I never invited him back to mine.

(Revised) Project X Schedule

~~September 1:~~ August 21: Announcement that you are, in fact, official ✓

September 3: GLAAD red carpet event, first public outing as official couple. I had to kiss major ass for these invites and move around the production schedule to get you two the day off so, don't fuck this up; prep with stylists starts 8am sharp

September 16: MC interview with InStyle magazine; slip in mention about how much you're in love with LG and what it's like to work with your boyfriend in a rom com film

September 29: LG interview with GQ; be vulnerable Gray, you want to be likeable in this one; talk about your rehab, how much you've been changing, how much you want to grow and change for Matt, etc.

October 12: MC to post on Twitter and Instagram platforms updating the world about relationship and how well it's going

October 28: Vanessa Stone industry Halloween party

MATTIE

DAVE'S VOICE ECHOES. "All right, folks. It's the scene we've all been waiting for."

I take a deep breath and release it slowly through my mouth. I knew this was coming. I met with Dave, Gray, and the intimacy coordinator, Jasmine, to go over everything we'd agreed on (no simulated sex, only bare chests shown), and ensure feelings hadn't changed since the initial meeting. Jasmine is waiting near, watching for any signal from either me or Gray that we need a break.

I was starting to think that this scene—and working with Logan—wouldn't be as awkward as I was afraid it'd be, but after Gray slammed me with his *don't forget, this is all fake* speech a few days ago, it's hard to feel comfortable and safe with him again. It doesn't help that the selfie we posted, and the photo of us holding hands as we walked off set together, is absolutely everywhere. It's inescapable. I should be able to admit it, right? It was embarrassing, to be told that we're not friends in that tone as if I'm deranged.

My sister freaked out at me when she saw the announcement. "*I knew it! I knew it!*" she screamed in my ear.

My mom wasn't as enthused. "Are you sure about this, Mattie?" she asked. "From what I can see of him online, Logan Gray—he's..." She never finished that sentence.

It's harder to keep up the act that I care about Gray when he rejected me. Is it crazy of me to want to be friends with him? Maybe I was wrong. Maybe he really has been the asshole he's claimed to be all along. But something tells me that he isn't as simple as he wants me to think. I want to ask him why he's pushed me away, but he'll most likely keep pushing—and I'm not in the mood to be insulted like that again.

These are the thoughts that filter through my head as I wait on set. We're in the constructed bedroom. I should be getting into the right frame of mind for Riley. This isn't very professional of me, to be wrapped up in personal drama.

Gray looks like he could care less. He's embodied Quinn already—I can tell, the way he leans against the bedroom's desk, eyes hooded. The lights feel brighter than usual. Anyone who was unnecessary to shooting this scene was asked to leave, so at least I'm not performing for dozens of extra people. I'm still struggling with shame at the thought of being attracted to another man, let alone kissing one in front of so many people, so it helps that the set is emptier than usual. But, still—it'll be awkward as hell, purposefully getting horny in front of Dave.

And with Gray.

Riley is afraid—unsure if this is a good idea. Quinn's already proven he can't be trusted, and Riley knows that he deserves a stable, unconditional love with someone who won't go out of their way to hurt him. But Quinn...he's irresistible, and at this point in the script, the two have been writing scenes back and forth with their own main characters becoming more and more attracted to each other. They've just finished writing a scene together where their characters have admitted they want to have sex, which has become explosive tension for Riley and Quinn. This time, when Riley invites Quinn over to write together...

"Action!"

The scene was blocked, but I still feel awkward, as if I'm standing in the wrong spot. I don't know what to do with my hands. Quinn is staring at me with those eyes, letting me know just how much he wants me. We've practically told each other that we want to have sex through our characters, our story.

"Maybe this isn't a good idea," I tell him, but my voice sounds breathless. Because, no matter how shitty Quinn has been, I can't deny that I want him, too.

"It's definitely not a good idea," he says, grin growing. He pushes off from the desk and walks closer. "But maybe it'll help with our writing."

"How so?"

"Our characters are probably going to end up together, right?"

I swallow. "Yeah. Probably."

"So, it'll help to figure out what they're like in bed if we do this. Consider it character development. We're getting into their heads."

Quinn stops right in front of me, staring down at me with a smirk. That challenge in his eyes. It's so similar to the way Logan looked at me while we were on that date, watching me carefully, waiting to see what I would do or say. I blink and look away.

"Cut!"

Shit. Gray immediately breaks the stare and returns to his starting position at the desk. He knows this one is for me.

I wave at Jasmine to let her know I'm all right as Dave

clears his throat and jogs over. "Everything okay?" he asks me. "You still feeling comfortable with everything?"

Jesus. I can't even get through a scene. "Yeah. I'm fine. Sorry, I just got pulled out for a second."

"Don't worry about it. Take your time. This is the one scene we need to get right." We have the entire day scheduled for just this, even with the recent schedule cuts. Makes sense. We can't have the sex scene in a romance film look or feel awkward, even if it fades to black.

I take a deep breath. "Okay. I'm ready."

Dave walks back to the director's chair. "Action!"

The lines are smoother this time. I can feel heat building. Quinn—*Quinn*, not Logan—smirks at me as he leans forward. The intimacy coordinator offered to have us rehearse beforehand, but Gray argued it'd be better to let everything physical be spontaneous anyway. I agreed, relieved to avoid as much awkwardness as possible until this moment.

His lips brush mine. I force myself to get into it. I grab Quinn by the collar of his shirt and pull him closer to me, pressing my mouth against his, only a little self-conscious about the moan that escapes. Quinn's body tenses. He pulls back, staring at me like he's starting to see a new person—someone I haven't shown him before, maybe. He yanks me closer and kisses me again, pushing me back onto my bed this time.

He pulls off his shirt and leans over me as he kisses my neck. I open my legs for him and he makes himself comfortable, and *Quinn's*—not Logan's—hard-on presses into my leg. He lets out a breath that's too close to my ear, and I arch myself into him.

"Cut!"

Gray pushes off me instantly. He's breathing heavier, and

his smirk is gone. At least he can't pretend to be unbothered. Dave hurries back over.

"It was good, it was good," he says, hands up, "but—just a little quick, you know? It was hard to feel that growing desire that Quinn and Riley would feel. They would be more tentative still. Try going slower."

I watch Logan as he leans against the desk again. He stares at me, refusing to look away. I've been attracted to him since the moment we met. I didn't think he would be interested in someone like me, but that heat in his eyes is undeniable. This isn't just acting. Maybe we've both had some pent-up attraction for each other. Maybe that's why he pushed me away. I could be overanalyzing, but it's possible, isn't it?

Lines again, before he walks over to me. He seems more unsure of himself. This might be closer to the real Logan. He lets out a breath, then leans into me—hesitates, continues. My eyes are still open when he kisses me. I close them as I return the kiss. Slow, like Dave asked, and—I don't know, it feels better, too. One of those soft kneading kisses, a rhythm back and forth. Logan pulls away, and my hand—I didn't even notice it, but I've already begun to pull at his shirt. He tugs the tee over his head and lets it fall to the ground.

I have a moment to take him in. I remember the photos I'd seen of Logan once, back in the days when he was in and out of rehab. He'd been so thin, so it's nice to see he has some more weight on him. I touch his stomach, which clenches, as if my fingers are cold. I bite my lip, then lean up to kiss him again.

I pull him backward onto the bed. He's on top of me again. I want to roll over, to straddle his waist, but this is the position we'd decided on, and I can't change it now. He kisses me again, taking his time from my lips to my neck and my collarbone. He pulls up my shirt and I let him take it off. His kisses continue down, over my chest and stomach and to my jeans. He looks up at me from between my legs and kisses the inside of my thigh. He can probably feel my hard-on against his cheek.

"Is this all right?" he asks me. His voice is so much deeper, almost hoarse.

I nod, letting out a shaky breath. He begins to unbutton my jeans.

The scene ends. "Cut!"

He pushes away and I sit up. Neither of us can look at the other as I tug my shirt back on. Makeup and hair return to the scene, powdering my face and fiddling with the strands of my hair—they probably got messed up from being on the pillow. Dave's back, and I hear his voice distantly. I try to snap out of it, to come back to reality.

"That was great," he's telling us. "It felt more intense. You can try playing around in the next few takes with levels of emotion. Sounds good?"

I chance a look at Logan. He looks at me, too.

"Can I have a break?" I ask.

Dave blinks, then nods. "Yeah, sure."

I get up from the bed and walk off set, away from the blinding lights and watching eyes.

Video begins:

A reporter, recording on a phone, hurries toward Matthew Cole, who's wearing an expensive suit and followed by an entourage as he leaves the Winchester hotel and approaches a black car where Logan Gray waits in the back. There's already a gaggle of paparazzi snapping photos of Logan. The reporter tries to push through the five, six men that are waiting.

"Mattie! Mattie!" the reporter calls. "Why are you dating Logan Gray? Everyone wants to know!" The reporter doesn't seem to care that Logan is close enough to hear. "Why would you date someone who spoke so badly about you just a few months ago?"

Matt has been ignoring the paparazzi, but this particular question makes him pause. "I really misjudged him, I think. Logan has told me that he misjudged me, too. We should've given each other a chance."

The reporter seems excited to have caught Mattie's attention. "Why *Logan*, though? Isn't there anyone else you could date? You're an attractive guy."

Logan glances over in the background. Matt hesitates. "Logan—well, there's something special about him." He seems to blush. "Besides the fact that he's really attractive. I think there's more to him than meets the eye. Maybe everyone should be willing to give him more of a chance, too. Sorry—sorry, excuse me, I'm going to be late."

He gets into the car.

Video ends.

LOGAN

THE SILENCE IN the car, as we're driven away from the hotel, is awkward as fuck.

I'm usually okay with silence. I thrive in silence. But Matt won't even look at me—not sure if he can—and I'm having a hard time looking at him myself. He's been pissed off at me for the past week. I mean, yeah—I get it if he didn't like the way I left things in his hotel room, but I was just being honest, right? And protecting both of us, too. It won't end well if we get sucked into this lie. Someone's feelings are going to get hurt.

His anger might've been bearable on its own, but then we had to spend hours on top of each other yesterday, kissing each other, grinding against each other, feeling just how turned on we both were, and—fuck, I have to admit I'm attracted to him. I hate that I am. I hate that I'm starting to get hard again just by breathing the same air as him, remembering his soft-as-fuck hands all over me. If we didn't have this red-carpet event tonight, I'd probably have ended up in a bar or club somewhere, just to have a quickie in a stall and get some of this out of my system. And then someone would've snapped a photo, and it would've leaked that I'm cheating on Mattie, and then I would've ruined the entire fucking movie and thrown myself back onto Hollywood's blacklist again. Shit.

He hears my sigh and glances over. Matt seems uncomfortable in his blue suit, sitting on the black leather seats stiffly, like he's afraid to wrinkle his clothes. I have to admit, the stylists did a good job on him. He's got the floppy-hair heartthrob thing going on. There's a beat when he looks like he's going to say something, then thinks better of it and looks away again, out of the window and at the passing lights of the city.

Fuck it. I can't take the tension. "You meant what you said back there?"

"What?"

"About misjudging me. Giving me more of a chance." Maybe he was just acting. Maybe he was serious, and he really meant it, even after I treated him like crap.

"Would you care if I did?"

Good question. I don't bother trying to answer it. It was a weird thing to ask him anyway. I guess I'm on edge, too. It doesn't help that we've been in prep for this red-carpet event for the past couple of days. Basically just drinking water, barely eating any food for a fatphobic industry, and then hours with the stylists today...

"I did mean it," Matt says.

I can't think of anything to say to that, so we fall into silence again.

~

The car slows to a stop outside of the Beverly Hilton and we step out, doors shut behind us. It's showtime. We're immediately greeted by someone who directs us forward, and ten camera flashes go off every second, so many cameras that it's hard to tell if they belong to paparazzi or news reporters or fans from behind the barricades—and we're not even on the red carpet yet. I force on a casual smirk while Mattie's face immediately glows with a smile. I put my hand around his waist, and he puts a hand on my back, and minders guide us down a lane separated by velvet ropes. We haven't been nominated for anything, but we're still getting a shit ton of attention, people calling our names, asking questions, someone even shouting at us to kiss each other.

We're led toward a partition, where Audrey's been waiting with Matt's manager under the big tent. Other actors, musicians, and stars mill around with their entourages, fluffing out dresses and brushing off invisible lint from shoulders and giving each other air kisses. Audrey gives me the same thin-lipped glare I'm used to getting from her, as if she's trying to telepathically send a message: *don't fuck this up, Gray.* We've worked together for the past three years now. She's the manager I've had the longest, by far, since the others tended to drop me after a few months. I don't know what the hell my father's paying her to stick with me.

Matt hugs Paola, because of course he does, and his eyes shine with excitement as minders direct us to the edge of the carpet. Our managers speak to some reporters, handing them tip sheets, and Matt and I are asked to step forward separately. I stand in front of the GLAAD backgrounds, turning one way and the other with my usual smirk. Matt does the same, following me up the carpet with a dazzling smile. We answer questions all the while.

"How's the filming of *Write Anything* going, Logan?"

"Better, now that I'm in love with my co-star."

"Logan, what is it like working with your boyfriend on set?"

"It makes our jobs easier, having the roles of characters who're in love."

"Mr. Gray," one reporter calls, "I can't help but feel that your responses to these questions are a bit practiced."

I stop posing. "What?"

The reporter continues. "There've been suggestions that your whirlwind romance with Matt has been a little too convenient, given that you began to date each other just as interest in the film was slipping. What're your thoughts?"

I freeze. I shouldn't. I need to be on my game, and Dave had prepped us to respond to questions like this, too, in case they came up. I should know what to do, but the words dry in my mouth. I usually have my lines memorized better than this. A few glances are exchanged, a few more photos taken. I swallow and look at Matt, who has been watching. He walks over and takes my hand. I wasn't expecting to actually feel comforted, when he glides a thumb over my knuckles.

"We're celebrities," Matt says. "There's always going to be speculation. Questions about why we're together and whether what we feel for each other is real. But I know what is true. I love him."

Maybe it's because I'm getting to know Matt more that I recognize the clench in his jaw, but only for a moment. A guy like Matthew Cole has to hate lying to the entire world like this. I squeeze his hand gratefully for saving my ass, but he doesn't acknowledge me. We're asked to take the last few shots together. He practically shimmers.

I don't know what possesses me to say it. It's been on my mind for the past few days, and it comes out with no warning now. "I'm sorry," I mutter, leaning in closer. "If I hurt your feelings, I mean, in the hotel the other night."

"Probably not the right time to talk about this, Gray," he whispers back. He meets my eye, grins, then leans up. I swallow, but I can't hesitate too long—I lean down, too, and kiss him. I would've thought that after making out with him for hours I would be tired of it, but the kiss sends a familiar spark through me, and I feel myself leaning closer to keep kissing him, keep touching him, even with so many people watching—but he pulls away, threading his fingers through mine.

We walk up the path, still holding hands, until we reach the front doors that lead to the hall, round tables set up with water glasses and flowers. The room is dark, even though the stage is lit up. Matt slips his hand out of mine, and under the cover of darkness, he stops forcing himself to smile at me every three seconds. It's embarrassing to admit to myself, but I want him to smile at me again. I want to go back to acting like we're in love.

"I wasn't trying to hurt your feelings," I mumble.

"Time and place, Gray."

"Fuck time and place," I whisper, leaning into him. "I'm trying to have a real conversation with you."

That was the wrong thing to say. He turns, glaring, like he doesn't give a fuck who sees or hears now. "No, that's what *I* was trying to do, Logan. I was trying to be real with you, and you—"

He cuts himself off, like he suddenly remembers himself. It was nice to see some anger from him, but I don't think he agrees. He stares forward at the stage expressionlessly, his face only lighting up when a woman taps him on the shoulder and says how much she loved him in *Love Me Dearly*. He thanks her, and when she leaves, his expression falls again.

"I was just trying to protect us," I tell him. "Something like this . . . It can get confusing."

"Are you confused?" he asks. "Because I'm not. I wasn't, anyway, before..." He sighs. "Forget it. I don't want to talk about this right now."

"I do. I'm tired of this awkward tension between us."

"You probably should've thought of that before you treated me like shit," he says, "at the hotel room, at the table read, and in that fucking interview."

Matt stands up with no warning and pushes the chair in.

"Where're you going?"

"Bathroom."

And he leaves without another word.

MATTIE

I HURRY DOWN the hall and to the bathroom, swinging the door open and shut behind me. It's a private bathroom, flowers everywhere, even a couch along the wall. I grip the edges of the sink and breathe as I stare at myself in the mirror.

I shouldn't have stormed out like that. Who knows if someone was watching, even listening to our entire conversation? But I couldn't stand being with Logan another second. His apologies—God, it's hard to believe anything with him right now, and it hasn't helped that I haven't been able to look at him all night without remembering the scene we shot yesterday. I could feel Logan glancing at me throughout the entire car ride, watching me like he was thinking of the scene, too. I wasn't sure if it was just my imagination, that I could practically feel his desire radiating from his skin. I had to keep shifting to hide my lap. It'd been torture, the hours of scripted foreplay without touching him the way I wanted to.

There's a knock on the door. I take a breath and splash some water on my face. Another knock. I turn around and open the door with a smile that instantly drops. It's Logan. His mouth is open, like he's going to speak but he's unsure of what he's going to say. He leans in and kisses me instead, and I tug him closer by the waist. He pushes me against the wall, slamming the door shut behind him, and grinds a leg in between mine so that I gasp into his mouth.

He pulls away again.

"What the hell?" I say, but it's more like a whisper.

"Sorry. I was just trying to make sure you're okay."

"That's a hell of a way of asking."

"Are you okay?"

"Why?" I ask. "You don't care."

He shuts his mouth.

"We're not actually friends, remember?" I tell him. "We can't forget that we're faking everything."

"Keep your voice down," he mutters.

Even with the door shut, I know that he's right, but I can't stop my rising anger. Maybe that's a good thing. "You're confusing the hell out of me," I tell him.

"I know. I'm sorry."

"What was that?" I ask him. "Why are you treating me like shit?"

"I don't—" He pauses. He stops and breathes for a long time. And I stand there, watching him and waiting. It's fine. I can be patient. He tries again. "I don't think you'd actually want to have any sort of connection with me," he says, "if you knew the real me."

"That's not for you to decide," I tell him. "That's up to me, right? And from what you've shown me, when you're being real and vulnerable . . . I wouldn't mind being friends with you, Logan. The real you. Not this person you pretend to be.

Trying to hurt me on purpose? It was messed up of you to do that."

He swallows visibly. "You have no idea who I am."

"Then show me."

His gaze drops. He seems so defeated. Maybe he's right. Maybe I shouldn't want to get to know him more, when he's already proven to me what he's capable of—the kind of cruelty that knocks the wind out of me, that leaves me feeling so unsettled and insecure. But I'm sure he's feeling the same way. Is it wrong, that I want to help him? Is it bad, that I want to kiss him again?

"You're not the monster you think you are," I tell him. He won't look at me. "If you don't want to be friends, then—all right, fine. That's your decision. But if you do want to try to have some kind of relationship outside of the acting and pretending to be boyfriends, then I'm here for it. But I've got a boundary, too. You can't treat me like that again. Not like you did the other day. Okay?"

He glances up. He looks like a puppy that knows he's done something wrong. "I do," he says. "Want to be friends, I mean."

When he says friends, I'm not sure which kind he means: the kind who sit together, chatting and laughing and sharing vulnerabilities? The sort who end up in bed together at the end of the night? Both?

He clenches his jaw. "We did the important job," he says. "The red carpet. Do you want to leave? We can go somewhere else."

The way he's watching me, I get what he's suggesting, what he's offering. I stop myself from pressing against him again. "Where? The hotel?"

"We can get a ride to my apartment. It's closer."

I take a breath. This feels like such a bad idea. A part of me even wonders if this is why he apologized—to make me trust him enough to sleep with him before he drops me again. But I want to believe in him more than that. And besides—I'm on the edge of desperation, too.

"Yeah. All right."

LOGAN

WE SLIP OUT without either of our publicists noticing and find the driver through the back exit, into the garage where he's smoking beside the car. When we're dropped off at my apartment, I ask Matt to wait outside for a second while I grab a garbage bag and throw away all the shit that's disgusting, the forgotten food on the countertops and empty takeout containers. I stuff the dishes into the dishwasher and throw all my clothes into the laundry basket. I even sweep and wipe off the sticky surfaces. I open the windows and spray some air freshener. I don't know why I'm so nervous.

Get it together, Gray. This isn't some high school crush coming over for movie night. I never even had that experience. I've only ever acted the role. My first film was when I was seven years old. The son of a real estate broker who kills himself. I walked into the office and found his body. Actually won an award for that one, even though I didn't watch the movie itself until I was about twelve. From there, I was cemented as one of Hollywood's child stars. My roles weren't as heavy after that. I was cast in action-adventure films for kids, had a couple of stints for shows on the Disney Channel as the cute love interest.

My biggest role, the one that made me a household name, was for my film as a teenage rock star in a boy band. My character never actually came out in the movie, but it was heavily implied that I was in love with the band's lead singer, another guy, before the ending gave me some throwaway kiss scene with a girl who'd been a groupie. It pissed me off that no one was brave enough to have an openly gay character on movie screens, so I came out myself. I was sixteen. Shit was pretty fucked up before, but I think that's the moment everything really started to spiral downhill.

I buzz Mattie in and he knocks on the door a minute later, bright smile on his face, like usual, as if we didn't spend all of yesterday dry humping each other and an entire evening fighting. Like we'd never had a problem where I treated him like trash because that smile of his scares me too much. I remember when I purposefully tried to piss him off in his hotel room while we were running lines, just to get some sort of reaction that wasn't . . . this. I refused to believe he's always this happy. Glad I've started to see some other emotion from him, too.

"Thanks for inviting me over," he says. His suit's jacket is over his arm. He looks around in awe. "Jesus. You live here? Well, I mean, that makes sense. Your dad's Jameson Gray."

My father's name shutters something in me. "I've been pretty successful on my own, too, you know." I say that, even though I've blown all my money and I *do* live here because of my dad.

He winces. "Sorry."

I shrug, reaching out a hand for his jacket so I can toss it on the back of a chair with mine. "I guess it's true that I had a step up over other people." I won't be one of those celebrities born with a silver spoon in their ass but tells the world they're self-made. "Something to drink? Wait—you only drink water, right?"

He laughs. "That's not what being sober means."

"I've got cranberry juice, lemon juice—some orange juice…" All chasers and mixers.

He raises an eyebrow at me. "Just water, thanks."

I grab him a glass and we spread out on the gray sofa's sectional. I try not to think about how, almost two months ago now, Briggs came over and we had a three-day spree of nonstop cocaine and sex, starting right here on this couch. Mattie's completely unaware as he sits down comfortably, still gazing around at the apartment. The place *is* a little much. It has a minimalist style of white shining walls, stark furniture, a ceiling that's two stories tall. The living room and kitchen are overlooked by the loft that acts as my bedroom.

My dad bought the apartment for me when I moved out of his place, the day I turned twenty. That's when I first went to rehab. I'd thought I was lucky then. Even when I was being a rebellious piece of shit, my dad was willing to support me. I should've realized that giving me a place to stay, where he still controlled all the money and the bills, was just another way to have power over me.

"Did you want to go over lines?" Matt asks, shyly, as if he doesn't know why he's here.

"Wasn't planning on it."

He hesitates. Takes a sip of water. "What were you planning?"

"I'm not going to fuck you, Matt." Well, maybe that's not completely true.

He snorts. "You really don't care about tact, do you?"

"Not at all."

"Fine. Why'd you ask me over?"

I shrug. "To talk. Apparently we're friends now. Isn't this what friends do?"

He laughs. "Haven't you ever had friends before, Logan?"

Clearly he means it as a joke, but... "No."

Mattie frowns. "Really?"

Briggs is a friend, when he wants to be, but he's only interested when he wants sex. I don't know if that counts as a friendship. Any friend I had as a kid, working movies and shows, wasn't really normal. They were my colleagues. Julie was the closest to being a friend, once, since we shared episodes here and there over at Disney. Now, the only time we speak is when we're in a scene together.

"I'm not sure how to do this," I tell him. This is what I'm supposed to do, right? Be vulnerable and shit?

He's watching me closely. "I've fallen out of touch with my old friends from high school," he says, "and now I'm this outsider trying to break into the industry, and... I don't know. I empathize. It can be lonely out here. LA really does fit that stereotype."

"Yeah. Maybe that's why I like to act like a piece of shit. At least I know what to expect."

I was joking—sort of—but he doesn't laugh. "Have you always felt like you had to have this guard up to protect yourself?"

No, I wasn't always this way. Everything started to change when I came out as bisexual. Angry messages from parents saying I wasn't child-friendly anymore. Castmates giving me the cold shoulder. There was the seedier side, too. I was only sixteen, but forty- and fifty- and sixty-year-old producers and actors would invite me over to their homes, pretending they wanted to be a mentor.

"It isn't easy to be out in this industry." It was hard to feel safe. Hard to feel like I could be myself. "What's the point in being vulnerable and showing your true self when you know you're only going to be hated anyway?" I ask him.

He's honest. "I don't know."

"I accepted the role I was given. If everyone's going to hate me no matter what I do, then fine. I'll give them a reason to hate me." I shrug. "It was what people wanted. I just gave them what they wanted."

"That isn't fair to yourself, though."

"Yeah, well." God, I could use a drink. I'd feel a little self-conscious drinking in front of Matt, though, with his sober holiness and everything. "What about you? Why do you keep a guard up?"

"My dad. All of that shame I feel. But I want to change. I want to be comfortable sharing the real me, and being loved for the real me. That's what I deserve." He meets my eye, even if it's a little shyly. "That's what you deserve, too."

I want to believe him. I really do.

He bites his lip. "Can I ask you something?" I nod. "How do you—" He stops himself and laughs a little. "This is a weird question, but how do you not give a fuck?"

I snort, and his grin grows. "Not give a fuck?"

"Don't laugh at me."

"I mean—shit, I think the first step is realizing that people are going to think what they want to think, no matter what you do. I had to learn that the hard way, I guess. No matter what I do or say, people will always treat me the way they want to treat me."

Matt nods. "What's that saying? What people think of you are reflections of themselves, right?"

"So, fuck it. I would rather be myself, free, than caged and treated like shit anyway."

Something shifts in his gaze. "I want to join you there," he tells me. "Feeling free. Sometimes I think it's about taking the jump and just doing it, not being scared about what happens next."

Is he flirting with me again? I think he might be. There's some heat in his eyes, and I have to admit, it's hard to get the expressions and sounds he was making on set out of my head. "Maybe I didn't invite you over just to talk."

He hesitates, then stands up. Mattie seems so shy and innocent, but he has more of a take-charge attitude than I would've expected. Even those scenes earlier...I mean, fuck. It was like a different version of him came out.

Matt takes his time as he straddles me, one leg on either side, and sits in my lap. "This okay?" he asks.

"We made out for the cast and crew. Why wouldn't it be?" He blushes, but he waits, watching. Forcing me to speak. "Yeah. This is okay."

He kisses me. The scenes we did earlier were torture. I think most people would assume I'd get off on it, but working on set in front of everyone, only for my body to take over? Not fun. I can't force my body not to be turned on. It's easier when I'm not attracted to the person I'm working with. It's better for concentration. But Matt—the way he surprised me every time he grabbed me...

His voice is low, hoarse. "How do you like to be touched?"

"What?"

"Do you like to be touched soft? Hard?"

Never would've expected words like that out of golden boy's mouth. "Rougher."

Fingers yank my hair, pulling my head back. My groan is

embarrassing, only because it's for innocent little Mattie. Not so innocent after all, I guess.

"Like that?" he asks, but the smile in his voice lets me know exactly what he's doing.

"Yeah. Like that."

He grinds into me and kisses my neck. "I really wanted to do this earlier," he says, voice heavier.

My hands slip into his waistband, but he pulls back. I stare up at him. Watch as the heat in his gaze cools with hesitation. He bites his lip. Something I'd like to be doing, too. "Are we— I just want to make sure we..."

I tilt my head to the side, waiting.

He sighs. "Maybe this isn't a good idea. What if it gets too confusing, like you said?"

"Actors hook up all the time, Matt."

"Right, but not all actors are in relationships as a publicity stunt."

"You think we're going to start to believe we're really in a relationship if we fuck?"

"Maybe?"

I'm not about to force him into something he doesn't want. I'm disappointed, sure, but I shrug. "All right. Let's stop."

He's still on my lap. Watching me with a gaze that lets me know how much he wants to keep going. My smirk grows.

"Don't laugh at me," he says.

A small laugh escapes. "I'm not."

He kisses me again. Slowly, pulling me closer by the chin. His hand runs into my hair and pulls my head back again so that he has access to bite my neck. I hiss, and he kisses me apologetically.

"I didn't realize you were this aggressive."

"I'm not aggressive."

"Sure. If that's what you want to think."

He might still be trying to decide if he wants to go through with this or not. My hands are on his waist, fingers pressing into his skin beneath his shirt. "Okay. Yeah. Let's go to your bedroom."

I lead him up into the loft and we sit on the edge of the bed together, taking off our shoes and unbuttoning our shirts. Shyness is still there, but it's easy to forget about that when you're horny as fuck. We kiss slowly as we lean back onto the bed, pressing our bodies together. Just doing what feels good. What feels right. We're freer without the stage directions and coordination. We don't have to worry about whether we're too loud for the camera or if we're making the right expressions. Don't have to worry about our characters. Our shirts are off and our hands are everywhere. I love losing myself like this. No more thinking necessary.

Matt's more thoughtful. His gaze is always on me, watching for my reaction. He straddles me again—he must love that position—as he reaches for my zipper. "This okay?"

"You ask that a lot."

"Yeah. I want to make sure you're all right. Consent and all."

"I'm fine."

He yanks off my pants and boxers. He isn't as shy as he's been when he looks at me lying beneath him, naked. It doesn't feel fair that he still has clothes on. He lets a hand trace over my chest and down my stomach and between my legs. He grips me—fingers tightening with just the right amount of pressure. He smiles when I gasp.

"You're more experienced than I thought you'd be."

He leans down to kiss the inside of my thigh. My breath is

hitchy. Usually I'm the one on my knees, making people gasp for me. "There was this one guy, a couple of years ago..."

He licks the tip of my dick. Fuck. I try to thrust up into his mouth, but he pushes me back down by my waist. Why is it always the innocent-looking ones who're secretly power whores? He grins at me. "Be patient."

"Come on, Matt. I hate teasing."

"Maybe I should just stop, then."

"Wait. Okay."

"Say please, if you really want it."

I snort.

He sits up, staring down at me with a playful grin, but his eyes—damn, his eyes are hooded. He's serious. He'll wait as long as it takes. I'm getting harder, breath rougher. I'm usually a total bottom for guys like Briggs. Didn't think I'm such a sub that I'd even end up begging to be controlled by someone like Mattie Cole. God. That's a new low.

"Fine." I'm a little pissed that I give in so easily. "Please."

He rubs a hand over my hair and kisses me again, before he gets back to work—head between my legs, taking his time with every lick, never taking me into his mouth the way I need it. It's been too long since I've come with anything but my right hand, and the pressure is building. I'm desperate for more contact.

"Please, Matt." I'll beg if I have to. "Fuck. Please, I can't—"

He takes mercy and starts to suck. I grab his head, but he yanks my hands away and pins them to my side. Shit. He and his friend must've had a fuck ton of practice. I'm just starting to think that I'm finally going to come when he stops. He wipes his mouth, smile gone but that same look in his eyes, as he unzips and pulls off his own pants and boxers. He sits on top of my chest, hand in my hair, guiding my head forward.

"Is this okay?" he asks.

Fuck, yes. I open my mouth. This is what I'm used to. Making other people feel good. I love this moment, messing around with someone new for the first time, figuring out their body and what they like. It doesn't take much to figure out Matt, the softer pressure he wants and the spots that have him bucking over me. As much control as Matt had before, he's lost it all now. He's squirming, practically crying, even cursing. Never heard so many fucks fly out of golden boy's mouth before. Unsurprising. I know that I'm good.

He grips my hair tightly, thrusting into me, then pulls back at the last second, right before I think he's about to come. He repositions himself again, pressing our dicks together and gripping them with a hand. We fall into gasping, moaning, skin sticking together and kissing in between breaths. He comes first, all over my stomach and chest, but I'm close behind.

He collapses on top of me. "Oh, my God." That's all he'll say. He kisses my neck, then rolls off to lie on his back. "Oh, my God. That was great."

The sex wasn't technically that special. We did the basics. Not a thousand and one different positions. No tying up and blindfolds and gags, no floggings and candle wax. And yet...It felt a lot more intense than the sex I've had in a while. I rub my eyebrow and turn away, lying on my side, my back to him.

Matt puts a hand on my shoulder. I almost shrug him off. "Hey," he says. "You okay?"

I don't know. I feel like I'm shutting down. There're some memories I'd rather not think about. Briggs helps me forget them, the way he slaps me around. Tells me I'm a piece of shit. I want to hear it. Matt's hand is too gentle, too tender, as he rubs my arm up and down, like he's trying to comfort me.

"Yeah. I don't know. Maybe you should go," I tell him.

His hand stops. "Don't do this again, Logan."

"Do what?"

"Treat me like this." He turns me over and forces me to look at him. "Talk it through, whatever's bothering you. But I'm not going to be kicked out of your apartment after having sex with you."

Matt frowns, watching me, waiting for my reaction. But I don't know what to say.

"What's going on?" he says. His voice is hoarse. He sounds more concerned now.

I shake my head. "Nothing."

He pauses for a while. He looks like he's thinking hard. "I can give you space," he eventually says, voice low, "if that's what you need. But something tells me you don't really want to be alone. Is that true? I'll leave, if you want me to."

I don't even know what I want. I sit up and put my head in my hands, elbows on my knees. "I'm sorry. Yeah. I think I need space."

A part of me is hoping he'll act like he did in bed. Tell me that he isn't leaving, not even if I beg. But he doesn't speak as he gets up and gathers his clothes. He hesitates at the top of the stairs. "See you at work, Gray." He turns away again. I hear the door slam shut below, and I fall into my sheets. Shit. Matt's probably not going to trust me at all after this.

Notes of Amy Tanner (Confidential)
Patient: Logan Gray
Age: 25
Diagnosis: CPTSD

Logan cannot speak about what happened without dissociating. I'm worried I may have pushed him too far this afternoon in asking if there was a link between the way he treated his romantic and sexual partners and the trauma, and he began to dissociate for several minutes.

There has been some progress in speaking openly about difficult memories. In group, he spoke about when he was sixteen years old and publicly came out as bisexual. Logan was under an immense amount of stress from the producers of a movie he had finished filming, and social media was abusive towards him as well.

Logan had no support system in place, as his mother had left the year before. His father returned home from a business trip and gave Logan the silent treatment for several days, which Logan has stated was one of his father's favorite forms of punishment. When Logan's father next spoke to him, he told Logan to go onto social media and announce that he had been confused or was only going through a phase, or something to that effect. His father stated that Logan "was only looking for attention by claiming he was bisexual" and that Logan would "lose the production company money."

When Logan refused, his father implied that Logan "took too much after his slut of a mother," which in particular implied Logan's traumas to that point were to blame on Logan himself.

There was a tense moment in the group, when Logan's roommate, Tom, asked if Logan had ever considered speaking publicly about the abuse he faced, which Logan took as an attack and suggestion that he would have spoken publicly if the abuse had been serious enough, or that, perhaps, the abuse was not so bad if he'd remained silent about it for so many years. Logan reacted angrily and sarcastically, and insulted Tom, digging into Tom's own wounds that he had shared in group. I was pleased to observe the open communication in the group as they investigated the assumptions made, and was particularly pleased when Logan admitted he made a mistake and apologized.

I will ask Logan next week if he feels comfortable being asked about his trauma, or if he would prefer to speak about what happened at his own pace.

MATTIE

I'VE BEEN AVOIDING speaking to Emma and my mom. I feel guilty, lying to them so much about this fake relationship with Logan—though, now, I'm not even sure if it's as fake as we think. We've had sex. Logan says this doesn't have to complicate things, but my feelings are already getting tangled. I care about him. I care as another human being, who is worried about someone who is clearly struggling with something, even if he won't say what. I care about him as a colleague, and as a friend. Pretending to be in love with him has only made things blurrier. I don't actually love him. I don't know him well enough to be in love with Logan. But when I force myself to feel emotions for the sake of acting, it can all get mixed up at times, trying to remember what is and isn't reality.

But the way he shut me out—literally and emotionally...By the time I get back to the hotel and have a shower, I'm feeling more alone than I ever have in this city. I feel tendrils of old shame curl through me. I had sex with another man again. I close my eyes and breathe through it. Remind myself that I'm worthy of love, even if some people in my life have acted like I'm not. I breathe until I can feel the shame fading.

I dry off and get dressed before I call Emma. She's already been at Sarah Lawrence for the past couple of weeks, and I've been texting with her on and off, asking how she's liking her classes and if she's settled into her dorm all right. Her text messages started out as enthusiastic, excited—but they've been getting shorter, until they became one-word responses. I assumed she was just getting too busy for her big brother, but when she answers the FaceTime, I see the shadows under her eyes. She looks like she's been crying.

"Emma?" I say, turning away from the balcony. "Are you okay?"

She shrugs. "Yeah."

I should've called her sooner to see how she was doing. My mom said she was fine, but Emma wouldn't have told her the truth, especially when our mom tends to worry so much. We really are siblings. I never open up to people when I'm struggling, either. Maybe I shouldn't judge Logan for that so much, for not being able to open up to me.

"What's going on?" I ask, sitting on the side of my bed. "Why do you look so upset?"

She won't look me in the eye. "I don't know."

"Come on, Em. Talk to me."

Emma sighs. "It's just...hard. Everyone's making friends with everyone else, and I feel like the weird kid sitting alone in the cafeteria." Em was in a bunch of clubs in high school, constantly surrounded with friends she'd had since she was little. She'd said she hadn't planned on telling anyone that she was my sister. She didn't want attention just because of me, from people who were more interested in my fame than who she was as a person.

"It's only been a couple of weeks," I say. "Maybe you'll get to know your classmates, and things will be different before you know it." She doesn't react. I feel my protective big brother urge come over me, and I wish I could be there to give her a hug in person and tell her it'll be all right. "Are you liking your classes, at least?"

"They're okay," she mumbles.

Sometimes I wish I had gone to college instead of immediately jumping into this acting career. Who knows? Maybe I would've learned that I love art, or music, or something else. But I'd decided this was going to be my dream, and I stuck with it. Emma isn't even sure what she wants to do yet. I'm excited for her to learn more about herself. But seeing her like this without that excited spark in her eye is killing me.

"I'm sorry, Em," I tell her. "I wish I could do something to help."

"It's fine," she tells me. "You can't fix everything, you know." I think she might be a little annoyed. "And besides, it's okay to just let someone be sad sometimes."

When did she get so wise? "You're right. I'm sorry."

She sighs. "It kind of sucks to realize I'm not as perfect as I thought I was. And it's like, now, I have to figure out who I am when I'm not surrounded by people who think I'm the best at everything."

I nod. I absolutely know what she means. It's almost painful, how much I can relate.

❧

The other cast members have met up for drinks after a full day of work a few times, and I've joined them twice, sipping ginger ale. Monica never seems overly enthused with me, but I think she might be that way with everyone. Keith is as funny in real life as he is in the script, and Scott has made me feel welcome...but sitting with them, I still felt like I had something to prove.

Julie especially has always gone out of her way to be friendly and supportive, as if she still feels bad for the way that Logan treated me at the table read. We only have one scene together: she's Lauren, the bitter ex-girlfriend who demands to know why I'm good enough for Quinn. We meet in my apartment when she barges in, enraged. "Quinn only thinks he's gay because of *you*," she says, pointing a finger into my chest. "Do you know how upsetting it is to be the last girlfriend of a gay man? Everyone is going to think that something is wrong with *me* now."

The scene runs smoothly, and at the end of it, Julie offers me a smile. "Coffee?"

I'm done for the day, so I nod. "Yeah. That'd be great."

Luckily, Logan isn't on set today, so I haven't had to deal with the awful awkwardness of avoiding him, trying not to remember what his dick looked and felt and tasted like, trying to pretend that I'm completely unaffected by the fact that he kicked me out of his apartment after having sex with him last night. I try to push all of that out of my mind as Julie and I leave the studio for the coffee shop around the corner, the same one we've been filming in. We place our orders and, after we have our cups, we sit at the same table where Logan and I filmed.

"It was great working with you today," Julie says, sipping her latte.

"Same. I'm sorry if this is weird fanboying, but I still can't get over the fact that I'm in a scene with you. I used to watch you on TV as a kid."

She laughs. "That isn't weird at all. Are you enjoying filming?"

"Yeah. It took a second to figure Riley out, but I think I've got him."

"I think so, too. You've really brought layers to him."

I'm hesitant. I have the feeling that Julie asked me here for a specific reason, but she isn't getting to the point or asking any questions. Maybe she really did only want to have a conversation. "How about you? How do you feel about Lauren?"

She sighs. "I'll be honest," she says. She leans in, glancing around to make sure no one is listening. "Lauren feels like a stereotype. I've been trying to figure out a way to bring her more depth, but it's kind of weird to have this role. I hate when women are pitted against gay men like this, you know?"

I nod. It's definitely a character I've seen before. "It's like women are turned into the enemy in any story with gay men."

"Exactly!" She leans back in her seat, smiling at me. "See? You get it, Mattie. I tried to talk to Dave about it, but he said his hands were tied. Lauren was the villain in the book, so this is the script." She sighs.

I'm curious, but I don't know how to ask this question without sounding judgmental. "Why did you take the role?"

She doesn't seem to be offended, but she doesn't meet my eye, either. "You could say that the Disney years are long gone."

Julie Rodriguez, having a hard time finding work? I'd assume everyone would jump at the chance to have her in their film. She's stunning, and talented, and hardworking, and kind, and—well, she's also a woman. I shouldn't forget my own privilege as a cis guy.

"It's like child stars have an even earlier expiration date," she says. "Expiration dates, as if we humans are products instead of living, breathing people. But it's true. If we don't manage to redefine ourselves, no one in this industry takes us seriously because we got typecast so young. I stopped getting auditions the second I turned eighteen. I'm twenty-five now. I probably have another good ten years before people decide I'm too old to be hired in any prominent roles just because I'm a woman, let alone because I'm also a former child star."

"I had no idea it was that hard."

"Oh, yeah," she says. "But there isn't any point in complaining. You've got struggles, too, I'm sure."

Everything she said makes me think about Logan. I wonder if he had any trouble finding work because of his history as a child star also. Maybe Julie can feel me wondering this, or maybe Logan just happens to be on her mind, too.

"How're things going with you and Gray?" she says, glancing up at me from her coffee.

The question catches me off guard. I sit up straight. "Great. Really great."

She nods slowly. "I have to admit, I was kind of shocked to see that you're dating him," she says. "Not that it's any of my business, but the way he's treated you so far hasn't been—well, it hasn't been the best."

That's true, more than she even realizes. "Yeah. He apologized for that, and we got to know each other pretty well."

"Really?" she asks, watching me carefully. "We'd been friends once, you know, when we were on set together."

"Oh," I say. He'd made it sound like he never had a single friend in his life.

She nods. "We got pretty close, and then one day—out of nowhere, he pulled away and told me to leave him alone. I was only fifteen at the time, so it really hurt my feelings." I want to tell her it still hurts, even at twenty-three. "I don't know why I'm telling you all of this. I just want you to be careful. Gray can be really hurtful."

"Do you know why?" I ask her. "I've always had the sense there's something else going on, but he just won't say what it is."

"I have, too," she says, "but—no, he never opens up about it. Anyway, like I said," she says, smiling again, "it isn't my business. I hope it works out for both of you. I wouldn't wish broken hearts on anyone."

"Thank you." I bite my lip in the growing silence as she finishes her latte. I've barely touched my cappuccino. This might be a mistake, but something tells me I can trust Julie. She seems open and genuine, and like she's the only person who could help me figure out how to handle Gray and this fake relationship of ours.

"Can I tell you something?"

"Yeah, of course."

I lower my voice. "Logan."

"Yeah?" she says, squinting in confusion.

"He and I," I say, looking around to make sure no one is nearby. "Well, we're not actually together."

The second I say the words, an *ahhhh, that makes sense* expression crosses her face. She really must have been trying to puzzle it out, why Logan and I would ever end up together.

I keep going. "It's a publicity stunt for the marketing of the movie. We didn't even like each other at first."

If Julie is judgmental of me getting strung along into a scheme like this, she keeps it to herself. "Right. I could tell."

"We've started to get to know each other more so that the relationship seems legit, but... Well, it's still not real, even though..." I shift in my seat uncomfortably. "We had sex."

She doesn't even blink as she listens. Logan must have sex

with everyone. She only nods with a small frown of interest, taking in everything I'm saying.

"But, like you said, he immediately pushed me away again, and now everything is a mess."

"First," she says, "thank you for trusting me with that. Seriously. It's hard to find people who're open-hearted. It's nice to have a real conversation with you."

"Same," I say, feeling comfortable warmth spread through me.

"Second," she says, "I'm really sorry that Logan is treating you badly. You deserve more than that."

I know this for a fact, but I can't stop thinking about him. "I think that I'm struggling because I still feel drawn to him."

"Why?"

I take a sip of my cappuccino. "I feel so . . . restrained. I never let myself go." I can never let myself be totally uninhibited. "Logan offers me a sense of freedom. He doesn't care what anyone thinks. I like to be close to him because of that."

"Even when he's hurting you."

She's right. I shake my head. "It's messed up, isn't it?"

"I'm not judging you. You can't help feeling pulled in by him. But I hope you can find that sense of freedom without Logan, too."

"I'm curious about him. It feels like there're so many layers, and when I was trying to get to know him better, I couldn't get past those walls."

"They're impossibly high."

I nod. "It's probably better if I just focus on myself. Figure out how to feel free for me, like you said, instead of wanting to rely on Logan."

Her smile is full of compassion. "Probably."

Julie is staying at her apartment instead of the hotel, but she takes the thirty-minute walk with me to the Winchester, chatting about nothing—favorite recent films and actors' performances, recent favorite games (she loves *Stardew Valley*, too). We say goodbye with a hug in front of the lobby.

"Thank you for listening," I tell her. "I haven't had anyone else to talk to about this."

"You're welcome, Mattie," she says. "Anytime. Seriously, okay?"

It's only when I'm upstairs in my room that I pull out my phone and see that I have a text from Gray. Sorry. I needed some time to myself. I shouldn't have kicked you out.

I hesitate, then type. It's okay. You needed space. I wish he would open up and tell me why, but I already have a feeling that he won't. I remember how he turned away from me while we were in bed. His entire body had begun to shiver. He'd scared me, and I reached for him as he pulled away.

I type again. Do you want to come over? We don't have to do anything. If you need to be with someone, I'm here.

He doesn't answer, so I start to get ready for an early night in. I order some in-room dining and watch a film. I've always enjoyed watching movies and dissecting actors and studying them. I'm not sure I'll ever be as talented as most of the actors I see on screens. It's just as I'm finishing up dinner that I see Logan had sent a text almost twenty minutes ago.

Okay. I'll come over. As the phone is in my hand, it buzzes again. I'm here.

There's a knock on the door. I open it. He won't meet my gaze as he stands in the threshold. He's showered, his hair still damp, and he put on a fresh black t-shirt and black jeans. His eyes are red. I can't tell if he's high or if it's because he was crying or if it's just allergies. I step aside, and he walks in. He stands in the middle of the room, like he isn't sure where he wants to go or what he wants to do.

"You can sit on the bed, if you want," I tell him.

His gaze snaps to me. He almost seems defensive. "You said you didn't want to do anything."

I frown. "I don't. And it's okay if you don't want to, either. We don't have to do anything you don't want to do, Gray. Ever."

This takes his defenses down a little more. He sits on the edge of the bed. Maybe I was right. Having sex yesterday was a bad idea.

I sit down beside him, careful not to touch him. "What's going on?" I ask him. "It's okay if you don't want to tell me, but—damn, Gray. I'm worried about you."

He swallows and sits straighter. He still can't look at me. "I think—uh, I don't know. Having sex with you fucked me up a little."

Did I hurt him? I always try to be careful about consent. Some of the guys I've had sex with have been annoyed with me, asking for permission every three seconds, but I'm more attracted to communication in bed. Making sure we're still on the same page together, still wanting to be touched in the same way. I don't like to assume consent can't and won't change from one minute to the next. But maybe I messed up. I could've gotten too caught up in the moment without realizing that Gray wanted to stop.

"Did I...I didn't force you to do something, did I?"

"No," he says. "No, nothing like that. It was—I don't know, different from the sort of sex I usually have, and it triggered me, I guess, bringing back different memories. Usually the feelings go away and I can go to bed and wake up and I'll be fine, but this time I started to get scared I would hurt myself. I didn't want to be alone tonight."

My heart clenches at the thought of him hurting himself. "I'm really glad you came over." I don't realize I've reached for his hand until I'm gripping it. He looks down at our hands for a moment, before he pushes mine away and stands up. He looks anxious, walking to the balcony and walking back again.

"Do you want to talk?" I ask him. "We don't have to if you don't want to. We can just watch a movie. I finished dinner, but I can order you something."

"Yeah," he says. "I want to talk. I haven't told anyone before, and you—this is so fucked up, but you're so innocent. Golden boy, right?"

Golden boy? I'm having a hard time following him.

"It's like I want to punish myself even more by telling you. No one else. To see how disgusted you are." He looks like he's either about to laugh or cry. I want to take his hand again, suggest that he sit down, but he walks out of reach. "Maybe I'm hoping you'll be kind enough to accept me anyway. Seems like you've been kind enough to accept everything else about me, right?"

I don't know what to say. I hesitate. "I accept," I say, slowly, "that you're struggling, and hurting, and because of that you're hurting other people, too. Purposefully, sometimes, because you're scared." I want him to tell me this secret of his, but I don't want to rush him and scare him off. "What's going on, Logan?"

I wait quietly as he keeps pacing, until finally he stops and sits on the edge of the bed again, farther away from me. "When I was seven, my dad was trying to get me a role on that movie. Won my first Oscar for it. My dad was struggling. The production company was going under. He needed to use me, I think. Use my success to bring back some attention to our family name. It ended up working for him. But he needed me to get that role, first, and there was this producer."

I think I know where this is going. My heart sinks so fast I feel sick.

"It's fucked up, right? It was only one or two times with that guy. I can't even remember what happened, exactly. I don't even know who he is. Just flashes. It was so long ago. How can it fuck me up so much, if I can't even remember? That first guy was probably the one who fucked me up the most. After that, there were actors or producers at industry parties. I knew what to expect, so it wasn't as hard to stomach over the years. I don't know. Maybe I'm lying to myself. People knew what was going on. They knew what would happen if I went into a bedroom alone with someone. No one batted an eye. That shit happens all the time. I don't know why it fucked me up as much as it did. Everyone else got over it fine, right?"

I feel so sick that I think I'm going to cry. I don't want to cry. I don't want to make this about me right now. I want to support Gray. I don't know if I can. "I'm so sorry," I tell him. That's all I can manage. "I'm so, so sorry that happened to you."

He shrugs. "Like I said. It happens all the time. But it's made me feel like I'm disgusting. I can't get out of my own skin. I can't escape my own body. And everyone who hates me— yeah, sometimes I think I deserve it because..." He doesn't finish his sentence.

"But you didn't do anything, Logan," I tell him. "All those disgusting creeps who abused you—" *Abused.* It's such a euphemism. I grimace. "They should be punished for what they did to you."

And his own father? His own dad sent him to be hurt, purposefully, for his own benefit. How fucked up is that? I struggle with my dad—and yeah, the shit he's done has hurt me, too, but *this* ...

I let out a shaky breath. "Can I...I don't know what to do. What do you need?"

Logan pauses. He looks at me. "What?"

"Is there anything I can do to help you?"

Logan blinks. "No one's ever asked me that before." He looks at me like he isn't sure if he can really trust me. "Maybe. I don't know. Just being here with me. Lying down together. We don't even have to talk, if you don't want to."

"We can lie down and talk. That's not a problem."

It's awkward at first. He lies down on his side. I don't touch him, but then he takes my hand and pulls it across him, so I wrap my arms around him. We try to shift around to find a comfortable position. I end up on my back, holding him as he curls into my side. We're quiet for a while. Just breathing, the movie still on in the background.

"Thanks for listening," he tells me. "Not a lot of people would've actually cared."

"I care, Gray." And I have a feeling a shit ton of people would care if he told them, too. But I can't force him to trust anyone. It's a shock, I think, that he's chosen to trust me with this. "I'm not going to judge you. I'll never ask you to do something you don't want to do."

He clutches my sides tighter.

"You're safe with me," I say. "Okay?"

"Yeah. Okay."

LOGAN

THE LINES WE'RE crossing are making things complicated. I was high and drunk when I went to Matt's hotel room and spilled the truth for the first time. I've never told anyone else about my past. No one. What was it about Matt? Maybe it was the image I couldn't get out of my head. The way he smiles at me. He didn't react the way I've always thought others would. He didn't look at me with disgust and say there must've been something I'd done. That I deserved what happened. Since the night I went to his hotel room and lay down with him for hours, and with the romance we're playing in and out of work, it's getting a little hard to remember what the lines between us are supposed to be.

We still do the public shit. Holding hands so that photos can be snapped. Eating together at restaurants for lunch. Something's different between us now, though. There was a silent comfort when we lay down beside each other in Matt's hotel room. The safe sort of quiet that doesn't need to be filled. The sort of easy calm where the two of us can meet each other's eyes and don't feel the need to immediately look away, holding the stare, seeing curiosity glint in Mattie's eyes before he reaches for my hand. Yeah. I don't think this is just an act anymore.

We start getting invited out all the time. All of the fucking time. Jesus Christ. Willow Grace reaches out to me for the first time in months, saying she wants me and Mattie to hang out with her and her new boyfriend. She just wants the attention Matt and I would bring her.

Matt's game, because he's too fucking innocent to know when he's being used, so I pick him up and drive him to the club in WeHo. One of those places where everyone's in tight dresses and heels and thousand-dollar jeans, and you've probably got to be a model or an actor or something to even get in. I hate it already. Matt winces at me. "We can always leave early, right?"

"We shouldn't have come at all."

He's been gentler with me since I told him the truth. It pisses me off. I'm not so fragile that I'll crack and break. "We're supposed to be convincing people that we're together," he says.

"You take shit too seriously."

The bouncer lets us in, and the music is loud, smell of sweet alcohol and perfume and conditioned air making me remember the days before rehab. I've fallen off the wagon, obviously, but I'm doing better than before. A couple of years back, I'd be on so much coke and Adderall when I came to a place like this that it's a wonder I'm still alive. Maybe that's partly why I haven't been going out so much. I know it'd be easy to get swept back into that old life of mine, and I'm trying not to. Really, I am.

Mattie takes my hand and we wander through the crowds, toward the VIP section where Willow said she would be. She's always been good at figuring out how to find the spotlight. Her golden dress shimmers when she turns to us with a squeal. She immediately hugs me, squishing herself against me, fingers against my ear. Probably purposeful. We had sex a few times, and the memory twinges through me, making me a little hard as she pulls away with a *fuck me* smirk.

She hugs Matt next. "It's so good to meet you!" she says loudly over the music. "I'm such a fan!"

Matt grins sheepishly. "Thanks."

Willow turns, introducing us to her boyfriend, a model named Ryan. He's hot, of course, in that white-man-with-chiseled-jaw way. He does the head nod with a smirk and eyes me in a way I recognize. A quiet invitation to follow him into a bathroom stall later, maybe. I forgot how obsessed everyone is with sex. But who am I to judge, right?

I sit down beside Matt, while he sits beside Willow. "Do you want anything to drink?" she asks him.

"Mattie's sober," I say, bored. I lean against him, arm behind his back. I realize as I'm doing it how protective it looks. Maybe that's okay.

Willow makes an annoying *that's weird* expression. "Oh!"

Matt meets my eye. I try not to laugh at how painfully uncomfortable he looks. "What've you been up to, Willow?"

"Oh, you know, auditions *everywhere*, but nothing's been good enough for me just yet."

She probably hasn't been offered any roles. Ryan leans forward. "You two look hot together."

Matt stiffens beside me. I don't think he's used to how straightforward this culture can be.

"Yeah," I tell him. "I know."

Willow frowns, not happy to be left out of the conversation.

"I'm one of the few people who can say what Logan Gray is like in bed."

Ryan laughs. "Personally, maybe, but half of this country knows what he's like in bed."

I don't like this fucking guy. Matt can probably tell. He speaks up. "Maybe Logan wouldn't want anyone to know without his permission..."

"Right. Maybe he shouldn't have leaked his own sex tapes three times."

I meet Willow's eye. So she told Ryan it was my idea, huh? Her forced smile is on the edge of threatening. "You should enjoy your time with him, Mattie," she says.

I'm pretty sure she's being sarcastic, but if Matt picks up on that, he doesn't show it. "I already am."

The music's too loud to keep shouting over, and Willow and Ryan eventually fall into their own conversation, her leg rubbing against his. We've only been here for half an hour, but I'm regretting coming. Matt's quiet, looking around, and completely out of his element. I nudge him with my shoulder. "Dance?"

"Huh?"

"Do you want to?"

He looks terrified. "Oh—no, that's..."

"You're so bottled up. Fuck."

Mattie clenches his jaw. "Yeah. I know."

"Let loose. We're here anyway, right?"

"I—I think I'm afraid I don't know how to. Let go, I mean."

"The only way to know how is to actually do it."

I sit there, waiting for him to make his decision, until finally he gives me a determined nod that makes me want to laugh. I take his hand for good measure as Willow and Ryan watch us get up from our seats. I guide him through the crowds of people grinding and tossing hair to the electro-pop beat. Matt looks scared. He's so afraid of what people think.

"What do you believe is going to happen if people start to judge you?" I ask him. "You think you're going to be killed or something?"

"It feels that way sometimes," he admits.

I laugh. "Come on." I loved dancing when I came out to clubs like this. Not something a lot of people expect out of sullen Logan Gray, but there's something about letting loose and just thinking fuck it, something about the beat of the music and all these bodies, the sweat and the touching. The energy feels like it's a piece of clothing away from an orgy. The only problem is, usually I'd be dancing with someone like Briggs, pressing my ass against them, or moving back and forth with their leg in between mine, before they invite me to the back of the club for a good time. I don't think Matt would appreciate that.

I put a hand on his shoulder and turn him around so his back is to me. I hold him by his waist and take a page from his playbook. "This okay?"

He nods. He looks like he needs my lead for the first time. "Yeah."

I press myself against him, only a little. He holds on to my arms as he grinds into me to the beat. Yeah. Dancing like this is basically sex. I have to admit, I've imagined what it'd be like to fuck him. To be inside of him. Matt starts to get into it. I press a hand against his stomach, pulling him in closer, and he lets his head fall back onto my shoulder. His eyes are closed. I love watching him like this. Love seeing him start to let go.

The song changes. He opens his eyes and pulls away and— fuck. That look he gives me. I almost want to ask, just to see what he'd say. Ask if he wants to go find a stall with me, or outside into the alley.

"Back to our seats?" I ask him.

He nods and takes my hand this time as I lead him. When we get to Willow and Ryan, I realize they'd been watching us. Willow eyes me like she's having a few memories of the times she came over to my place.

She leans over to me when we sit down. "Ryan and I would totally be up for a foursome, if you and Matt want to join."

I might've, once. A small part of me wants to ask Matt. Maybe he'd want to also. No shame in sex for fun. There's another part, though. Even bigger and harder to ignore. I can't fucking stand Willow, and I don't like her boyfriend much, either. I'd rather spend my time with Mattie, I guess.

"No, thanks."

As I drive back to the hotel, I'm lost in my thoughts. My memories of Willow. She'd tricked me, during our fake relationship. I started to think she was a friend. I believed she wasn't only interested in the spotlight and the attention. I don't know. Maybe I'm falling into the same mistake with Mattie. Maybe not.

"Thanks for pushing me to dance," Matt says. I glance over at him. "I don't know. I kind of wanted to, but I was afraid, so it was funny that you asked me at that exact moment."

"You really care that much about what people think, huh?"

"Yeah. I do."

"Sounds like a shitty way to live."

"It can be, sometimes. I always feel so self-conscious. I've gotten pretty good at pretending to be confident."

"There're some moments that shine through. I can tell when

you stop giving a fuck." He looks beautiful when it happens. Like a god. Giving in to his pleasure and power.

He grins. "This sounds crazy, but I—uh—well, I've always wanted to run through a field ass-naked. Like that's the ultimate symbol of freedom for me."

I don't say anything. I understand, wanting to let go so completely and find a burst of freedom like that. He falls quiet for a while. Lost in thought too, maybe. It's only when he glances up that he frowns.

"Logan, where're you going?"

I glance at him. "A field."

"What?"

"I'm finding you a field."

"Logan, stop messing around."

Griffith's closed, but it's easy enough to pull onto the side and walk up the road. We could jump the fence into the golf course. Matt's mouth falls open comically. "Logan, come on. I'm not running through the park naked."

I laugh. "Why not?"

"Because—shit, that's crazy! I'll get arrested!"

"Not if no one sees you." I slow, pulling to the side by one of the entrances. I turn off the engine. "I'll do it with you."

Matt's laughing. I don't think he believes me. "No. No way in hell."

I can't help but grin, watching him. "You said it was your dream, right? Just trying to help it come true."

He shakes his head, sitting back in the seat. I think he's actually considering it for a second before he shakes his head again. "I think I might be starting to think of another dream," he says.

We hold each other's gazes for a second too long. It's the kind of look I practice for movie screens. That stare where it

165

seems like we're wondering, for just that moment, if we really might be starting to fall in love. But it's more likely we're both amazed that we don't hate each other as much as we thought.

I start up the engine again. "All right. Your loss."

MATTIE

"QUIET ON SET, please! Action!"

Mrs. Evans clutches my hands painfully tight. "Please, Riley. Whatever you do—don't break my son's heart. I don't think he can take much more of a world where hearts are always broken."

"Cut!"

"Take thirteen. Action!"

Lauren flips her hair as she glares. "Riley isn't good enough for you, Quinn. He doesn't love you. Not like I did."

"Cut!"

"Ready? Action!"

Jake Powers smokes a cigarette as he looks over the manuscript. Paul stares over his shoulder. "You two managed to come up with this, huh?"

Quinn glances at me hesitantly. He takes my hand, and I turn back to Mr. Powers. "Yes. We worked all night on it."

When Logan is heading onto set for a scene with him and Keith, he catches my eye, walks over, and kisses my cheek before he keeps going. I don't have to act out the blush that heats my face. Things have shifted between us, since Logan told me about his past. He showed me a level of vulnerability that I've never seen from anyone I've dated before, and it feels like an honor, that he trusted me with this. It's not an honor that I take lightly.

I lean against the coffee table and watch as Dave speaks to them. This fake relationship has become more overwhelming than the movie. We've started to become a sort of celebrity power couple. People still trash talk Logan on social media, but more people are deciding that Logan is surprisingly soft and cute, using photos of us holding hands and kissing cheeks as evidence. He isn't the only person benefiting. People don't look at me like I'm the actor of the week anymore. Articles aren't as dismissive of me.

Besides the official schedule he handed us, Dave expects us to go on at least one public date each week, and we've started to get requests for interviews on set.

"What is it like acting with your boyfriend?" the reporter for the *Inside Hollywood* blog asks. "Is it difficult to focus?"

"No," I say—a total lie, of course. "It's helpful. I can pull from my real emotion for Riley, who is falling in love with Quinn."

The reporter asks, "Is it possible that you've mistaken your character's feelings as your own?"

Wow. They really go for the jugular, huh? "Well, that's certainly happened to other Hollywood couples, but I know that this is real love for me and Logan. I started to get to know him, not Quinn, and it was Logan that eventually won me over."

It's uncomfortable that this is a little closer to the truth than I'd like to admit.

Julie invites me and Logan to dinner with her, Scott, Monica, and Keith. Logan practically begs me not to make him go. "You'll be the only person there that doesn't hate me."

Ever since he told me what'd happened to him as a kid, I feel like I've been handed a jumble of puzzle pieces, and I'm slowly putting things together. Is this why he'd pushed Julie away when he was young? Maybe he didn't feel like he had anyone he could trust.

I hesitate. "Scott doesn't hate you."

Logan gives me a look.

This is the kind of thing that Dave would expect us to say yes to for our fake relationship. "We'll stay for an hour, tops," I tell him. "It'd look bad if we say no." Besides, I want to spend more time with the rest of the cast outside of set—but his pained expression makes my heart twinge. There's so much I don't know about him still. Maybe something that doesn't seem like a big deal to me and most people, like this dinner, would feel like torture for him. "You don't have to go if you really don't want to."

He sighs. "You want me there though, right?"

I can't lie to myself about that—or that I'm grateful when he agrees, insisting that it's okay, yes, he'll go when I ask him if he's sure.

Logan drives, and we end up at the sort of restaurant that has fairy lights strung up along the outdoor space. We get a large table near a firepit, which feels nice tonight, since the breeze is a little colder in the chilly fall air. Julie sits next to Keith, and I notice the way she leans into him. I don't think that they're officially dating, but maybe they've started to see each other privately, too. I feel a spark of jealousy at the idea of allowing a relationship to grow organically, outside of the spotlight. I glance at Logan. Then again, we probably wouldn't even hang out at all if it wasn't for this publicity stunt of a relationship.

"So, Mattie," Scott says after we've given our orders, leaning forward on his elbows. "It's been—what, three months since you moved here?"

"Just about."

"Feeling settled in?"

"I am, yeah," I say with a nod and grin. I've always liked Scott, and I like him even more after spending time with him on set. He's offered a few pointers and some advice for surviving this industry. "Don't take the franchise jobs," he said one afternoon at the coffee table. "It's good money, but you'll be stuck playing Bug Man or some shit for the rest of your life."

"I'm sure Logan has something to do with that," Scott says, smiling at Logan.

Logan sits silently, glaring off into space. I'm usually the front man of this fake relationship, taking on all the questions. I don't even mind it, not really. Those are just the roles we ended up with. But sometimes I wish he would try, even just a little. I know he's a lot kinder than this. I wish he would show that other side of himself so that others could fall in love with him, too.

Monica has never had much patience for Logan. She purses her lips in an expression that practically screams *we'll see how long that lasts*. She picks up her glass of wine and starts to drink, as if it's the only thing that will get her through the night.

Keith leans back in his seat. Keith scared me at first. He looks like the sort of white frat boy that would go out of his way to make my life a living hell in Decatur, but he's funny and has always been welcoming. Still, I also know he can't stand Logan, either. He's passive aggressive when he speaks. "I think it's safe to say that Logan is the lucky one. Seems like Matt's been keeping him on track."

Logan has no comment.

Julie takes a breath and decides to change the topic. "The new production schedule is kind of ridiculous, isn't it?" she asks.

Logan changes his mind. "What do you mean by that?" he asks Keith. *"Keeping on track."*

The silence is tense. Keith picks up his own glass. "Oh, you know. The last time we worked together, you'd come in about five hours late?"

Logan shrugs. "Yeah, well. I'm always on time now. Haven't been late once."

I feel a hit of shame. Out of everyone here, I'm the only one that'd come to set an hour after I should've. Julie notices. "Everyone's late to set at least once in their life," she says.

"Yeah, but with Gray it was every fucking day," Keith says to her. "He'd show up drunk or high on coke. So excuse me for not jumping for joy just because he's actually doing his job and behaving like an adult."

The quiet is painful. I look at Logan, who's started to shut down. I can see it in his eyes. I take a sip of water and clear my throat. "I understand being pissed."

"You don't have to stand up for me, Mattie," Logan mutters.

"I mean—no, I'm not standing up for you," I say. "I'm just trying to say that everyone fucks up at some point."

"Or a lot of points," Monica says beneath her breath.

"Or a lot of points," I amend. "But we've got to allow space for someone to change, too, right? Logan's always on time. He works harder than anyone I know—harder than me." It's partly this act we're putting on, and partly me, I think, that has me reaching for the hand he has on the table. I cover it with mine. He tenses for a second before he takes a breath and relaxes. "I'm a better actor because of Logan, so from my perspective, this movie is as good as it's going to be because of him."

I'm not sure if Logan's just playing a role also when he turns his hand over. He lets me intertwine my fingers with his and he meets my eye, my heart warming. I understand why he was so uncertain that night, when he told me we shouldn't be friends. Everything's so blurred now.

Scott leans back in his seat. "That's really sweet, Mattie."

Logan and I let go. I grin. "That's what happens when you act in romantic comedies."

Monica's on her second glass already. "I have a hard time believing those two are actually in any kind of relationship," she says.

We all freeze. Logan glances at me.

"Why would you say that?" Julie asks. She looks at me with worry.

"I have a nose for bullshit acting," Monica says. "I've been in this industry for longer than you've been alive," she tells me, "and you and him look like people who're acting the way they think they're supposed to act if they're in a relationship. It isn't real."

My breath is caught in my throat. Keith frowns, looking between me and Monica closely. "I think it's because things are still new," I tell her. "We're still trying to figure it out ourselves and what we want our relationship to look like."

Julie's nodding a little too strongly. *Good answer*, her eyes say.

"I mean," Logan starts, and my heart drops. Maybe he'll get sick of this secret and decide to spill everything. "Yeah, this relationship is kind of bullshit, because we do have to put on an act for everyone. We're in the spotlight nonstop. It's hard to figure out who we really are with all these eyes on us."

I blink at him. I didn't expect him to speak from the heart.

"Well," Monica says, reaching for her wine again, "that's the one thing that isn't bullshit. You two are definitely in love. That's something that can't be acted easily, I'll tell you that much."

My face gets hot, but Keith is staring at me now, so I smile at Logan while he gazes at me openly. He's not forcing himself to look like he's in love with me or anything, but he's watching, as if he's curious. Am I in love with Logan? No, I don't think I am—I haven't had a chance to get to know him. Could I fall in love with Logan, the way things are going now? I look away again.

"Come on, Mon," Scott says, clapping his hands together. "It's not up to us to judge these kids and their relationship, right?"

She just purses her lips and takes another sip.

We chat a little longer until the food arrives, and then we break into separate conversations. I overhear Monica complaining about healthcare and agents while Scott listens, nodding patiently. Keith talks to Julie with a low voice, and she's smiling at him flirtatiously. Logan and I are quiet.

"Are you okay?" I ask him.

He still seems upset from earlier. "I said I didn't want to come."

"I'm sorry. I hoped you'd have a good time. We have fun together sometimes, right?"

"Yeah. That's us. Not everyone in the cast."

I look up and see that Julie's noticed. She frowns at Logan,

173

but she meets my eye. "Matt, I feel like you're not really getting a taste for what hanging out with the cast can be like."

"What's it usually like?"

"Oh, man," Keith says loudly now, "the fucking parties at hotels can get crazy as hell. Remember when Alexis invited us over for that one episode?" he asks Julie.

She laughs. "I can't believe we still managed to make it to set the next day."

Scott makes an apologetic face. "Sorry. I'm too old for that."

I grin. "It's okay. I prefer things like this anyway. Sitting and eating and actually talking, getting to know each other."

"Me, too," Julie says. "I've never been good with partying."

Keith barks a laugh. "Could've fooled me."

We all talk as we eat. Logan didn't order much, and he's barely touching his meal of quinoa something or other. He's silent—not necessarily sulking anymore, but staring off, lost in his own head. God. I hate that he's so uncomfortable and unhappy.

I take his hand under the table. "Do you want to go soon?"

He smirks. "I wanted to go about an hour ago. But it's all right. Take your time. Seriously," he says when I hesitate. "I'm fine." I get the feeling he's used to this: being in a setting where he isn't welcome and doesn't feel safe, so opts out of interacting altogether.

I bite my lip, then turn back to the table. "We should get going."

Julie looks genuinely disappointed, but she nods and stands to hug me goodbye, and I shake Keith's and Scott's hands while Monica tilts her wineglass at me. Logan barely waves as we leave, and I say over my shoulder that we'll see everyone bright and early.

"I said I was fine," he says, but I can hear the relief in his voice.

We crunch down the gravel path together, toward the street where cars are parked. "Well, I like it when we're both enjoying what we're doing. I'm sad that I pushed you to come and you didn't have a good time."

"You didn't push me to do anything."

"I knew you didn't want to come and asked you to anyway." Guilt threads through me. I'd promised him I would never force him to do anything he didn't want to do, but I pressured him into coming to this dinner. Maybe I'm not as good at respecting boundaries as I'd like to believe. Maybe that's something I can work on.

"I could've said no, if I really didn't want to be here." He hesitates as he opens the car door. "I'm dreading going home alone. I can get wrapped up in my head sometimes, and—I don't know. Would you want to come over?"

I raise a brow. It sounds like an invitation for more. Maybe that's how Logan means it, too, as he watches me, waiting to see what I'll say.

I wouldn't mind more right now. "Yeah," I say. "Sure. Let's go."

Inside Hollywood Blog

Matthew Cole and Logan Gray have been seen around town as the new Hollywood "it" couple. Interest in the pair has grown as their private romance gives audiences glimmers of the chemistry the two will share onscreen. The recent photos of public displays of affection have continued to build excitement for their film, though some continue to express their concern for Cole, given Gray's track record for cheating on partners. We'll have to see how the ending to this particular story plays out, and if Cole and Gray will have their own happily ever after.

Love in the Club

uwuhearts99

Summary:

Mattie Cole and Logan Gray can't keep their hands to themselves.

Notes:

OH MY GOD??? Did you see those photos?? They actually WENT TO THE CLUB!!!! Here's a celebratory post!

Chapter 3: The Blood Sucker

Matthew Cole was shocked. How could he have not realized the truth sooner? It was obvious, now that he thought of it, that Logan Gray was a vampire. Hadn't Gray's teeth always glimmered and seemed extra pointy? And Gray always had a particular affinity for Mattie's neck, too.

They stood at the back of the club, Phillip holding the stake that he meant to use to kill Gray. "Don't think I won't be afraid to use this," Phil said. "I will protect Matthew with my life."

"But I don't even know you," Mattie said. "Who the hell are you?"

"I am the love of your life," Phillip replied. "You simply do not know it yet."

"Bullshit," Gray growled. "You don't get to waltz into this club and demand that I hand over my boyfriend."

"Some boyfriend you are," came Phillip's retort. "You didn't even tell him the truth!"

Mattie looked between the two, uncertain. Phillip *did* have a point. Gray should have revealed that he was a vampire much, much sooner. However, he also knew he had to put a stop to this. "I don't want either of you to kill one another," he said. "Why don't we make a truce? And I know just the way to forge peace between vampire, human, and werewolf…"

He stripped off his shirt. He might have been the human, but he looked at both Gray and Phillip hungrily.

LOGAN

MATT HAS COME over to my apartment every day for a week now. It was pleasantly surprising, finding out that his sex drive is almost as high as mine. He was awkward at first, the first couple of times after I told him about my trauma—like he was afraid to touch me, afraid to be rough with me. I shut that shit down. "Don't treat me like I'm going to break. You didn't act this way before, right?" There was a glint in his eye at that one. He took it as a challenge. Had a few bite marks after that, something makeup had to spend a few extra minutes powdering.

We order Thai takeout since I don't know what the fuck to do in a kitchen, and we sit together on the couch after we've showered. We're not snuggling, exactly, when he sits with his back leaning against my arm and shoulder, feet up on the sofa. I've never had friends over in this apartment, except for people like Briggs, so it's awkward for me at first—but then one day I suddenly can't imagine being in this apartment without Matt anymore. I can't stop thinking about him. When I'm figuring out what I'll eat for dinner and want to text Matt to see what he's in the mood for. When I'm taking a shower and wonder if he'd want to try having sex in here sometime, too. Even when I'm pulling on a black t-shirt and wonder if Mattie will like it.

It's a fucking black t-shirt, Gray. Same as all the others. I think I'm losing my mind.

We lay in bed together, Matt holding my hand and rubbing a thumb over my knuckles as he stares at me. He didn't reject me when I told him about my past. He didn't tell me I was disgusting, and that he doesn't want to see me again. But the more he looks at me like that, the more my chest tightens.

He kisses the palm of my hand. "Something's different with us, right?" he whispers.

"Yeah." I'm having a harder time looking at him.

We've only got a couple more weeks of shooting when the cast is given our first public outing. It's at Vanessa Stone's annual Halloween party, though no one ever dresses up. It'll be a chance to reenter the world and schmooze as we get ready for the publicity and brutal promo tours. There'll be bullshit with social media for the others in the cast—thank God I don't have to deal with that—and interviews and sneak peaks for the film and photoshoots and red-carpet events and talk shows and . . . I'm already exhausted just thinking about it.

I'd get invited to these industry parties all the time, whether I was in a film or not, but after a while I learned to avoid them. Usually I'd end up as the party's unpaid entertainment by being wasted and having some guy offer to take me home. I'm nervous. Old habits die hard.

The party is in a sleek mansion in the Hills with all-white walls and glass, glowing lights shining and people glimmering in their makeup and outfits that cost thousands of dollars, holding glasses of wine. I hate it. Everyone's trying so hard to make everyone else believe they're more important. I want to leave as soon as I step inside.

Mattie looks downright terrified. It'd be funny if I didn't feel bad for him. I take his hand. Half continuing the act, half wanting to comfort him. I lean into his ear to whisper. "Don't worry. You don't have to impress anybody."

He doesn't seem so convinced. "If I fuck up, I could ruin my career."

I shrug. "That's true."

"Thanks, Gray."

"We could always leave."

"No. It's all right." He takes a breath and gets that look of determination in his eye that I've been growing to love. "It's part of the job, right?"

Across the room, I see Phillip Desmond nursing a glass of wine as he talks to Julie and Keith. Phillip is the star of that rival film that's trying to beat us to the release date. It's another queer romantic comedy. Two guys who fall in love while walking their dogs or some shit. What is it called? *Good Dog?*

"Isn't that Phillip Desmond?" Matt asks.

"Yep."

"Have you met him?"

"Nope."

Mattie looks at Phillip curiously.

"You should go over," I tell him.

"Are you sure?"

A part of me, a small part, was hoping he would say that he didn't want to leave me behind. But why would he? The point of this event is to meet new people, right?

He hesitates. "Why don't you come with me?"

I don't want to deal with Phillip, Keith, and Julie. Can't think of a more awkward group to stand with, all of them grinning through their teeth. "It's all right. I'll catch up with you in a second."

He still seems unsure, but he nods and approaches the group. He's greeted with warmth and love. Julie pulls him in for a hug. I grab a glass of wine from a passing waiter and walk over to the balcony to drink alone. This is usually how I end up at these events. I sip the wine and stare out at the landscape, the twinkling lights of manors and downtown LA in the distance.

Dave walks up to me. He sighs and leans against the railing. "I hate these things," he says. He found a nice suit, but he looks like he's itching in it. "It's impossible for creatives to just create. No. Now we have to kiss ass and schmooze to get our projects greenlit. And you end up directing bullshit, soul-sucking romantic comedies just to earn a production company some money, waiting for the chance to do something that makes you feel alive. No offense."

Dave's obviously already had a glass or two. I don't give a fuck. "None taken."

He sighs. "I wonder when the end of the line is, you know? How do you know when it's time to move on from an industry that doesn't want you anymore?"

I've never considered it. Walk away from acting? It's the only thing I know how to do. The only path I can see that would get me enough money to escape my dad and his control over me. But maybe getting away is as easy as leaving. Leaving my apartment, leaving the city. I don't know what the hell I would do then. Become a barista in New York, maybe. I'd just need to get comfortable with the realization that I wouldn't be living this lavish lifestyle anymore.

Dave claps a hand on my shoulder. "Just promise me one thing, Gray. Don't become a bitter old man like me, stuck in a world where you're walked all over and treated like shit. No matter how much money you make. Okay? Fuck money. Money is bullshit. These billionaires are ruining the world."

I like drunk Dave. "Yeah. Okay."

He leaves. I turn around, back leaning against the railing. I can see inside. Mattie's smiling, speaking to Phillip. Phillip Desmond is the whitest man alive. Pink skin and yellow hair, eyes so pale I can't even tell what color they are. He's laughing at something Mattie says. He leans in, a hand grazing Matt's arm. Makes sense, somehow, that they flirt the exact same way. Matt doesn't pull away. He looks a little shy. It's like that magical moment when you see two golden retrievers meet for the first time. Fuck.

I down the rest of the wine and put the glass on the railing before I head to the group, grabbing a fresh glass from a server on the way over. I stop beside Matt and take his hand. Phillip looks at our intertwined fingers, then up at me.

"Great to meet you, Logan," he says. He has a British accent. Not a fake one, like some people in this city tend to have. "Huge fan of yours."

I raise my wine to him with my free hand. "Wish I could say the same."

The silence is painful. Keith shakes his head and leaves. Mattie looks at me. Why should he be surprised? He knows who I am.

Julie rolls her eyes. "I'm sorry, Phil. Gray's socially inept."

Phillip shrugs. "That's all right. I have enough confidence that I don't need validation from strangers. Besides," he says, "it's been a nice enough evening, speaking with you and Matthew. Nothing can ruin that."

"I'm glad I met you, too," Matt says, like he's trying to make up for what I'd said. I let go of his hand and sip my wine.

"I still think we should pitch the idea," Phillip says, grin returning. He and Matt are looking at each other with that joy that makes me uncomfortable, the same happiness that Matt shows whenever he looks at me....

"What idea?" I ask.

"A rom-com pitch," Matt says, gaze a little more uncertain now. "It's great that there're two romantic comedies starring gay men coming out around the same time. But there could be more stories, you know?"

"It's a change to what we normally see," Phillip says. "We usually only get to watch tragedies, or thrillers with murder mysteries. Death follows us everywhere in these films. We should get the chance to see ourselves have a laugh, too." He meets my eye, raising his glass to his lips. I feel the strong glimmer of dislike coming from him. "Don't you think?"

"Right. Yeah. A laugh."

"The idea's actually really great," Matt says, looking at Phillip with excitement. Completely unaware that Phil and I can't stand each other. "We'd be ex-boyfriends forced to live as roommates, who still secretly have feelings for each other."

"I was thinking it could either be a feature or a series," Phil says with a shrug.

I look at Matt. "Can I talk to you for a second?"

Mattie frowns. "Okay."

We walk away far enough that we're out of earshot, though when I turn I see that Phillip's and Julie's gazes have followed us. Matt bumps a shoulder into me. "What the hell, Logan?"

"What?"

"Why were you so rude to Phil? That was really embarrassing."

"I hate the British accent."

He tilts his head to the side in confusion. "What?"

"People only give a fuck about white British men because of colonialism and racism."

"You're drunk, Gray."

"Doesn't mean it's not true."

"Phillip's really nice, if you'd give him a chance."

"Sure. The way everyone gives me a chance, right?" Why should I give him a chance when he's probably just going to treat me like shit?

"Logan," Matt says, and he sounds frustrated now—no, not just frustrated. Pissed. "Not everyone's out to get you. Not everyone automatically wants to hurt you. If you treat someone like shit right off the bat, then, yeah. Chances are they're not going to be too pleasant in return. I think you owe Phil an apology."

I've never really heard Mattie speak like this before. He isn't yelling, but his words are firm. Reminds me of when he's in bed with me, telling me what to do and how to behave. It's not as much of a turn-on right now.

"I'm going to get another drink."

"Logan. Hey."

I ignore him as I walk away. I'm only criticized by people who want me to know how much they hate me. Strangers online. My father's phone calls. It's taking me a second to separate Mattie's words from all the people who have attacked me. How do I know he's safe, and isn't trying to hurt me like everyone else? Maybe I started to trust him a little too quickly. Got wrapped up in feelings and daydreams. That's the thing with romances. They're supposed to look a certain way, right? They've got story beats they're supposed to follow, according to the movies I've worked on. They can't have heroes and love interests with the kind of trauma that takes over their body, trapping them so they don't know how to move forward. Can't have fucking rape victims. Who the hell wants to watch serious, depressing shit like that? And they absolutely must have a happily ever after. I guess that means that romances, by definition, are not for someone like me.

Another glass of the same wine from another person with a tray. In the corner of my eye, I see Matt's returned to Phillip and Julie. They're all laughing about something. My phone buzzes. When I check the screen, I see that it's Briggs.

You around?

I hesitate, then start typing. At some industry party. You're back in LA?

Yup. Only for a few days. He's probably been here for weeks already. He just didn't bother to text me. Wanna meet up tonight?

He knows I've got a boyfriend. He's never given a fuck about that.

He doesn't have to know that Matt and I aren't really together. That our relationship is bullshit, and I can do whatever the hell I want.

And I need to get out of here. I'm starting to feel stuck in my body, anxiety crawling through me.

Yeah. I'll meet you at my place.

There're a few lingering glances as I leave. Matt, across the room, does a double take. I get the feeling that he's going to try to follow me and ask me where I'm going. I put the empty glass on a table and walk fast. I pull out my keys as

I head into the night, cars parked along the circular concrete driveway, rushing past a few people who linger. I jump into my car and slam the door shut. I get a text from Matt. Where are you going? I drove him here so that we could play into the role, getting out of the car and walking into the house holding hands. It hits me as I start up the engine that it probably doesn't look great, me abandoning him at a party, but fuck it. That's expected, right? We're still playing the roles people want from us.

I peel out, hitting the curves fast. My apartment is only ten minutes away, and there's barely any traffic this late at night. Briggs is already outside, leaning against his car, arms crossed. He smirks as I step out and slam my door shut behind me. Briggs is typecast into antagonistic roles. He's most well-known for being the head of a white gang in *British Streets*, an 1800s period show, even though he's Aussie. He tends to swing baseball bats hard enough to knock people's heads off. He looks like he could do it, too. He's a foot taller than me, with muscles bulging through the t-shirt that presses against him. He buzzed his hair for the role, but the reddish-blonde fuzz is coming back in, light beard on his face.

"Good seeing you, Gray," he says.

We're not the type of friends who hug when we see each other for the first time in months. I nod toward the door and he accepts the invitation, following me into the lobby and the elevator. He shoves me against the wall and presses against me as the elevator doors shut, kissing me, hands grabbing my ass so tightly I can already tell I'm going to be bruised in the morning. He bites my neck hard enough that he might break skin. That's okay. I like pain. It's a distraction. This time, though, I remember Mattie kissing my neck. Fuck.

The elevator opens again, and Briggs follows me down the

187

short hall to my apartment, hugging me from behind so that I can feel just how—uh—excited he is as I struggle with the keys. I must be drunker than I thought. Briggs tsks in annoyance and grabs the keys from me, unlocking the door and shoving me inside. I almost trip. He shuts the door, locking it behind him.

"I've missed you," he says, walking over to me and tipping my chin up. I'm pretty sure he missed my body more than anything else.

"How's shooting going?" I ask. My words sound strange in my head, mixing together. I realize they're slurring. Briggs starts to guide me over to the couch. He puts a hand in my hair and pushes down.

"You really want to ask how the show is going right now?"

We never really talk about anything personal or private. He pushes harder, until I give in, sinking to my knees. I struggle with his zipper.

"Come on, Gray," Briggs says. "Get it together."

He always talks to me this way. I should be used to it by now. I get the zipper undone and pull out his dick. It's already half hard. He grabs a fistful of my hair and my chin, squeezing my mouth open and holding my head in place, before he starts to shove himself in my mouth. I block his dick with my tongue the first time, but I struggle to breathe when he rams it to the back of my throat. I feel like I'm going to throw up. I put a hand up on his waist, trying to push him back.

He frowns at me. "What's going on, man? You can usually take it." He grins as he thrusts and I cough, trying to pull away. "What? Is the boyfriend making you soft?"

I push him back hard enough that he lets go. I wipe the corner of my mouth. Just the mention of Matt makes my chest buzz. There're too many emotions for me to unravel, and my head's fuzzy. I start to get up.

"I don't think—you know, sorry, Briggs," I say. "Maybe you should go." He reaches for me, and I snatch my arm back. "I'm serious. I'm not in the mood."

He stares at me before he snorts, like he thinks I'm joking. When I don't laugh, he sticks his tongue into his cheek in annoyance. He pulls up his boxers and jeans, buttoning and zipping. "I just drove here for this shit?"

"Yeah. Sorry."

"You're a fucking asshole, Gray."

I frown. I don't know. Maybe being around Mattie has had an effect on me after all. "I'm an asshole for not wanting to have sex with you?"

"For being selfish, yeah."

"Sure. Okay." I turn away, toward the kitchen to get some water.

"You should be happy," he says. "Isn't this how you made your whole life? Your whole career? Letting yourself get fucked by whoever wanted to—"

I turn back around and shove him. He stumbles for a breath. And then he shoves me so hard I fall over my feet, landing partly on the edge of the center table. "Fuck!" I put a hand to my abdomen, checking for blood. I didn't break skin, but the muscle and bone there aches so much I'm not even sure I can get up again.

"You're a piece of shit, Gray," Briggs says. "You know that? You can't see how pathetic you really are."

"I have a pretty good idea of how pathetic I am," I say, wincing as I try to stand.

He doesn't like my dismissive attitude. He grabs my arm and yanks me up, tugs my arm behind my back as he pushes me into the couch. I don't even know what's happening, not really—my brain shuts down and I don't have any thoughts.

Whenever I was with those sick fucks as a kid, they pretended I wanted it. I didn't fight back. It was what they expected. I was afraid. I blame myself for that shit. I can already hear Matt in my head at the thought of even saying that out loud. God. He'd want me to know it wasn't my fault. That the focus shouldn't be on me and whether I fought back. It should be on the assholes who raped me.

Briggs is pulling down my boxers. My body reacts without me thinking. My elbow slams back. He shouts, and I twist, pulling my pants up. I got him in the eye. His brow is bleeding. And I don't know. Something takes over. I throw myself at him and punch him again and again. I hear myself screaming so hard my voice tears my throat, but I don't realize it's me. Not really. Not until Briggs manages to throw me off him. His nose, his lip, his eyes—blood is everywhere. I'm breathing hard. There's a cut on the corner of my mouth. He must've gotten a punch in and I didn't even feel it. Shit.

He stares at me. He's breathing hard, too. He might kill me. I'm pretty sure he's considering it.

Then he gets up. He opens the door and doesn't bother to close it as he practically runs down the hall.

I sit on the couch for a while. I don't know how long. At one point, I consider texting Mattie, but the idea slips away. I just keep sitting, trying to fight off the thoughts that eventually find their way to me again. Don't they always?

MATTIE

IT'S MORE HUMILIATING than I would've imagined, being abandoned at a Halloween party by my drunk fake boyfriend. I decide to pretend that it was intentional—that he told me he would leave early, and I was okay with his decision. I smile at anyone who looks at me with a raised eyebrow, silently questioning why I would ever want to be in a relationship with someone like Logan Gray.

I'm not fooling Phillip or Julie. They saw the whole interaction.

Julie shakes her head. "I don't know what's up with him," she says. "I'm sorry, Mattie. You deserve to be treated better."

"It's okay," I say, though I'm not sure that's true. We're not even in a real relationship, but I know I'm worth more respect than that. At the very least, he could have come over, told me that he was leaving, and asked if I'd be okay getting home on my own.

"He used to be different when we were kids," she says. "I have no idea what happened to him to make him become such a shitty person."

I feel a flare of defensiveness for him. Gray isn't a shitty person. He just makes a lot of shitty mistakes. Knowing the root of it all softens my anger for him.

"Oh, right," Phil says, nodding. "You were on that show together. What was it again?"

"*It Takes Two*."

"God, I loved that show growing up," he says. Phil is very charming, I'll give him that. He gives off a warmth that feels safe and loving, even if we only just met. "It's hard to imagine Logan Gray being different," he says.

"He was actually nice, once," Julie tells him. "Kind."

"What happened to him? What made him change?"

I know the answer to that, but it isn't my story to tell. Logan told me how, one day when he was seventeen, he suddenly realized how messed up everything he'd experienced had been. He'd convinced himself it was normal, but when he couldn't lie to himself anymore—that he'd been abused and assaulted—he became angry, angrier than he'd been with the years of bullying, the biphobia, all the shit he had to survive on his own. It'd been silently building until he finally couldn't keep the rage bottled up anymore. I'm quiet, but Phil and Julie don't seem to notice.

"That—well, that *film* he posted," Julie says, lowering her voice. I know she means the one when he was eighteen. "He was always sarcastic, but he never went out of his way to be hurtful, or controversial for the sake of controversy. After that, it was like he became a different person. It was hard to be around him, especially as he started to pull away for no reason. I tried to see if there was something I could do to help him, you know? But some people can't accept help from others. They need to save themselves. We can't be responsible for another person when they need to learn how to be better."

I feel like she's trying to say something to me, specifically—

and yeah, maybe she's right. Even if Gray isn't really my boy-friend, I've felt like it's my responsibility to help him. Phil is watching me quietly.

Julie puts a hand on my arm. "I'm going to get another drink. Do you want water?" she asks me. I love that she remembered I'm sober and is kind enough to offer without judgment.

"I'm okay, but thank you."

She leaves. Phil and I are silent for a second. I wonder if that's why Julie suddenly became thirsty—to leave me and Phillip behind and give us a chance to talk more. Julie's been smiling at us all evening, like she thinks we would make a much better couple than me and Gray. She might be right. We'd certainly look better together, anyway. Compared to Gray, I know the public would prefer Phillip Desmond as my boyfriend, with his clean-cut look and easy smile. Plus—well, he's white.

"She's right, you know," Phil says. "You certainly deserve to be treated better."

The fact that he's white would make people think of him more highly. They would automatically see him as more attrac-tive. Logan was right, earlier, too. The history of colonialism would also mean that people would say Phillip's accent is "sexy." People would like Phil much, much more than Logan Gray, with no hesitation.

I've gotten to know Logan. I've learned that he has layers, hurts and pains that he hides from the world—this world that has enjoyed attacking him for entertainment for most of his life now. If Logan wasn't half-Black, and had two white parents, would everyone have treated him differently? Would they have had more patience and tried to get the full story? If he was white, they might've tried harder to learn about his past, his history with being abused in this industry. They might've had more compassion from the beginning, and he wouldn't have had to spend his entire life fighting, growing in anger and fear until he learned to push everyone else away. I'm angry at Logan, while I'm also angry for Logan.

Phillip sips his drink. "I broke up with my boyfriend a few months ago," he says. I wish Logan were here. He would've smirked and met my eye. Not everyone can be as amazing at flirting as Gray is, apparently.

"Oh," I say. "I'm sorry to hear that."

"Thank you. It was a little hard for us, I think, with me coming all the way to Los Angeles, and him staying in London. We decided we weren't fit for a long-distance relationship."

I've gotten the sense that Phillip's been flirting with me on and off all night. He slowed down once Julie told him that Gray was my boyfriend. He said he didn't usually keep up with the tabloids and social media, so he didn't know, but I'm not sure if I believe him.

"You mentioned Logan was your ride home," Phil says. "Do you need a lift?"

He's still smiling, but his eyes are luring, too. I'm pretty sure it's a silent invitation.

I hesitate. "No, thank you," I say. "I should probably get an Uber or something."

He laughs. "Your driver will be excited to find Matthew Cole sitting in his backseat."

Shit. How do I always manage to forget that I'm a celebrity? "Right." I laugh a little with him. "I think I still have the number for the car service that takes me to set."

I pull out my phone to check. I have twenty missed messages. Most are from Emma. I frown. "Excuse me," I tell Phil. "Sorry, my sister's trying to get in touch."

Phillip nods. "No worries."

I step away, pressing the dial button and putting the phone to my ear. Emma picks up on the first ring. "Mattie," she says. "Where've you been?"

"At an industry event. What's going on?" I ask. The panic in her voice is scaring me. "Is everything okay?"

"The news. Have you looked at the news yet?"

She tells me to hang up, to go to social media and look at the trending topics right away. It's an emergency. I frown, telling myself she's probably just being dramatic, but my heart speeds up as I think about Gray, leaving the party by himself...He'd been drinking. Did he get into an accident? Is he hurt? I should've stopped him, but before I could take a step in his direction, he was already out the door. I open the Twitter app, and I don't need to see any of the trending topics, because I've been tagged hundreds of times already. People ask, over and over again: What do you think of this? Are you going to say anything?

Briggs Stevenson is tagged a lot, too. He usually plays minor roles on TV shows, but he's famous enough that I recognize him immediately. He's posted a video. The still frame has him bloodied and bruised. I frown as I walk across the floor, to the balcony. I can feel people's stares following me. Gossip has probably already spread here, too. I put the video to my ear.

Briggs's voice is hoarse. "I just left the home of Logan Gray, where I was physically assaulted. Gray had been drinking. He attacked me. Look at my face. Look at my fucking face."

I turn the video off. My hands are shaking. Would Logan really do something like that?

"Mattie?"

I spin around. Julie walks onto the balcony behind me, phone also in her hand. She looks tentative. "Did you see?"

"Yeah."

195

"Are you okay?"

I look back at the screen. "I'm not sure. I—I think I need to go see Logan."

She hesitates. "Maybe that's not the best idea. If he's already attacked someone, then..."

I shake my head. "I don't know. I just need to hear what happened from him."

She still seems uncertain, but she nods. "Okay. I can drive you."

We're quiet on the ride over. I can't stop scrolling through the comments—hundreds of thousands of comments, building with every minute. Most people are calling for Logan to be arrested. He could be, technically, if he's really assaulted someone. It wouldn't have been his first time, either. There've been multiple videos of him getting into fights with strangers. But this—it really looks like someone put this Briggs Stevenson's face through a meat shredder. Like Logan was trying to kill him.

Julie pulls up to his apartment building after I've given her the address. I'm not expecting her to get out of the car with me.

"I'm not letting you go up there by yourself," she says.

We walk into the building together, Julie gripping my hand. By the time we've reached Logan's apartment, I'm sweating and feel faint. I knock on the door. "Logan?"

He doesn't answer. There're some shuffling sounds.

"Logan," I call. "Please open up."

The door cracks open. Logan is on the other side. His face is pale. His gaze skims from me to Julie. "Didn't realize I was hosting the afterparty."

I push open the door further. The place is a mess. It's like he just trashed it. Bottles everywhere. Drugs on the central table.

Enough for him to overdose and kill himself. Julie makes a sound of disgust to my left.

"What the hell happened?" I ask him.

He rubs his face with stress. I can't tell if he's sober or high. "I beat the crap out of Briggs."

Julie speaks. "You do realize that's *assault*, right?"

Logan glares at her. "Why the hell are you here?"

"I'm here for Mattie. To make sure you're not going to hurt him."

Logan turns away and falls into the couch. "I would never hurt Matt, all right?"

I swallow. I want to believe him, but I don't know what to think right now. I need to hear what's happened. I need him to tell me the truth, and I don't think he'll do that with Julie here. I turn to her and put a hand on her shoulder. "Thanks for helping me," I say. "I'll be okay."

She frowns. "Are you sure?"

"Yeah."

She hesitates for one long moment. I think she's considering telling me that she refuses to leave, but she finally nods. "All right. You have my number. I'm not far away. I'll come back if you need me, okay?"

"Thanks."

I walk her to the door, then shut it behind her. Silence echoes for a moment. I'm not breathing, and I don't think Logan is, either. I walk and stop in the middle of the living room, looking around at the scene. Logan's sitting, head back, staring up at the ceiling blankly.

"What happened?" I ask him.

He doesn't answer.

I sit down on the couch, where we've spent so much time together. I've seen flashes of this Logan before. This version of

Logan comes out when he doesn't feel safe, when he needs to protect himself. But this Logan—it's the same one that'll harm anyone, including himself. I don't know what to do, to get through to the real Logan beneath it all.

"I want to listen," I tell him. "I want to hear what happened." I pause. "I still care about you, no matter what. You know that, right?" But if he really attacked Briggs...I don't know. There'd have to be consequences for that, too.

He clenches his jaw and swallows, so I know he's listening.

I wait. I've always been patient, waiting.

Finally, he speaks. His voice is so hoarse it cracks, and I can't understand what he said.

"What'd you say?" I ask, voice quiet.

"He tried to rape me."

A sharp breath. "What?"

Logan sits up. He still doesn't look at me as he talks. "He texted me. He wanted to meet up. I left the party. Met him here. We usually fuck whenever he's in town, but—I don't know, I changed my mind. That pissed him off."

The way he says it—it's like he's suggesting he thinks it's his fault. "Jesus, Logan."

"He tried to rape me. I beat the shit out of him. He left."

I don't know what to do or say. My voice sounds hollow when I finally grasp at words. "You were allowed to change your mind."

His gaze meets mine. "You're not angry I almost had sex with him?"

"No. No, that was—" I do feel a tug in my gut, a pinch of hurt and disappointment, but that's nothing now, nothing in comparison to what's happened to Logan. "It was your choice, if you wanted to or not. Jesus, Logan," I say again. "He assaulted you."

"His dick never actually went in."

"That's still assault." I'm about to start crying, but he shouldn't have to deal with my emotions right now on top of everything else. "I—I think you should go to the hospital. Press charges."

He snorts. "If everyone tried to press charges for every rape and attempted rape in this industry, there wouldn't be any more movies."

I don't understand how he can be so dismissive of this. Is it because of his past? Does he think this is normal, somehow? Expected? "You don't deserve to be treated like this, Logan. You deserve to be safe. To feel safe. To not be attacked—"

"Done with your sermon?"

I close my mouth. I know it's only because he's hurting. He shouldn't want to hurt me in response, but I want to have patience for him—compassion, especially now. "It's your choice," I say softly. "You don't have to go to the hospital or file a report or anything."

"Yeah. Thanks. I know that."

"But I want to be here for you. So," I say, slowly, "please don't push me away. I don't want to leave you alone like this."

He doesn't speak. His eyes look like they're about to well up.

"I'm here, Logan. Okay? For as long as you want me here—for as long as you want me to stay. I promise I'm not going anywhere."

He looks at me for long enough that I think he's going to tell me to get out, until he closes his eyes and leans back against the couch. I understand his silent message. He's done speaking, but he doesn't want me to leave.

Twitter.com

Trending for You

#CancelLoganGray
#LoganGrayIsOverParty
#FuckGray
#BoycottWriteAnything

@facinwashere
This is FUCKING CRAZY Y'ALL. We BEEN trying to
warn you about how dangerous Logan Gray is for
YEARS and now he actually out here beating people
up?? He needs to be ARRESTED. #CancelLoganGray
💬 908   🔁 9.1K   ♥ 15.6K

@everydayhustlin
god this dude is sick in the head, fr fr.
#FuckGray
💬 201   🔁 1.2K   ♥ 4.7K

@angelsky4033
We need to #BoycottWriteAnything so that these
asshole celebrities can't continue to think they can

get away with everything. The world has real life consequences.

💬 189   🔁 1.7K   ♥ .9K

@robertklingon
Lol I could find logan's address and send someone to take him out so we don't have to deal with him anymore

💬 103   903   ♥ 2K

LOGAN

THE TEXT MESSAGES don't stop rolling in.

Dave's flipping out. What the fuck is going on Gray?? Answer me

Audrey's threatening to quit. How can I do my job and assist you in this matter if you won't return my phone calls?

Reynolds wants to fire me. This is unacceptable. You have destroyed the film.

Mattie slept over. He's cleaning up the apartment now, walking around with a garbage bag. I lie on the couch, scrolling through the messages, music streaming from my phone and to the TV, like usual.

"You're not looking at social media right now, are you?" Matt asks me as he passes by.

"Nope."

A new text from Willow. What happened? This is pretty shitty, even for you.

My phone starts to ring. It's my dad. I freeze. I don't want to answer it, but if I end the call, he'll know I'm ignoring him, which will only make him more pissed off. It's only as the voicemail starts that it hits me. Mattie will be able to hear this, too.

"Logan," my dad begins, his voice booming over the speakers, "you fucking disgusting piece of shit—"

I end the call. Mattie spins around. Why does he have to look so shocked?

"What the hell?" he says. "Who was that?"

I don't want to answer him. I sit up. "I should take a shower."

I feel his eyes on me as I walk down the hall. I open the bathroom door. There's a giant steam shower that takes up half the room with a tub inside. Even though I never take baths, I want one now. I strip and turn on the water.

Fuck. Why am I embarrassed? Mattie already knows the worst of my secrets. But this . . . I feel like Mattie's just found a stash of drugs or something else I was trying to hide from the world, and now he's discovered yet another layer of me that I hadn't meant to show. It was private, somehow. The way my dad speaks to me. We both know it's shitty of him, the things he says. We also both know that I deserve it. To let anyone else see that feels like I'm allowing them to understand just how horrible I am. Mattie thinks he understands me, but he doesn't. Not really.

I sink into the tub and close my eyes. It'd be easier if I weren't alive. Easier if I didn't have to deal with this body and all the trauma I can't escape. The memories and triggers. The disgust and self-hatred. I don't want to deal with any of it anymore. I can already see what everyone would say. It'd be the ending I deserved.

There's a knock on the door, interrupting my thoughts. "Logan?"

Sometimes my body shuts down. I can still think and hear and see, but I can't move or speak. I don't have the energy.

Mattie calls again. "Logan, are you all right?"

When I don't answer, the doorknob turns. I didn't lock it. He walks in, sees me naked, sitting in lukewarm water, crying. How pathetic am I?

He says my name again, softer, and walks to my side. He doesn't bother asking if I'm okay or what's wrong. I'm grateful. Wouldn't have been able to answer anyway. The water isn't that cold, but my teeth have begun chattering and I'm shaking.

"I think we have to take you to a doctor," he says.

I can tell he doesn't want to force me to go, is trying to leave it up to me—but I don't think there's any point. What the hell is a doctor going to do? Un-rape me? Figure out a way to reach back through all the years and take away the memories so that I can feel, for once, what it's like to be a person without any trauma? I wonder who I would be if people had never taken advantage of me and my body. Maybe I'd be different. Someone who could figure out how to be loved. Mattie's crying with me, and I realize he must be scared, too, sitting there without me saying anything. He just wants to help. I know that.

"Is it okay if I pull you out of the tub?" Matt asks. "Take you to your bed?"

I nod. He helps me up. He's a lot stronger than he looks. Water splashes on the floor. I'm shaking so violently it's hard to walk. He takes me up the stairs to my loft and lets me lean on him until I get to the bed. I lie down on the mattress and sheets, though I'm still wet, and Mattie gets a towel to dry me off. He opens up a dresser and grabs me a t-shirt, some boxers.

"Can I stay with you?"

When I nod, he helps me move over and takes the wet patch I left on the bed. We're under the comforter. He doesn't touch me. He's probably afraid. Scared that he'll touch my skin and I'll start to splinter and crack until I finally shatter open. I reach for his hand, and he holds it tightly, watching me. Looking for an answer.

"Thank you for letting me be here," he says.

⟵⟶

When I wake up, my mouth is dry and my body aches. I forget what happened for a second, before it comes back to me, and I roll over, wanting to go to sleep again. Mattie's not in the bed. I hear him speaking and realize he must be on the phone when no one answers him for a pause and then he keeps talking.

"Okay. Love you, too, Mom. Bye."

I push myself out of bed and walk down the stairs. Matt's on the couch. He looks up with a natural smile, even though there's still worry in his eyes. "Hey. You're awake." He stands up, then hesitates. There're new rules, now, for us to figure out. I'm not even sure I want to be touched. "Are you hungry?" he asks.

"A little, yeah." Good to know I haven't completely lost all ability to speak.

"I can order something," he suggests.

I'm not even sure what time it is, or how long I've been out. We end up getting food from one of my favorite Thai restaurants. We eat in the living room quietly, spread out on the floor. It reminds me of the days when we started to spend time outside of work, comfortably together, getting to know each other. I always manage to fuck things up, huh?

"I was thinking," Matt says. He seems uncertain. He won't meet my eye, anyway. "I know that you don't want to go to the hospital or press charges or anything. Though—you know, I really think you should, but that's the last I'll say about it."

Thank God. I don't want him to push me on that right now.

"But I was thinking," he says again. "Maybe it would be a good idea for you to tell your side of the story."

He chances a glance up at me now. The worry in his eyes grows when I don't say anything.

"I mean," he adds, "I don't think you should have to say anything if you don't want to. What happened...it shouldn't be anyone's business but your own."

But the truth lingers. It shouldn't be anyone's business, but the public has forced their way into my life, like usual, using me for their entertainment. It shouldn't be their business, but everything Briggs said could stay with me for the rest of my life. This could end my career. It could fuck up the movie, too. I don't think Matt cares that much about the film right now, but the thought crosses my mind anyway. This will affect him and Julie and Dave and everyone else who's worked their ass off for *Write Anything*. I shouldn't have to deal with the thought of talking to the public about this now, but, well, here we are.

There can only be one reason Matt's bringing it up. "How bad is it online?" I ask him.

He moves rice around in a circle on his plate. "Pretty bad," he finally admits. "A lot of people are calling for you to quit the movie. There're other actors, too, who're coming out in support of Briggs. People are planning to boycott the film. I don't care about the movie," he says, looking at me again. "It can be boycotted or cancelled or whatever else. It's not as important as you. But for you—I think it's best for you to tell the public your truth. It isn't fair to you that Briggs can destroy your life like this and get away with it. You don't deserve that, Logan."

"What do you think I should do?"

"You could make a statement. Written, or maybe a recording. Anything you're comfortable with. Do you think you would want to?"

"I don't know. I don't think I can do it right now."

"Whenever you're able and whatever you're most comfortable with, even if it turns out that you don't want to do or say anything—I'll be here with you, okay?"

"Thank you."

The silence stretches. I think Mattie might be waiting for me to speak. He's trying so hard to take his cues from me, to make sure I'm comfortable and feel safe and—God, I don't think anyone's ever treated me with so much patience. No one has ever had to. I'm an adult. I'm my own responsibility to exist without being loved and accepted by other people. That's how I've gotten by all these years. But it feels good, I think, to know that I can still be loved anyway. It feels good, and it also scares me. I'm waiting for the moment Mattie changes his mind.

"I want to make a statement," I tell him. "A recording. Post it onto socials."

His eyes shine with—pride, maybe? Some fear, I think, for me. "Do you want to talk to the team about it first?"

It's shitty we have to keep up the bullshit of our fake relationship. Though I'm starting to wonder if it's actually that fake at this point. "No. I'll say what happened. They'll deal."

Mattie grabs his phone. I sit on the sofa. He tells me when he hits record. I'm not inside of myself when I start to talk. I hear my voice, distantly, as if it belongs to someone else as I describe what happened.

"I made a huge mistake when I decided to have sex with Briggs. I was hurting Mattie. I shouldn't have. Briggs and I came over to my place. I changed my mind." I start to freeze again as I get closer to having to say the actual words. Mattie's watching for a moment in my silence before he moves closer to me, holding up the camera still, but sitting next to me in the frame, holding my hand. His comfort brings me back into my body enough to speak again.

I can't say the word, the r-word, the one that still makes me feel sick. "When I changed my mind, he assaulted me. I acted in self-defense. I know that a lot of you won't believe me," I say. "But, well, that's the truth."

Mattie ends the video. His hand is still in mine. "That was brave. You shouldn't have had to do this in the first place, but I admire you."

When he puts up the video on social, I was right: there's instant backlash, an onslaught of people calling me a liar, saying it's convenient that I would say this now after Briggs called me out. Mattie's dragged into this, too. People accuse Mattie of being the doting boyfriend too naïve to see how harmful I am. Refusing to acknowledge that I cheated on him. Blink twice if you need help Mattie a comment reads. The way they're treating me is all right. It's what I expected. But Matt? I don't think I can take it, people treating him like shit because of me.

"I wish there were a way to prove it," Mattie says.

There is a way, I realize. The security camera is still installed. It's supposed to show the living room, the couch. I hadn't thought of it. I haven't been able to do much thinking at all. I nudge Matt and point up, at the corner. The camera is so small that it isn't surprising he didn't notice it.

He doesn't get angry for not mentioning the cam before now. There's some hesitant hope on his face. "How do you get access to the footage?"

"It's downloadable."

We end up on my laptop, checking out the files on the security company's website. There's a lot of rewinding. It's painful to see me over the past two days, frozen—Matt moving backward in triple speed, cleaning and going back and forth with trays of meals. He's been taking care of me more than I've realized. I squeeze his hand, and he looks at me, surprised, before he threads his fingers through mine. He goes back to concentrating on the recording.

And then the door opens, me on the couch—Briggs walking backward, toward me. The fight. Him pulling off my jeans.

Matt presses pause. He takes a deep breath and lets it out slowly. "Are you okay?" he asks me, voice low. Pissed. He's actually pissed off, I realize, watching this.

"I will be," I tell him.

"You could press charges with this."

"Yeah. I know."

But I already feel exhausted at the thought. Exhausted, thinking about the many months and maybe even years I'll be forced to confront this over and over again, speaking about it publicly when I can barely talk to Matt about it without freezing, when I can't even think about it without feeling like I've left my body. My words would feel slow and heavy as I think not only about Briggs, but about the different men who have assaulted me throughout my life. My father, who knew what was happening, but just didn't care—who let me be abused, if it meant money for his films. I can't press charges. I can't deal with the media frenzy this would become. Dealing with strangers' opinions on what happened. Saying that I'm lying for attention, or that I deserved to be raped. That I probably wanted it, because I'm such a slut. I wouldn't survive that.

I don't know how to explain any of this to Mattie. I land on saying, "I don't want to."

It's a testament to him that he only bites his lip. He doesn't ask why, and he doesn't argue. "Okay. It's your choice."

"But I do want to send a copy to Briggs. Show him I've got proof. I could put this out to the entire world. I'll tell him to say what really happened. Not that I was—" I swallow. "But that he attacked me first, and I fought back."

"Do you think he'll do it?"

"If not, I'll tell him I'm going to post the recording."

I don't think that I'd really be able to do it, and I don't think Matt believes me, either, but he nods. I text Briggs a copy of the footage, cut and edited for the thirty-second fight. I tell him what I expect. I want the post up within the hour. He doesn't respond. Mattie and I wait together, not speaking much. Lost in our own thoughts, him running a hand through my hair.

I've figured out that there are cycles. Repeating patterns that began when I was seven years old, patterns I haven't been able to escape. I've been through this cycle before. These memories will become old nightmares, stored away in my body, something I'll push deep down. After a while, life will feel like it has returned to normal. My normal, anyway. The normal where I never really felt safe. Waiting for the next attack.

"Have you ever had a therapist?" Mattie asks.

I snort. "My therapist would need a therapist just to deal with me."

"It might help, you know?" he says. "I don't want to pressure you into anything, but—"

"Then why bring it up?"

His hand pauses, before he continues. "You don't have to see one if you don't want to."

A few more seconds of silence. "Sorry for snapping."

"It's okay."

I get a notification. Briggs's texted a link. I press it, and it takes me to his social. He has strips of tape on his cuts, and his bruises have gotten darker over the past few days. His expression is sullen.

"I have an apology to make," Briggs says. "I was angry at Logan Gray for the way that he attacked me when I posted my original video a few days ago. I did not, like Gray said, *assault* him, but I might have been inappropriate. I don't think it excuses his response, beating the shit out of me like he did, but I apologize if I misled anyone."

Matt's pissed. "That's his apology?"

"I think it's the best we're going to get."

It doesn't matter, in the end. The video is enough to stop the onslaught online. The focus shifts to Briggs, and a new conversation begins: what does it mean to be inappropriate? Some people suggest it's possible Briggs made a flirtatious comment and I started to beat the shit out of him, but enough people acknowledge what I looked like in my video. The bruises I have, too, and the hollow look in my eyes that was strange for me to see from the outside. More than a few people guess correctly what I really meant by assault, but at this point, it's pure speculation. Any other actor, and there probably would've been an outpouring of apologies, but I think people assume I deserve whatever happened—that the character I play as Logan Gray deserves all the hatred that followed.

"I'm not even sure who I am," I tell Mattie. "It's like all the shit that happened when I was a kid stripped away who I might've been. I don't even remember who I was before."

Mattie hugs me. He hasn't kissed me since he came over. I didn't want to be touched like that at first, but I want his comfort now. A reminder that I don't have to be afraid of another person's body. He hesitates when I begin to lean in, but he presses his lips to mine softly, for just a moment.

AN APOLOGY

This back and forth with Logan Gray and Briggs Stevenson has been CONFUSING, to say the least. Accusations are flying left and right, and I don't know what to believe, so I will be pulling my latest blog post about Gray's assault on Briggs.

I apologize to my fans for moving forward with assumptions without having the full scope of information. (TBH, I don't know if you can exactly *blame* me. Logan Gray has always been a trash fire of a human being, so it's not very hard to believe.)

But, still, maybe there's more to the situation than meets the eye...

Until next time,

Angel

Happily Ever After: A Memoir

by Matthew Cole

I never did well with fame. I always felt uncomfortable with others placing me on a pedestal. I wanted love from others, but fame meant that their love was conditional—that I could only be the Matthew Cole others expected me to be. I would not admit it, but I was afraid to fall.

I eventually learned the hard way that conditional love is never truly love. I realized that the pedestal I was placed on was never about acceptance. As I grew in fame, I became a reflection to other people: a person that others could look at, instead of looking at themselves.

We don't like to look at the truth within us—the ways that we hurt others, the pains we need to heal, how we each need to grow and learn. It feels easier, better, to look at a celebrity's flaws rather than our own—or to put a celebrity on a platform as if they're a god, as if fame makes them extraordinary, when the fact is that we are all human beings. I've always hated the sense that I am praised and idolized by the very people who should be praising and idolizing themselves, loving themselves unconditionally instead of giving that love to a falsely perfect Matthew Cole that they created in their imaginations.

Project X Schedule

November 15: Wrap party. Rest up on your months off.
You'll need it.

February 5: Joint interview with Us Weekly—you love
each other, excited for the world to see your film,
etc.

February 9: Joint interview with People—standard
photoshoot, look hot together

February 17: MC interview with Cosmopolitan, drop
hints that things are not as perfect as they seem

February 20: Some gossip about you two fighting to be
leaked

March 7: Promo tour begins

March 12: MC breaks up with LG for one last attention
boost. Celebrity breakups = big money. ☺

MATTIE

I KNOW THAT Logan also got Dave's newest schedule handed to him on set, but neither of us talk about it. It seems that's the story for everything right now: no one's talking about what happened with Gray and Briggs. It's been a week, but no one's talking about how Keith and a bunch of other actors went online to post their support of Briggs, but when the truth came out, they only took their posts down without making a single apology to Logan. Even Dave pretends nothing happened. I know that, behind the scenes, he and Reynolds and the PR team were likely scrambling to figure out what to do—fire Gray and hire Phillip Desmond to reshoot all of the scenes? Cancel the movie altogether and cut their losses? But now that the heat is off Logan, it's like no one cares enough to ask if Logan is okay.

When we're on our lunch break, I knock on his trailer door. He opens it a crack, then lets me in without a word, closing the door behind me. The trailer is a lot cleaner than I thought it would be. Logan's still in his white shirt and slouchy sweatpants from the scene. He gestures at the couch opposite him. I sit, and we're silent for a moment together.

"How're you?" I ask him.

He swallows. "Pretty fucked."

My heart hurts, hearing the pain in his voice. He was given the week to rest, last scenes that didn't involve him shot instead, though the schedule still ended up delayed. I'd suggested that he tell Dave that he needs more time and offered to continue staying with him as he recovered, but he refused. "I need this," he said. I'm still not sure what that means.

I take a breath. "Is there anything I can do?"

He sighs, like he's letting out the breath I took. "What're we doing?"

"What do you mean?"

"You," he says. "Me. What is this? What are we?"

That's a hell of a question. I don't know how to respond.

"This shit was already complicated enough, and—you know, I don't want to sound ungrateful. I'm grateful for you, Matt. Everything you've been helping me with."

"I'm grateful that you're letting me."

He eyes me for a second, and his expression looks strangled. "Did you get the new schedule?"

I hesitate. Maybe a part of me liked that we were ignoring it. "Yeah. I did."

"They want us to break up," Logan says.

I nod slowly. I don't like the direction this is going.

He leans back in the couch, hands on his knees. "Maybe we should stop...this. Whatever this is. We'll have to eventually anyway, right?"

I sit straighter, tension in my back. My heart's pounding, beating harder and harder, until I force myself to say the words. "I don't know what we are," I tell him. "But I do know I love you."

His gaze snaps to mine. He blinks, looks away with a clenched jaw. "Come on, Matt. Don't do that."

I knew he wouldn't react well, but it hurts just the same. "It's true. I love you."

He doesn't believe me, that much is obvious. "Why would you love me?"

I could list all the reasons, I guess—tell him how he's helped me feel less shame, to break out of my fear and to feel uninhibited and free; because I've seen him at his most vulnerable, seen through the role he'd created and all the layers of hurt to *him*, and what I see is beautiful...But it's hard to get the words out when I take in Logan's shuttered gaze. The more I speak about how much I love him, the more he will want to reject me.

"It's all right if you don't feel the same," I say, even though my heart clenches at the thought, "but—if you do, we don't have to stop our relationship just because of a movie, or Dave's schedule. We could figure something out."

He runs a hand through his hair, messing it up. "Time. Fuck. I need time, all right? I need time to think." He runs his hands over his eyes. "Shit, Matt. Why did you have to say that?"

I will my tears not to come. It isn't fair to cry right now and make him feel guilty for possibly not loving me, for not wanting to be with me. "Because it's the truth."

"I don't know if I love you," he tells me.

His words hurt so much it takes my breath away. Maybe I should've thought this through. Figured out a better way, a better time, to tell him how I feel. But it's too late to take back now. "Okay. I get it."

"Let's take a break from seeing each other," he tells me. "I need to figure some shit out."

"Are you pulling away again?"

"Just for a little while."

I'd practically moved in with Logan this past week, both of us abandoning our hotel rooms. I'm afraid to leave him alone. I'm afraid that he'll stop answering calls and won't show up to set, afraid of what I might find when I open his apartment door.

But maybe he sees my fear. "I'll be all right, Mattie."

"If you start to feel—you know, the way you were feeling, please text me or call me. It doesn't matter what time it is. Okay?"

He nods, and it relieves me a little, that I believe him. "Okay. I promise."

I hadn't thought things through enough when I decided to tell Logan that I love him. Quinn stands in the doorway, drenched from running in the rain. He's breathing hard, tears in his eyes. I stand in front of him, my heart splitting open, because I don't want to hear the words that're about to come out of his mouth.

"I'm sorry," he says. He steps inside and hesitates before he reaches for me. I force myself not to pull back. "God. I'm so sorry, Riley. You were right."

"What're you doing here, Quinn?" The anger in my voice is real. The hurt, the confusion. I've felt this enough times with Logan.

"I—" He lets out a shaky breath. "I couldn't say it before. I have to say it now. You were right. I love you. I've never loved anyone like this before—but you. Riley, there's no one else like you."

I swallow. These words are hitting a little too close to

home right now. Quinn's eyes look hollow as he turns into Logan, clenching his jaw. I haven't been Riley for this entire scene. I can't get into character. Dave doesn't seem to notice. He hasn't said anything from across the set. Maybe it's one of those moments when my character blends with who I am so perfectly that I don't have to act. Maybe it's the tighter production schedule.

"How can I believe you?" I ask him. "I can't believe you, Quinn. You hurt me. You broke my heart." I lose my breath for a second, real pain clogging my throat. "I trusted you. I let myself be vulnerable with you, just for you to reject me."

"Riley," he says, "I know I don't deserve your forgiveness. I'm sorry I told you I don't love you. That was just the character I made up to protect myself. I was scared. That's all. But now, I see how much you mean to me. I can't lose you. Not again."

I take a shaking breath, and I let him pull me into his arms. His body is familiar, his skin and his hair against my cheek. I want to sink into him, like when we'd hold each other in his bed, whispering in the dark. We kiss. I'm afraid to touch Logan, but he told me that this was okay beforehand, and he pulls me in even tighter. "I love you," he says.

I let myself believe it's Logan telling me this, not Quinn—just for a moment.

Filming wraps for *Write Anything*. The production schedule was tight, but I survived it, somehow. I can't imagine how difficult these past weeks have been for Gray if they were hard for me.

"I'm worried about him," I tell Julie. We're undercover,

which is a nice change from the very public lunches and dinners Logan and I have had together. We're at the back of a dark restaurant in the neighborhood she lives in, over by Los Feliz. "I'm not sure if I'm the best person to help him, and I don't know if he's actually getting the help that he needs." He said he needed space, and I've given him that—but it's been over a week since I told him how I feel; over a week of worrying about him, unable to stop thinking about him...

"Logan's never been the sort of person to accept help," she says. She's been apologetic for immediately siding with Briggs, but even knowing that Logan told the truth hasn't helped her opinion of him. "He doesn't open up to anyone and tell them what's really going on, and he keeps bottling it all up until he finally self-destructs. I can feel bad for him, sometimes," she admits. "But feeling bad for someone doesn't mean I should open myself up to getting hurt by them over and over again."

She asks me if I'm going to the wrap party tonight. I already know Logan isn't going, from what I've heard on set. He's probably gotten angry phone calls about it, but no one can force him. He's been focused on the job the past couple of weeks since the assault—coming in to set, delivering an incredible performance, and leaving—but there's a quiet tension everywhere he goes. I don't know how he's able to handle that stress. Maybe he isn't actually handling it, not really.

"I don't know."

"It's not going to look great if the movie's two stars don't show up." She pauses, then shrugs. "Maybe it doesn't matter how it looks."

"I just want to be ready at the hotel in case Logan texts me."

Julie has known that this relationship is just a publicity

stunt, but I think she's caught on that, even if Logan and I haven't decided to become privately official, things are just a little more complicated now. "I know your relationship is your business, but...It's okay for you to have needs separate from Logan, too."

I lean back in my seat as her words hit me. She's right. I want to be supportive, but my life has only revolved around Logan recently. Before he asked for space from me, we would leave the set together and go back to his apartment. Sometimes we didn't even talk for the entire night. I'd just sit beside him or hold him. I loved being by Logan's side. But it's true, I think, that I've started to lose myself. For the past two weeks, I've only gone to my hotel room and thought about Logan, wondered if he's okay, hoped that he would text or call.

This wrap party is something I would've looked forward to, once. It'll be a final chance to say goodbye to a lot of the people I've been working with for these past few months.

"You're right," I tell her. "Yeah. I'll go."

The party is at a restaurant closer to Santa Monica. The whole place has been shut down for us. Karaoke machines are hooked up, though no one is using them. Music plays in the background. People stand in the groups they're more comfortable with. I end up with Julie, Keith, Monica, and Scott. Even though I'd pushed myself to come, I'm not feeling present. I look up when everyone laughs, and I realize I've missed half of the conversation. I force a strained smile and shrug when Keith asks, "Where's the boyfriend?"

Julie frowns and asks if I'm all right. "I'm fine."

I push myself to leave the small group of actors to walk

around the set, thanking everyone I see. After about an hour of mingling, Scott shakes my hand and says he hopes we'll work together again soon, and even Monica gives me a tight hug. I hang out with Julie and Keith for a while, and when they say they're going to head out, Keith slaps me on the back and Julie pulls me in for a hug.

"This is only goodbye for now," she says. "We're going to keep hanging out even after the promo tour, right? And we'll have the photoshoots and the red carpets, so this isn't really goodbye."

"Yeah," I say. "Of course."

I should probably head out, too—but the thought of going back to my shadowy hotel room alone depresses me. I wander for a while until I find Dave over by the open bar. "There you are," he says, grin widening. "I was afraid you weren't going to show."

"I'm here." I ask the bartender for some water.

Dave watches. "Maybe that's the secret to making it in this industry," he says, raising beer to his lips. "Don't drink."

"It probably takes more than that."

"Have you spoken to your manager?" he asks me. "About the tour, I mean."

"Paola sent over the basics." The cities, which outlets, that sort of thing. I'll have some time off as the film moves into post-production. I was planning on going back to Atlanta. It'll be the holiday break, so Emma will be home, too. It'll be a sudden shift, a change from everything I've been experiencing here in LA.

The movie's expected to come out in eight months, but publicity will begin soon. We've been doing a few interviews here and there, but the real work has barely begun. The promo tour as one of the lead actors is going to be rough. I'll have to speak openly about being a gay man, and as much as I've learned to breathe through the shame, there's still a flinch of fear.

Dave seems especially interested in his drink now. "So ... They didn't mention anything else?"

I don't like that he won't meet my eye. "No. Was there something else?"

He shrugs like it isn't a big deal, but his frown deepens. "There've been some talks about Gray. Whether he'll be a benefit on the tour."

I almost laugh. "This is a promotional tour for a romance movie. I'm not even the main character."

"Gray's had a lot of negative press lately," Dave says. That's putting it gently. "There's some concern that this entire situation with Briggs Stevenson will be a distraction from the film."

There's a spark of anger, hearing that one. "Has anyone even bothered reaching out to Logan? See if he's doing okay?"

I already know the answer to that. Dave shifts uncomfortably. He hasn't spoken to Logan besides the usual greetings on set before jumping into work. That's a hell of a lot more than the EPs or any of the studio execs have done. They don't care about Logan at all.

"Look, it's not up to me," Dave says. "I hope they'll reconsider and have Gray on board. It might do him some good, and if he shows himself in a positive light, then ..."

That's frustrating to hear, too. I know that these promo tours would expect me and Gray to sit still for interviews for twelve hours a day, grinning happily and excitedly, not showing a hint of exhaustion. It'll require almost as much acting as for the film itself. But if Logan can't force himself to pretend to be happy for the sake of the film and the audience, then why isn't it okay for him to show that? Would it really be the end of the world if he was given space to be honest about what he's going through—to be listened to, and accepted for once in his life?

Dave shrugs again, then offers a hand. "Good luck to you, Matt. It's been good working with you."

It hurts to head back to my hotel room alone. The air feels stale, the sheets musty. I open the balcony doors and sit on the edge of my bed and try not to wait for a text or a phone call. I should take some time for myself—take care of my own needs, like Julie said. My entire existence and all my happiness shouldn't depend on Logan.

My phone vibrates against the wood of the nightstand. I pause, then turn it over to see Logan's name with a flourish of emotions—relief, excitement, love. Do you want to come by?

Logan opens the apartment door when I knock. He's given me a key by this point, but I feel like it'd be more polite to ask to be invited inside. He's wearing a white t-shirt and gray sweatpants. His hair is a mess, shadows under his eyes. He's been looking thinner recently.

"Are you all right?" I ask him, concern flooding my voice.

"Yeah. I'm fine." He pushes the door open more. "How was the party?"

I follow him in, close and lock the door behind me. "It was okay. I missed you."

I've been trying my hand at saying things like this to him. I missed you. I love you. A part of me wonders if he's ever had someone who has told him that before. If anyone in his

225

life has gone out of their way to let him know that he's wanted.

I can't save him. I know that I can't. But it also breaks my heart to think that he was never gifted these basics, of knowing that he's loved and wanted and deserves to be here with the rest of us. I want to be safe for him. That's okay, isn't it?

He doesn't say anything. Maybe he doesn't know how to respond. He doesn't push me away, which is progress. He doesn't lash out in fear that I'll hurt him. It scares me a little, I think—the pressure. What if I do or say something that hurts him without meaning to? I'm a human. I'm inevitably going to make a mistake.

Logan plops back down on the couch. "I was thinking," he says. I sit down next to him. "Maybe it'd be nice to get away from the city."

Logan and I haven't spoken about our plans now that the movie's done. It was a subject I think we were both avoiding, afraid to talk about what comes next.

"Where're you thinking of going?" I ask him.

"My family has a cabin near San Francisco," he says. "It's my dad's, but he never goes there anymore." He pauses. "Thanksgiving is next week."

"Right."

He shrugs. "I don't really celebrate Thanksgiving."

"Me either."

"It's a fucked holiday."

"Yeah, it is."

"But—I don't know. Thought maybe we could spend some time together." He chances a glance at me. "Would you want to come with me?"

He asks this like it isn't a big deal, but the two of us going away on vacation? Maybe I'm not the only one who's started to think of this as a real relationship. Even if he hasn't said that he loves me, too, maybe he cares for me more than he'll say out loud.

"Yeah. I would love to."

LOGAN

WE TAKE A flight, shades and ball caps on. We only get a few lingering stares, a single "Is that...?" whisper. But most people ignore us. Actors getting away from LA to San Francisco isn't new. I only have a duffel while Mattie has a backpack. He looks like a fucking Boy Scout. I laugh at him, and Mattie grins at me. "Shut up."

I haven't wanted to tell him the truth. How much I've missed him. Having Mattie around—I don't know, he always kept me out of my head. That bright-as-fuck smile, his laughter. I kept hearing his words, over and over again. His voice shook a little, when he said that he loved me. I didn't react well. I know that I didn't. I guess I invited him out to my father's cabin to make it up to him. Give myself a little more time to find the courage to tell him that I'm pretty sure I'm falling in love with him, too. But—fuck, what's the point of any of this if we just have to break up anyway? Matt seemed confident that we could make it work. I want to believe him. I really do.

The flight is only an hour, and when we land, I rent a car to drive another two. I haven't been to the cabin since I was a kid. I used to spend my summers here. It's like I can't escape my father wherever I go, but this cabin, at least, has some happier memories for me. My mom would pull out of her depression the farther we were from LA. She would hug me more often and let me sit with her by the lake as she read.

The more we drive, leaving the city behind, the more buildings disappear, replaced by towering trees and a winding road. I pull off onto a rocky path that leads down to a lake. The "cabin" is basically a smaller contemporary mansion, gray and silver paneling. Matt's close behind me, staring around in awe, as I fiddle with the keys and try the wrong one to unlock the front door. Shit. Why am I so nervous? I look back at Mattie. He isn't annoyed. He only raises his eyebrows with a *what's wrong?* expression. He's always so patient.

When I finally manage to push open the door, I pause at the threshold. Dust floats through light. I'd called the old house-cleaning service in the area and asked them to freshen up the place before we arrived, but I guess they could only do so much with the cabin abandoned for a few years now. The place hasn't changed much. The furniture is contemporary, gray—the kitchen open with glistening white cabinets, appliances all stainless steel. The windows are floor-to-ceiling.

"God," Matt says as he walks in. "This place is amazing."

We go to the bedroom we'll share, king-sized bed taking up most of the space, sitting area in a corner. It's an ensuite. An open door connects to the bathroom that really looks more like a sauna, benches included, with a porcelain bathtub. The bedroom's sliding glass doors open to a patio that has a pool, though it's covered by a tarp. I never questioned it as a kid, but why does there need to be a pool right next to a lake? This is the sort of thing that happens when people have too much money, I guess.

I drop my duffel to the floor and fall onto the bedroom's couch. I shut my eyes. Not looking at Mattie gives me courage. I didn't expect this to be so terrifying—him being here, knowing we'll have to talk about *us*. He's already said that he loves me. He's already said that he wants this relationship. What's the big fucking deal, Logan?

Matt sits down beside me. "Thanks for inviting me."

I peek open an eye. He's watching me, completely unembarrassed, as if he really doesn't mind that he told me he loves me, and I haven't told him how I feel yet. Like he'd be happy to stay in this gray area for the rest of our lives.

"I was afraid I scared you off," he says. "With—you know, me telling you that I love you and everything."

Just diving right in, I guess. "You kind of did."

He nods. "Yeah. I could've chosen a better way to say it. I shouldn't have sprung it on you like that."

"There isn't really another way to do it, I guess." Perfect opening. Perfect chance for me to just say the fucking words. I swallow and look away. "I didn't think you'd agree to come."

"Why not?"

"I don't know. Haven't seen each other in a few days, since you said what you did."

"You needed space. I understand."

"Maybe a part of me didn't believe you," I tell him. It's not like I think Matt's playing a cruel joke on me, but maybe he's tricked himself into thinking he's got feelings, and the second I decide to be vulnerable about how I feel, too, he'll only see that he doesn't love me after all.

His expression looks like he might feel bad for me. It pisses me off a little. "Why don't you believe me?"

A small laugh escapes me. Why *would* I believe him? "I

don't know. No one's ever said they're in love with me before. I've never had anyone stick around this long, either. Usually people realize they've got what they needed out of me and leave, or they figure out I'm too fucked up to deal with." I pause. "Not saying that because I feel sorry for myself. It's just the truth."

"I don't know if it's feeling sorry for yourself. It's self-compassion, maybe. That's okay, too, isn't it?"

I shrug, eyes closed. "People say I'm just playing the victim."

"You are a victim," he says. "It's like you've been in survival mode your entire life. It's okay to—I don't know, grieve that."

Shit. I can feel tears growing. I don't want to go down that path. "The only reason you stuck around is because you were told to. It was a job."

He nods. "Yeah. That's true. I probably wouldn't have given you as much of a chance as I should have, if it weren't for this publicity stunt. But I'm glad I had to. I'm glad I got to know you, to see you. I would've missed out on you, Logan."

I can't answer him. I don't trust myself to speak, because if I do, I might release all the emotion I'm struggling to keep in. It's enough to be vulnerable by inviting Matt to my family's vacation home, to talk about all this crap, without me starting to sob in front of him, too.

I guess it doesn't matter. He can tell I'm about to cry anyway.

He takes my hand. "I'm not going to leave."

I don't answer him.

"You trust that, right?" he says. "I'm not going to leave you. Not unless you want me to."

I rub my free hand over my face, keep it over my eyes so I don't have to look at him. "How do you know that?"

"I don't," he tells me. "But getting to know you. Falling in love with you. That means learning to accept all of you. If I accept you, I don't see why I would ever want to leave."

"You could get sick of me." I swallow, letting my hand drop. "I could—I don't know, hurt you. Push you away again."

Matt bites his lip. "You could work your way through it. Talk to me, if you're feeling that way."

I could, sure. The question is whether I will, or if I'll feel so trapped in my head that I won't be able to.

Mattie rubs the back of his neck. "I should be honest about what I need to work on, too," he says. "I'm always preaching at you to open up, right?"

"Yeah."

He takes a breath. "I feel like I start to lose myself, after a while. Wanting to make sure you're all right. I stop thinking of my own needs, and I start to forget my own feelings. It's like I'm becoming a shell of a person sometimes. I don't think that's healthy for me."

This is new. I sit straight up, listening, still unable to look at him. Yeah, I want his honesty—but I can't ignore the fear, either. The fear twisting through me, making it just a little harder to breathe. I'm toxic, so toxic I'm starting to fuck up Mattie's life, too. I'm hurting him just by being in pain, just by asking for his help.

Matt plays with my fingers. "We need to be honest with each other, right? This scares me so much. You're afraid I'm going to leave you—but I've been just as afraid that you'll push me away again."

"I mean." I shrug. "I don't know, Matt. I might. I don't know what I will and won't do. I can't promise you anything. You get that, right? I can't promise you I won't mess up, if

232

we were actually going to try to...make this, whatever this is, work."

"But that's a relationship, isn't it?" he asks. "Making mistakes and trying to learn from them together."

"Is that what you want?" I ask him.

"Yes," he says, without even a pause. "I want to be in a relationship with you. A real one. Not just this publicity stunt."

I close my eyes. It really is easier, talking this through without looking at Matt. "Maybe it'll be worth trying, you and me."

I feel him lean closer. When we kiss, our lips linger. We haven't kissed like this in a while—slowly at first, growing more intense with every breath. Matt pulls back. He rests his mouth against my neck and breathes. "I want to slow down," he says. "I don't want to feel like we're only connected through sex."

That's also new. Not for Matt, but for anyone who has ever been with me. People have only ever been interested in me for sex. It's uncomfortable, maybe too new, to sit here with Matt, arms around each other, touching without the goal of ending up in bed.

"Can we stay like this?" he whispers.

I resent him a little, too. I don't want to be coddled, just because of the shit I've been through. "I don't need you to protect me from sex," I say.

He jerks back, eyes wide. "I'm sorry," he says. "I wasn't trying to protect you. It just felt nice, to be here with you without..."

I don't know why the moment's shifted, why this doesn't feel okay. Maybe I'm too used to feeling like my only value is my body. It's almost like a security blanket, I guess. Having sex with people to feel like they need me, want me, won't abandon me. That's pretty sad.

"Don't you want to have sex?"

He's watching me too carefully. "Yes, but we don't have to."

I lean in closer. "But I *want* to."

MATTIE

LOGAN LETS OUT a shaky breath as we kiss. I think he's just as afraid as I am. I force myself not to comfort him. He seemed angry, that I was trying to be gentle. I have to admit that I'm nervous about triggering him. I've wanted to protect him. That's all I want to do whenever I'm with Logan. I end up on top, Logan on his back on the couch. His hands reach under my shirt. I pull away a little. "Are you sure?"

He nods, not meeting my eye. I put a hand on his, and he looks up at me. "You don't have to force yourself to do anything if you're not ready," I tell him.

His voice is low. "I want this. I don't want to be afraid of my own body for the rest of my life."

I believe him. I lean forward and kiss him again. He moans into my mouth as I reach under his shirt, roam his skin. He takes my hand and guides it in between his legs. I pull back and look at him.

"Let's get undressed and take showers," I murmur before I climb off. He nods and stands and begins to walk.

"Where're you going?" I ask him.

He hesitates. "The shower."

"Get undressed here."

I sit down and lean back in the seat, waiting. I'm enjoying this take-charge attitude that's developed with Logan. It lets me explore my unashamed power. He has a flit of surprise—a smirk at the challenge. I'm nervous about pushing him too far right now. I want to keep an eye on his expressions and body language, make sure he's still with me and isn't starting to disappear into his head, his thoughts, his memories...

He faces me. "You're bossier than anyone would believe."

"Do you like that I'm bossy?"

He hesitates. The answer is on his face. Yes. He just doesn't want to admit it.

"Take off your shirt, Gray."

"You know," he says, "what's hilarious about this is that you can't make me do shit."

"No, of course not," I say. "I don't want to make you do anything you don't want to. But that's the point, isn't it?" I ask, leaning forward. "You *do* want to. You love being told what to do."

He clenches his jaw.

I smile. "You love begging. You love getting on your knees."

Something flickers in his eyes. There's a glazed look in his expression. I stand up, walk to him, and put a hand on his cheek. "You still with me?"

He nods, but he isn't looking at me.

"What happened?" I ask, voice low.

"Being on my knees," he says. "Briggs..."

He doesn't need to finish. "I'm sorry." I'm going to need to learn his triggers. Maybe that should've been a conversation first. Maybe he won't even know until it happens. That's a scary thought. I don't want to potentially trigger or hurt him every time I touch him. "Are you all right?"

He nods. He meets my eye and begins to pull off his shirt. I put a hand on his. "It's okay. We don't have to keep going."

"But you're right," he says. "I do love being told what to do."

He's watching me again, at least, even if his expression still feels like he's shut down.

I rub a thumb over his mouth. "Then do what I tell you, and wait until you feel present. Tell me when you do. Tell me when you're ready to keep going. Then we'll start again."

He frowns. "But I want to now."

"So you don't feel triggered anymore?"

He rolls his eyes. "No, but—"

"Are you whining?"

He smirks. "A little."

"You like being told what to do, right? Then do what you're told."

Logan practically laughs. "You get off on being strict, huh?"

I eye him. "Yeah. Maybe. But I also like to give rewards, if you listen."

His grin fades. I think he might be coming back to himself more now—from that shine in his eyes, he might be imagining what I mean by *rewards*. Still, he isn't happy when he grumbles, "Fine." Maybe he's being a little dramatic. We are actors, after all.

We have quick showers separately. When he's finished, I prep a little, just in case, not with any expectation of what could happen. Feeling less grungy from a day of travel and in a fresh t-shirt and shorts, I find Logan out in the kitchen, refrigerator open.

He glances over the top of the door. "Nothing's in here. We have to go to the store if we want to eat."

I'm excited to explore a different town, especially one so

off the beaten path. I like smaller town atmospheres, and I've felt stuck in LA for so long. We grab wallets and walk out to the rented car. The green of trees and twitter of birds and yellow sunshine, glistening on the still lake, is peaceful. Even the breeze feels like it enters my skin and relaxes me from the inside out.

We play music in the car ride over to the town, twenty minutes away. Logan sighs but agrees when I ask to take a break from the heavy metal station, and we turn to some relaxing Solange instead. The town feels more like a series of spread-out buildings and houses in the middle of a forest, until we reach the grocery store. It's small, not one of those big-chain supermarkets, but it has everything we need. We get a few glances, but if anyone recognizes us, they don't say anything. It feels like we're ordinary people—no fame, no movies. Just two boyfriends walking through the grocery store, his hand touching mine. I'm afraid to let myself get lost in this moment, knowing it could end.

Logan plays some alternative rock in the kitchen as we cook spaghetti together. Neither of us are very talented chefs.

"What do you think you would do if you weren't acting?" I ask him.

He leans back as he considers. "God, I have no idea. It's the only thing I've ever done."

"Do you ever imagine walking away from all of it?"

He shrugs. "Sometimes. But I have no plan. I'm afraid of what's on the other side."

It seems he's given this more thought than I was expecting. "Do you want to leave the industry?"

He nods slowly. "Sometimes I think this whole industry is a trigger. If I left...I don't know. Maybe I'd feel safer."

"That's what I want for you," I tell him. More than anything.

He grabs a glass of water. "What about you?"

"This was always my dream," I say. "I love acting. I'm not sure about the fame. That's not what it's supposed to be about, right? I don't know. Maybe one day I'll want to escape, too."

We spend hours doing nothing. We take a walk by the lake, the rocks smooth under my feet. I stand in the cold water up to my ankles while Logan collects stones that he likes. We lounge around in the living room while he reads one of the yellowed and forgotten books from a shelf, and I lie down next to him, falling in and out of sleep and mixing up reality with dreams.

The sun is going down by the time I've woken up and stretched. Logan isn't beside me anymore. I get a glass of water and wander the house until I find him in the bedroom, lying down under the covers. I think he might be naked. His shirt is off, anyway. He watches me as I finish my water, putting the glass on a table. I go into the bathroom to splash some water on my face. When I walk back out, Logan's still staring.

"That was one of the best naps I've had in a while," I tell him.

"Mattie."

"Yeah?"

I recognize the look on his face. It's the same one he's given me in a few scenes we've shared, like he was thinking of all the things he wanted to do to me.

"What is it, Logan?"

He's still unexpectedly shy sometimes. "I'm ready."

"Ready for what?"

"Stop messing with me."

I wait for him. He knows what he has to say.

He takes in an impatient breath. "Please."

I sit on the bed beside him and kiss him. "You sure?"

He nods his yes, and I believe him when he grabs me and pulls me on top of him. I breathe a laugh as I kiss him again, sliding the covers away. I was right—he already took all his clothes off. That's disappointing. It might've been nice to play with him, telling him to undress slowly, but I can think of other ways to have fun. His hand grips at my shirt, trying to tug it off.

"Patience. Be patient."

"You promised rewards."

I laugh again, but he's serious—practically squirming beneath me, trying to press his hips up into mine. "Please."

He's getting better at begging. I smile as I kiss him. "Okay."

LOGAN

MATT REALLY SHOCKS the hell out of me and uses a belt to cuff my hands. It's like he knew the one way to torture me. Really get at me, not being able to touch him. He grabs my jaw, forcing me to look at him as he grips my dick, taking his time going up and down. If I try to pump up into his hand, he pulls away completely. I could cry, I really could. Just when I think I might get close, he presses a thumb to the tip, making me jerk under the pressure.

"Not yet."

I can't even beg properly, since he's stuffed my mouth with a sheet. I give a muffled "Fuck you," and he laughs at me. He straddles me, sitting in my lap, my dick rubbing against his.

"Is it okay if you go inside me?"

Always asking questions, always asking permission. It drove me crazy, once—but I look forward to it now. It's a constant reminder, maybe, that he's thinking of me and my safety. That he wants me to want everything he does. It makes me think that I deserved more than the shit I've gotten before. The edge of a memory starts to twist its way in, but Matt puts a hand against my cheek, watching me closely.

241

I nod. He grabs the lube, which I'd taken out from my duffel earlier, and plays with himself. He's torturing me again. Making me watch as he pushes in one finger, and then another. He's totally unashamed. Unembarrassed. This is the Matt I wish I could see more of. Unapologetically himself, not trying to please anyone but him. He looks free for once. He's fucking powerful like this, grinning as he spreads his legs so that I can see. I've never come without touching myself, from just watching something so hot my body wants to explode, but there's a first time for everything. I have to breathe slowly and close my eyes to stop myself.

A hand grabs my chin and holds my head up. "Watch," he says. My words are muffled. He pulls out the sheet. "What was that?" he asks.

"I can't," I say, gasping. "Please. I'm—" It's embarrassing to admit. "I'm close."

He tilts his head. "I didn't say that you could come yet."

"I know. That's why I—"

Matt stuffs the sheet back into my mouth. "Fine. Let me put it in."

He slips on a condom. Just his fingers and even the grip of latex is torture. He positions himself, and—fuck, I almost come with just the tip pushing into him. He's warm and tight, but not painfully so. The lube lets me slip in, and he wraps around me. I buck my hips, and he doesn't stop me this time. He meets my rhythm, pushing up and back down on me, both of us moaning loud enough that I'm glad I don't have any neighbors. He pulls out the sheet from my mouth and leans forward to kiss me. The pounding slows to a grind, and he sits up again, rocking back and forth.

"You feel good," he tells me. "You feel so fucking good."

I thrust up and hit a wall. He clenches around me as he cries out.

"You okay?" I ask. My voice is hoarser than I'm expecting.

"Yeah. It only hurt a little." He leans back on one hand as he rides, other hand gripping his own dick, his eyes closed as he bites his lip. It's too much. I pulse in and out until my body tenses and my brain glitches. My body shakes as I come, eyes squeezed shut. When the waves end, my chest heaves for air, skin coated in sweat. Matt's still on top of me, watching me hungrily. He's still pumping his hand around his dick, and I open my eyes just in time to see a spurt of white fly forward, hitting my cheek and neck and chest. His body spasms, ass clenching around my dick, but I don't mind. He's so fucking beautiful as he moans, almost cries, losing control.

He gasps and falls forward on top of me. I can feel my eyelids growing heavy. Whenever I come I'm ready to pass out. I'm worried Matt's going to fall asleep like this, too. "Can you untie me?" I whisper.

"Yeah. Yeah." He reaches up and undoes the belt. There are red marks around my wrists. "You okay? Shit. I should've been more careful."

"I'm fine." I rub my wrists, but I don't know if I really am all right. I can't even look at him. I reach down and pull off the condom, absentmindedly tying the ends and tossing it.

"Hey," he says. He leans forward so that I can see him clearly. "You're pulling back."

He's right. I always feel a wave of shame after I have sex. Usually I've got someone like Briggs to treat me like shit and distract me, but now just the thought of *Briggs* sends a knife of anxiety through me, and Mattie is here with his questions about if I'm okay, brushing a hand against my cheek like he loves me, and—shit, it's mortifying for my eyes to start to well up now. Am I really going to be that guy that cries after having sex? I blink, try to look away so he won't notice, but of course he does.

"Logan?" he says, worried. "What do you need?"

I don't want to speak. I don't want to be touched. I'm feeling too hot all over, trapped with him on top of me. "Get off. Get off me."

He does without hesitation, sliding off, a hand hovering over me like he isn't sure if he should touch me or not. I'm not sure either.

I hate that I'm this fucked up. I hate that I can't have sex without wanting to cry, without hating myself and my body and my mind. Around now I would just let myself become numb, but this time I can't escape the emotions. Maybe it's because Matt is here, and he wants me to know that he's safe and that he cares. The tears keep building. I start to lose control in a different way. There's no warning. I sob so hard that I think I might be sick. I hear my own voice—distant but loud, almost screaming. "I hate this shit." I say that over and over again. "Fuck. I hate this."

Mattie's holding me. I don't push him away. He's holding me tight, saying that he's here. "Let it out. Let it out." His voice is calm. It helps. Like it's okay to let him be the anchor. The screams and sobs slow down until I'm lying on my side, crying, Mattie holding me tightly from behind.

"I'm here," he keeps saying. "I'm here. I'm not going anywhere."

I think I'll do it. I think I'll let myself trust him. Let myself be vulnerable, knowing I'll be safe. Maybe it's this cabin. Getting away from everything, having the space to be myself. Maybe it's just that I'm tired of the way I've been living. "I'm so tired, Matt."

"I know. It's okay."

When I wake up, I smell food cooking in the kitchen and hear music playing. I peel myself out of the bed's sheets and pad to the bathroom to take a shower. I stand under the hot water that stings my skin. He saw me last night. Matt saw a version of me that I didn't even know was inside of my body. He might know me better than I know myself at this point, since I was so out of it that I'm not sure what happened. I'm already feeling the heat of shame crawl through me as I turn off the water and dry myself with a towel, grabbing a fresh pair of boxers.

I head out into the kitchen. I try not to feel overtaken by embarrassment. I still can't meet Mattie's eyes. "Hey."

Matt turns with a smile. "Hey. You're awake." His smile starts to fade. "How're you feeling?"

I nod. "Better." It's true. After last night, there's nowhere else to go but up.

He sets out plates of eggs and toast. We sit quietly. I'm not even hungry.

I clear my throat. "What do you think happened last night?"

"What do you mean?"

"I freaked the fuck out."

He puts down his toast and thinks for a second. Maybe he's trying to figure out the best way to say what he wants so that he doesn't hurt me. "I think it's all the trauma," he eventually answers, slowly. "Stuck in your body, you know? I thought it was a good thing, seeing you cry like that. I don't know. I can't tell you what your experience was."

"But?"

"It just made me wonder if you don't let it out enough. All of the pain that's built up inside of you."

I barely cry on my own if it's not for a film. The last

time I remember crying was in scene with Mattie. It's ironic. I remember getting on him, saying that he needs to let himself feel anger. That it would let him become a better actor. I was hiding emotions from myself, too, in the end.

"Sorry," I tell him. "It was embarrassing."

"I was happy you felt safe enough for that to happen."

"Yeah. Maybe it was a mix of being with you and getting away from the city."

"Good. It's important to release that kind of thing, you know?"

We're quiet again for a while, long enough that we both finish eating. I get up and grab our plates to take them to the sink. "Whatever happens," I tell him, "I hope we can keep coming back here."

"Do you want that?" he asks. I look over my shoulder at him. "I'll come back. I'm game."

"Once a year," I say. "Same month and date, next year."

He's giving me that look again. All vulnerability and trust and love. "It's a promise."

Notes of Amy Tanner (Confidential)
Patient: Logan Gray
Age: 25
Diagnosis: CPTSD

Logan has increasingly made positive breakthroughs. Without prompting, he speaks about how his history with sexual abuse, assault, verbal abuse, and neglect has affected his ability to create secure attachments. He speaks with awareness on his various trauma styles, ranging from fight, freeze, and fawn. He has displayed a range of emotions, expressing more anger for his father and mother in particular, who he says "should have done more to protect" him.

Today, Logan spoke about his regrets with former partner Matthew Cole, and the way that their relationship ended. He stated, "I wish I had worked harder to heal before now, to make our relationship work."

Logan expressed a desire for more closure with Cole. When I suggested he reach out, Logan said, "I doubt he would want to hear from me." I did not push him to see that this was said in fear. I trust he will come to this realization on his own with time.

MATTIE

WHEN I FLY into Atlanta, it takes my brain a second to get used to the slower pace. I get into a car and begin the drive back to Decatur, the sleepy neighborhoods with front yards, sunlight shining through the large trees. I'd invited Logan home with me for the holidays—I didn't want him to be alone—but he promised he'd be all right in LA for the rest of the month. I texted Logan to let him know I landed safely and that I miss him, but I still haven't gotten an *I miss you, too*. We've been texting, calling, or meeting up every day for the past couple of weeks since the cabin, but I noticed when his messages slowed down and got shorter, when we only kept in touch because I reached out first. It's hard not to give in to insecurity. We got so close so quickly because of this movie, but now that filming for *Write Anything* is over... What if he starts to realize the feelings he'd had for me were because of his character? With some space, he could realize he doesn't care about me after all.

I pull up and swing into the driveway behind my dad's car. The house has pale blue siding. My mom's garden and hedges are doing well. I step out and slam the door shut just as the front door opens and Emma runs out, tears in her eyes as she leaps into my arms and hugs me so tightly I can't breathe. I laugh, eyes also welling up.

"Did you get taller?" I ask, pulling away.

"No," she says, wiping her cheeks and grinning. "Just gained weight."

"You look really great, Em."

"I know, right?"

My mom's come out, too, waiting in the doorway. She's radiant as I walk up to her and give her a hug, the sort of hug that could last a full minute and I still wouldn't want to pull away. "Welcome home, Mattie."

***

I settle in so quickly that it feels like I never left. I return to my old childhood bedroom. The closet's been taken over as storage for some of my mom's old clothes, but that's okay. I have more than enough space for my t-shirts and jean cut-offs. I go back to playing video games on my old Switch and watching TV in the living room and messing with Em, like I did when I was in high school, flicking Cheerios at her when our mom isn't looking.

"Stop being so immature!" she yells, but she's laughing, too.

Something else hasn't changed. My dad barely leaves his office now that I'm back. He's a warm brown and has those freckles that grow around the cheeks and eyes with old age and a mouth that's set into a scowl. I don't remember him ever laughing. I used to wonder why my mom would marry my father, but there were smaller moments peppered throughout my childhood, too: them sitting together silently in the living room, holding hands for hours without any need to speak.

When I first got back, my dad and I had a quick hello—serious, stern. We avoid each other when we can. We were never the type of family to sit down and eat meals together, which is probably for the best. He stays in his office while I eat on the living room floor with Emma. If we run into each other in the hall, we grumble an "excuse me" and pass by without meeting each other's eyes.

I want to say something to him, but I'm not even sure what. I want to ask him, maybe, why I wasn't enough for him to love me. I want to ask why me being gay changed his view of who I am, and the fact that I'm his son. It hurts. It still hurts, after all this time, but maybe I've gotten so used to the pain that I've learned to push it to the side.

I remember holding Logan as he screamed, releasing all the pain that'd built up inside of him, everything that he'd been hiding from himself. He'd scared me, the way he screamed, though I didn't want him to know. He screamed like he was dying. Maybe he was. Maybe holding in that pain was ripping him apart. I wonder if I'm doing the same.

This change of pace is what I needed. I can pretend, for a few days at least, that I'm not the actor Matthew Cole, star of one of the most anticipated films. I'm just Mattie, sitting at a table with my mom and my sister, talking and laughing and loving their company. It's good to hear how Emma is doing in school. She's a lot better now. As I suspected, she just needed a couple of weeks to get to know her classmates, and now she's friends with a group that she always hangs out with.

"We eat at the cafeteria together and we have movie nights and we study together in the library."

"That's great, Em."

"Oh, and I'm gay," she says.

I almost choke on my water.

My mom laughs. "Blessed with two gay children, huh?"

"When did you find out?" I ask her.

"Well, I don't know if I'm gay," Em says, "because sometimes I still like guys, too. Like, it's constantly going back and forth. But one of the girls in our group, Ayana, is really beautiful and so smart and funny and I have the hugest crush on her." Emma says all of this like she doesn't care what we think, but she isn't really looking at us, either.

"Thanks for telling us, Em," I say.

No one ever has to tell another person about their identity if they don't want to. It's a gift that she invited us in, a sign that we're trustworthy and safe enough for her to tell us. I hesitate. I wonder if she plans on telling our dad, too.

Maybe my hesitation makes my thoughts obvious. "I don't know if I'm going to tell him," Emma says. Her voice lowers. My mom smooths down her curly hair. "The way he treats you, because you're gay...I don't think I want him to know, just for him to treat me badly, too."

"You don't have to tell him anything. Not if you don't want to."

Emma shrugs with a twinge of sadness. It hurts, knowing she'll have to deal with the same thing that I did. A part of me hopes that if our dad ever found out, he would realize that he can't lose Em, too, and he would finally start to change. But maybe that's too optimistic.

I slide off the counter's stool and walk over to Emma and hug her. I pull away and she rolls her eyes at me with a grin, but I don't mind. "I love you, Em. Okay?"

"Yeah, yeah," she says. "I love you, too."

It's only been a couple of weeks, but I'm getting comfortable in Decatur. On Christmas morning we exchange gifts, and Em and I help our mom cook the traditional dinner. Cousins and my mom's friends come over, pinching my cheeks and ruffling my hair and saying how proud they are of me, the movie star. Dad even comes out of his office and sits on the couch the whole day, though he barely speaks.

After Christmas, I sleep in until ten in the morning and play games on the living room floor day after day. It's like the more I rest, the more tired I become, as if my body still has months of sleep to catch up on. I have to remind myself that, in just a couple of weeks, publicity is going to ramp up for *Write Anything*, and I'm going to be thrown back into the fast pace of LA. Besides Dave's "Project X" schedule, I've gotten a separate schedule for the red-carpet premiere, six different photoshoots, multiple TV and radio appearances, interviews in magazines, and of course the promo tour, which will have me traveling to ten different cities. I got confirmation that Logan won't be on the tour. I'm going to be trained on how to handle questions, especially surrounding him.

I've been texting with Logan on and off, trying to ignore the increasing panic when he doesn't text me back as often. It's possible that the excitement for our relationship has begun to wane. I have to ask myself, seriously, if my excitement has started to fade, too. I miss him, but it's easier to see how consumed I was by him—consumed with wanting to save him. I already know that I can't *save* Gray. He has to help himself, ultimately. But I can be there to support him, can't I? As long as supporting him doesn't become my entire life, my reason for being, overtaking myself and even my dreams—then we could make this work.

⌣

I get a text from Julie when I'm lying in bed, playing *Animal Crossing* on my Switch. We've been texting even more than I have been with Logan, but her latest message confuses me when it pops up on my phone. I'm so sorry, Mattie.

I frown as I type a response. What's wrong?

She doesn't reply right away. In the silence, my heart starts to pump harder. Something bad has happened. I'm afraid it's about Logan. I still don't spend a lot of time looking at social media. My only posts have been the obligatory photos on Insta, quick snaps of me around set with Gray. The notifications are way more overwhelming than usual, and I squint as I begin to scroll. My eyes blur.

Matthew Cole is a piece of shit.

Who the fuck lies about something like this?

I thought you were better than this, Mattie.

There's a mix of emotions—relief that it isn't news that Logan was found hurt or dead, and fear of what the hell happened in the last hour. My phone buzzes. It's Paola. I pick it up on the first ring.

"Hey!" I try to sound cheerful and not confused and scared. "What's going on?"

"Hey, Matt," she says slowly, carefully. "Have you been online today?"

"I just started to scroll through Twitter."

"Don't," she says, quickly. "It's not good." She takes a breath. I close my eyes and, somehow, in that moment, I know what she's going to say. "It leaked. I don't know how. It somehow got out that your relationship with Logan isn't real."

She told me to stop, and I know that she's right—I should stop—but I keep scrolling on my laptop.

I thought you were different than other celebrities.

This is so disappointing.

You're just as bad as Logan Gray.

My phone buzzes again. Another text from Julie. I think I know who leaked it

This is too much. I feel like I can't breathe.

"Mattie?" Paola says. She sounds worried. "Are you there?"

I nod, even though she can't see me. "Yes. Yeah, I'm here." My breaths are short, rapid—I force myself to take one long inhale and let it out slowly. "What now? What do I do?"

"I've tried to get in touch with Reynolds. He's already discussing damage control with PR. The best thing might be for you and Logan to come out as a united force and say that this leak is just a rumor. You're together, and you're in love."

I bite my lip. It's true now, technically, that we are together—but that doesn't change the fact that our relationship was first a lie. I don't know if I want to continue telling it. Paola says she's getting another call, and after we hang up, I scroll to contacts and try to call Logan. I'm sent to voicemail. I text him. Can we talk?

He doesn't answer right away. Maybe he doesn't plan on answering at all. I sit with my phone, staring at Julie's text message. I start to type. Who do you think it was?

Bubbles appear and disappear. My phone starts to ring, and my heart jumps, thinking that it might be Logan, but when I look at the screen I see that it's Julie.

When I answer, her voice is soft. "Are you okay, Mattie?"

"Just a little shellshocked, I think," I say.

I've seen the way people treat celebrities. Humans so often decide as a collective to hate one person—decide that they have the right to treat another person horribly. I've never liked to see it, but I've also never been on the receiving end. Maybe I was too comfortable, thinking of myself as the golden boy of Hollywood, the Southern sweetheart that everyone loved. I didn't accept the fact that people could decide to hate me just as easily, too. What's worse is that I know I messed up, agreeing to lie about this relationship in the first place.

But I also know I don't deserve to be treated this way— not by anyone. Even if I've made a mistake, I'm still a human being, and I still deserve compassion and respect.

"I feel awful," Julie says. I can tell she's been crying. Her voice sounds stuffed up. "I'd—God, I've been seeing Keith," she tells me.

I'm confused by the sudden tangent, before things start to click into place.

"I was drinking with him last night, and I told him about you and Logan," she says. "I'm so sorry, Matt. It wasn't my business to tell, especially when it was supposed to be a secret."

"It's okay," I say, voice low. And I mean it. I really do. Julie made a mistake, too. She must have trusted Keith not to hurt me, even if he'd be tempted to hurt Logan. "How do you know that it was him?"

Julie lets out an annoyed breath. "He says it wasn't," she tells me. "I don't know. Maybe it's just a coincidence that I told him last night, and today it leaked. He says he wouldn't put the movie at risk just because he can't stand Logan, but I don't know. I'm so sorry," she says again. "I never should've told him in the first place."

"It's all right. Really. I promise, Julie. I forgive you."

"You're too kind to me," she says, and I think she might've started crying again. I hate that she feels so torn up about this. "What're you going to do now?"

"Paola says that Reynolds will probably want me and Logan to continue the lie. Say it's just a rumor. I don't know."

"I'm here," she says. "If you need me to get onto Instagram Live and swear up and down that you two are in a relationship, I'll do it."

I laugh, even though I feel like crying myself. "Thank you."

"I love you, Mattie. Okay?"

"I love you, too."

After I've hung up, I sit in my room for a few long minutes. I wait for Logan to call or text, and I'm not surprised when he never does.

There's one thing I dread, more than anything else—one thing I dread even more than the social media and the anger from the fans and Reynolds's potential plan, but I have to do it. I force myself to get up, open my door, and walk down the hall.

My mom and Emma sit together on the couch. They're both bent over Emma's laptop, open on her knees. Emma snaps her laptop shut the second she sees me. I know what she was showing my mom. They both look at me, and I look at them.

I take a deep breath, then step into the living room and sit down beside Emma.

"So," I start. "I know it's probably disappointing to hear, but it's true."

Neither of them say anything. They only watch me with surprised expressions, which is probably more heartbreaking than anything else.

"It started because the film wasn't getting good publicity," I say. "The producers needed the world to think that Logan and I liked each other—loved each other—to turn things around for the movie. I eventually really did fall in love with him, but I know that doesn't excuse the fact that I lied."

Emma is watching me, and God—I hate that I'm sitting here, telling her that I've messed up so badly, when I'm supposed to be the person she looks up to. She blinks and looks away. Even she doesn't know what to say.

My mom stares forward at the blank TV screen. "Why would you agree to something like that, Mattie?"

The disappointment in her voice might just shatter me. "I really—" I pause, clear my throat. "I needed the film to work. I felt like this was my chance to make it."

"And you were willing to give up your integrity?" she asks, looking at me finally, though now I wish she hadn't.

My gaze drops. My mom stands up, and I think she's about to walk out, unable to stand being in the same room with me—but she stops in front of me instead and rests a hand against my cheek. "I love you, Mattie," she says. "No matter what. But I know you were raised better than that."

I swallow and nod.

"You don't let go of who you are and your understanding of right and wrong for anything or anyone," she tells me. "You made a mistake. Now make it right."

She bends over, kisses my cheek, and leaves. I stare after her, probably more because I don't know if I can even face Emma, but I look at her when she pokes my arm. "It's kind of nice to see that you're not perfect for once," she says.

"Thanks?" But even as I try to force the sarcasm into my voice, I can't stop the real gratitude that peeks through.

She grins. "So what're you going to do now that you've fucked up so badly?"

"Like Mom said," I tell her. "I have to make it right."

LOGAN

AUDREY WON'T STOP calling me. She has the highest number of missed calls and texts, right after Mattie. I haven't been answering him much in the past few weeks. I don't know. Thoughts have been finding me recently.

My apartment's been steadily becoming worse. I pay more attention to cleaning when I know someone's going to come over, and I haven't seen Mattie for almost three weeks now. He's the only reason I bother to clean this apartment in the first place. I don't have enough energy to put shit away. I sit on the couch instead.

One of Audrey's voicemails told me that the truth leaked. I'm used to seeing people trash me on social. I'm not used to seeing it happen to Matt. I think they're going after him even more than me. Maybe because they thought he was better. Had him up on a pedestal.

I was the one who talked shit about him in that interview, got everyone talking about how we don't like each other, made the producers decide we needed to be in this fake, fucked-up relationship. And now, because of me, Matt's getting hurt.

These fucking people online. They're tearing him apart. The way things are going, this might mess up his future chances in Hollywood, and that's all he's ever wanted. I've managed to take his only dream away from him, too.

I'm too afraid to pick up when he calls or answer him back when he texts. Too afraid to face him, knowing how much I've fucked up his life. It's easier, isn't it? Easier to just scroll through social and listen to my phone every time it rings.

I'm not expecting to see Mattie's post. I hesitate, mouse hovering over the arrow. His face, his eyes, makes my heart jump. I haven't seen him in so long. I click play.

"I want to start by apologizing. I know I've disappointed a lot of you, and rightfully so. The producers of *Write Anything* wouldn't want me to say this, but I have to tell the truth."

I feel a spark of pride for him. Mattie going against Reynolds and Vanessa Stone?

Matt takes a breath. "It's true. At the beginning of filming, Logan and I both agreed to pretend to be in a relationship to boost the film's publicity. I shouldn't have lied. I shouldn't have agreed to it, for the benefit of the movie and myself. There isn't anything I can say in my defense. It was wrong, and I'm sorry.

"But as time went on, and as I got to know Logan more, I started to develop feelings for him. I fell in love with him. Though it started as a lie, Logan and I really are together. It isn't an act. I wish our relationship had begun differently, but in a strange way, I'm also grateful, because I don't know if I would've had the chance to get to know the Logan that I do now. The Logan he hides from the world—the Logan who's sweet, and caring, and generous, and deserving of so much more than anyone has given him." He looks up, his eyes into the camera, and it feels like he's trying to speak to me directly.

Like he's asking me to listen, to hear him, to stop running away. "I love him. I love Logan."

He rubs his neck. "I understand if I've lost your trust forever," he says. "I understand if you don't want to support me or *Write Anything*. But, if you are able to forgive us, I promise you I'll do better. I'm a human, and I may mess up again, but I'll do everything in my power not to."

The video stops. The silence of my apartment is overwhelming. I hadn't realized how much of a comfort it was, to hear Matt's voice.

But the whispering thoughts begin again.

MATTIE

AT FIRST, THE producers were pissed I went out on a limb on my own, but within a day of my post, there was a surprising turnaround. A lot of people still say what Logan and I did is unforgiveable, but many others have shown support, applauding my "courage to tell the truth" and "give a genuine apology." Conversations have sparked around whether we should show more compassion to people when they mess up, including celebrities. Other actors have shown their support, too, with some retired actors even sharing their own publicity schemes from back in the day.

I've done all that I can. I decide to unplug—rest my brain from the stress of social media and publicity. Holiday break ends, and Emma flies back to school in New York. It's nice to have my mom to myself for a while, even if the house is so quiet. But without Em around, I also find myself running into my dad more. It was like he felt outnumbered with both of his children here, but without Emma he feels safer to leave his office and roam the halls. He even comes out one night to sit in the living room with me and my mom as we watch TV.

The channel is on some Hallmark movie, my mom's favorite kind to watch, when the commercials begin. The trailer for *Write Anything* starts playing. Seeing myself and Logan on the screen is like a shock of ice-cold water. Makes sense, schedule-wise, since we've been in post-production for a while, but that world—the movie, LA, Logan—felt separate from my life here in Decatur.

My mom claps with excitement and grabs the remote to turn the volume up. I glance at my dad. He's staring at the screen, expression blank. I overheard my mom telling him about the trouble I'd been in one night, while they were sitting in the kitchen and I was passing by in the hall, but when I paused to hear what my dad thought of it all, there was only silence.

Romantic, inspirational music plays as different shots appear on the screen. Logan running through the rain. Me, turning to look over my shoulder at the viewer. A split screen as we furiously type, engulfed in anger for each other.

The voiceover: "But can the power of story transform their hatred into love?" A shot as we turn to each other, contemplating kissing. I wish Logan were here so that he could say something sarcastic, and so that I could laugh with him. "*Write Anything*. Rated PG-13..."

My mom shakes my shoulder excitedly. I grin up at her from my spot on the floor, and we bend to each other for a hug as she tousles my hair. "I'm never going to get tired of seeing you on my TV screen," she says.

"Thanks, Mom."

I look at my dad to see if he's going to say anything just as he stands up and walks past without a word.

"I'm sorry, Mattie," my mom says. "Habits are hard to let go."

I have a flinch of anger, hearing that. It's a habit to hate your son? But I'm not really upset at her. What do I expect her to do? Divorce him for me? A part of me wishes she would make a mighty stand like that, but it wouldn't be fair to expect that she destroy her entire life because of the way my father treats me.

I need to figure out my relationship with my dad—that isn't my mom's responsibility—and after everything with Logan, I'm feeling more and more like I need to speak. Say something, instead of sitting silently. My father has made me feel so ashamed to be *me*. Not only the fact that I'm gay, but ashamed of my entire existence. It's like his hatred of my identity has begun to sink into my layers, poisoning my body and my love for myself. I'm tired of having so much shame for who I am and hiding myself away in a shell.

My mom's mumbling that she has to call so-and-so to see if they've seen the trailer yet. I tell her I'll be right back. I follow my dad down the hall and to his office. He hasn't closed the door, so he sees me when I step into the threshold. He looks like he's just getting comfortable at the desk when I walk in.

We watch each other for a long moment. We're used to silence with each other, but this time instead of looking for an escape path, I'm trying to find the right words.

"I know that you don't accept me," I tell him. "That really messed me up for a long time. Made me ashamed of myself."

He sits straighter in his seat, raising his chin. I'm afraid. I shouldn't have to be. Not of him—not anymore.

"But I want you to know that I've let go of that shame." I pause. "I'm working on letting it go, anyway. I deserve to love myself and who I am. I deserve to be respected and loved and to feel free to be me. I deserve better from you."

I stand there, waiting. It feels like an eternity. I'm just

starting to think he's refusing to speak when he opens his mouth. "You—being gay was never right when I was young," he tells me. "It was always a sin. I still think it's a sin now."

"If you don't accept this part of me, then you don't love me."

He looks away. "You're my son," he says. "I love you because you're my son. I don't love *this* part of you."

I'm going to cry. I'd feel embarrassed, I think, of my emotion once—especially here, in front of my dad as he rejects me. But maybe it's a little act of rebellion that I let my eyes well up. "No. You can't love me if you don't love that I'm gay. And if you can't love me, then I can't have a relationship with you."

We never had much of a relationship to begin with, but saying it out loud—it feels like I've taken some power back from him. He's made his hatred and disgust obvious. Now, I've made my love for myself just as clear.

He's never liked losing power. "Fine. This is my house. You can leave."

I watch him for a second, before I decide that there isn't any point in arguing. There isn't any point in trying to change his mind—in convincing him that I'm worth more than this. I deserve a safe space, and right now, this house isn't it. I leave the office for my bedroom without another word and begin to pack, grabbing my backpack and opening my drawers. My mom is confused when she looks up at me as I walk into the kitchen, pulling her reading glasses off.

"Where're you going?"

"Dad told me to get out." I lean in to kiss her cheek good-bye, but she pulls away.

"What?"

"It's okay," I tell her. "Well—it's not okay that he's doing this, but I want to leave now, too."

"No, no," she says, hand on my arm. "Wait. Let me speak to him."

I sit down at the counter, but only because she asked me to. I can hear the argument escalating in the office, until finally my mom comes back. "You can stay, Mattie," she says.

"Has he told you that he accepts me?"

She hesitates. "No, but—"

"Then I have to leave," I say, standing up from the counter. "I deserve better." I might've felt guilty, once. I might've been afraid that I was tearing the family apart. But my dad is the one who has decided not to love me. I can't take responsibility for what he does.

"Where're you going to go?" she asks, exasperated.

"I'll just stay in a hotel in the city." My flight back to LA is in a couple of days anyway.

She looks like she's considering arguing. A part of me is annoyed with her. I'm not the one who needs to be convinced to put my energy into making peace. My dad is the one she should be focusing on. Maybe she figures out the same thing.

"All right," she says. She's getting teary-eyed. This is a stressful way to end our visit. "Call me when you're settled in the hotel, okay?"

I hug her goodbye. It's only when I'm back in the car I rented, engine on, that I sit for a second. My adrenaline is pumping, so I don't think I'm even aware of my emotions. I let myself feel the anger and the fear and the broken heart. I'm heartbroken that my dad doesn't love me. One thing that's not there, though? Shame.

I turn my music on, roll down the windows, and start singing as I pull out of the drive.

LOGAN

NOT SURE HOW much time has passed. Maybe a couple of days. I don't have enough energy to do anything but lie on the couch. When depression hits, it's too late to realize I'm caught in it.

There's no hope for me. No chance I'm going to change. I'm just going to be the same miserable fuck for the rest of my life, caught in the same repetitive cycles, this hell I've created.

Last night, I wondered what the least painful way would be to die. I thought I could give the housekeeper a call so my body wouldn't rot too much before I was found. Sorry, Sandra. I drank myself to sleep. But by the time I woke up again, something shifted inside me. Daring to have some hope, I guess, that things could be different. I just don't know how. I don't know how to change.

There's a knock on the door. Who the hell is that? My dad only leaves voicemails. He never comes to visit. Another knock, and then a jingling of keys. My heart beats harder when I think of the possibility. Mattie, walking in through the door. I want to see him, even though I shouldn't. I shouldn't want him to be anywhere near me.

Audrey calls my name. "Logan?"

I manage to force myself up from the couch enough that she sees me. Disgust is smeared across her face as she looks around the apartment. I must smell like shit, too. It's kind of sad, maybe, that I'm not even embarrassed. She's seen far worse.

"Where the hell have you been?" she says, heels clacking closer.

"Here." My voice is hoarse.

"I've been calling you for a week straight, Logan. I was afraid I'd walk in and find..."

She doesn't finish that sentence, and I don't say she was close to that happening.

Audrey takes a handful of bottles from the center table. "You need to get up. I got a call from Reynolds."

I stare up at the ceiling. "I'm already off the promo tour, right?"

"Yes, but he has another request. Another way you can help the film's promotion."

They already cut me from all publicity. What more could they possibly want?

"Reynolds let me know that he and Vanessa Stone thought it might be as good a time as any to publicly end your relationship with Matthew," Audrey says. "He wants to move up the scheduled breakup."

I flinch. I haven't spoken to Matt going on a month now. "Why would they want that?"

"There's been surprisingly good response to Matt's message, but it's not enough. The numbers for the film took a hit. Reynolds thinks there's still a chance to save the film if you two break it off. Lean into the bad publicity instead of trying to avoid it."

"That's the stupidest fucking thing I've ever heard."

She ignores me. "Audiences will be interested in the drama. Sales always go up around celebrity breakups."

"That isn't the whole reason, is it?"

Audrey purses her thin lips. "Reynolds has never been happy with you," she says. "He doesn't want you publicly attached to the film going forward."

"Besides being the lead actor, you mean?"

"He says detaching you will lessen the chances of another . . . incident."

"And being Matt's boyfriend attaches me too much, I guess."

Audrey's face softens. She smooths down the back of her dress and sits on the couch beside me. "This is a perfect opportunity for you to take some time for yourself. You can regroup. Work on your image, try to prepare for potential auditions."

I rest my head on the back of the sofa. "You really think anyone will be interested in me for auditions right now?"

"They might be," she says, "if the film does well enough. The relationship has served its purpose and run its course. The attention of this breakup could turn focus back to the film while Matthew is on tour."

I've been in this business long enough to understand what she means. Matt's interviewers will inevitably fish around for questions about me, this scandal with Briggs, the assault— things that could sour the movie's image. But if Mattie and I have broken up, then he can have more power to say that he doesn't know how I'm doing, we haven't spoken in weeks, is it okay to focus on the movie? Maybe he could even rev up some pity points. He could say that the celebration of this film is bittersweet, because even though I've broken his heart, he still loves this movie so much. There's plenty of upside for publicly ending this relationship. It'd be good for Matt, too, in the end. Better for him to not be connected to me.

Audrey asks me if I'm still listening.

"Yeah. I'm listening."

"This is a good thing," she says. Always trying to put a positive spin on shit.

"Right. What do they need me to do?"

MATTIE

PAOLA PICKS ME up from my hotel and gives me a tight, warm hug. I check my phone as I pull on my seatbelt. I texted Logan a few times—after my fight with my dad, when I found a hotel in Atlanta, and when I landed in LA yesterday. Nothing. At least in person, I'm able to look him in the eye and tell him not to push me away, but now...

"Everything all right?" Paola asks me, looking over her shoulder as she pulls into traffic.

"Yeah. I think so." I don't want to get into my personal life right now. She doesn't need to worry about my relationship with my father or with Logan.

"It's amazing how much you've turned everything around with that post," she says. "There's just something about you that people want to love, Mattie."

I try not to think about the fact that I wish one person in particular wanted to love me, too.

She meets my eye. "Are you ready?"

Vanessa Stone got in touch with Paola to request a meeting in her office. Vanessa's production company is one of the highest earning in the industry. She could end my career with the blink of an eye. Not only do I have to deal with the stress of impressing her, but I'm nervous not knowing why she wants to meet in the first place.

"As ready as I can be," I tell her.

Vanessa is waiting for us in a conference room when her assistant guides us in through the glass doors. I'm surprised to see Reynolds there in his business suit and Dave standing awkwardly by the tall glass windows. He spins around when we walk in. Vanessa stands up. She has a short, sleek black bob, a dark gray dress, six-inch heels. Her handshake is firm, and she gestures to the seats opposite her at the table.

I try to swallow down the nerves, sitting opposite Vanessa and Reynolds. My old childhood stage fright isn't as bad as it usually is. A lot has changed, since I've started to learn to stand up for myself and let go of my shame. But it's still scary, sitting opposite such powerful people in the industry. Dave rejoins us at the table, giving a quick, friendly nod. It's strange to see him again after over a month, when we'd been working with each other almost every day.

Vanessa begins. "It's great to see you. I haven't had a chance to watch the film yet, but I've heard it's expected to be well-received. Are you looking forward to the promo tour?"

I flip through the roles I'm used to playing and snag the confident, up-and-coming movie star. I put on a charming grin. "Yeah, of course. That's the fun part of the job, right?"

Vanessa chuckles in the back of her throat, lips still tightly pressed together. "We wanted to have a chat with you about our plan. A quick prep to your prep sessions, I suppose you could say."

I'm reminded of the initial meeting I had with Dave and Reynolds, except this time, Logan and his manager aren't with us. "Okay," I say, overly aware of how uncertain my tone sounds.

"Focus on *Write Anything* is beginning to wane. *Good Dog* is getting a lot of attention due to Phillip Desmond's growing popularity."

"Have to admit, he is pretty attractive," Dave mutters. "In that basic white boy way."

"Yes, well," Vanessa says with a barely disguised annoyance, "audiences have been trained to love basic white boys, so inevitably, the film is starting to gain more attention."

My heart sinks. It isn't surprising that there would be more publicity and buzz around a film starring two white men, versus a film starring two Black men, even with me and Logan benefiting from colorism. It's discouraging, but it's the sort of racism I knew I would have to deal with in the industry. I decided to make acting my dream anyway. All of that, plus the issues we've been having with publicity...I can see how *Write Anything* won't stand a chance against its rival.

"We need to make a play to turn attention back to you and our film," Vanessa continues. "We need you to break up with Logan Gray."

I sit straighter, fully startled, mouth opening. I don't catch myself fast enough. "What?"

"We went through different options and ideas with various teams," Reynolds says. He sounds bored, as usual. "This seemed like the most efficient route. You would've had to break up eventually anyway, after the promo tour began."

"No," I say.

Everyone's eyes land on me. Vanessa raises a finely threaded eyebrow.

"No," I say again. "I can't." I look at Paola, whose mild look of panic translates into *please, stop talking*, but I shake my head. "It might be a shock, but—well, Logan and I are in a real relationship now."

The silence is stunned, but it's quickly interrupted by Reynolds's barking laugh. He thinks I'm joking.

"I thought that was a part of the act," Dave says. "That message you posted. I thought you were just doubling down on the lie. You're really dating Logan?"

"More than dating," I say. "We're boyfriends."

Vanessa frowns. "That was an unwise choice," she says. "We agreed that the relationship was for the purpose of publicity."

"Technically, that was a verbal agreement," Paola says for me, always ready to fight. I always love her, but especially now.

"Besides, we can't help that we began to—well, start to have real feelings," I tell them.

Vanessa doesn't like me pushing back. "You need to publicly end this relationship with a social media post to your followers. The post has already been written. The draft will be shared with you tonight."

"I'm not doing it."

"Mattie," Paola whispers.

"You'll essentially say that you've discovered Logan Gray is more harmful than you've expected. You've grown tired of the negativity that follows him."

"I refuse."

"Matt," Paola says, more firmly this time. "You could break up with him publicly and continue the relationship privately."

"That isn't an option," Vanessa tells her. "We can't have paparazzi snapping photos of them together and blasting the news that they were lying about the breakup on top of everything else."

"This is ridiculous," I tell them. "You can't control my love life." I might have a dream of being successful in this industry, but I'm not willing to give up myself and what I want for anyone.

"We kind of already did, kid," Dave says, leaning forward, but I'm sick of this role he's been playing, too—pretending to be this fatherly mentor figure who gives a shit. He doesn't. He's been hired by Vanessa. He only cares about the film. "You already agreed to play along for the sake of the movie. Don't back out on us now."

I shake my head. "Logan deserves more than that. I care about him. I'm not going to toss him and our relationship away for a publicity stunt."

"Communication has already been sent to Logan," Vanessa says.

My heart drops. Is this why he's been ignoring my texts? Has he already agreed to this without even talking to me about it?

"He knows what to expect," Vanessa says. "You need to be the one to publicly end this relationship by the end of tonight."

"No. I'm serious," I say, cutting Paola off when she tries to say my name again. "I won't do it."

I stand up. I'm trembling, but I do a good job of hiding it as I turn away from the table without another word. Paola catches up with me in the hall.

"Are you sure about this?" she says, her voice lowering. I can hear raised voices echoing behind us. "Vanessa is not going to be happy."

I'm tired of being controlled by everyone around me because of my fear. I have to be willing to walk away from Hollywood if it means freedom. My dream has been acting—not this bullshit behind the scenes. "Yeah. I'm sure."

But even as I say the words, anxiety drifts through me. I'd feel better about this if I knew I had Logan by my side to make a stand—to fight Vanessa and the rest of the team and say that we're going to continue our relationship, no matter what they demand. But he hasn't replied to me in weeks. It's possible he broke up with me in his head before Vanessa even made this decision. I'm starting to feel twists of regret. What if I fucked up my entire career over this, and Logan doesn't even feel the same way anymore? Maybe I'm relying on just a little too much faith.

LOGAN

Can we talk please?

Please give me a call. We can talk this through.

Remember what we agreed to, in the cabin? We said we would try to work through this.

We said we'd talk things out instead of pushing each other away.

I love you, Logan.

Please call me.

I think about it. But the idea of hearing Matt's voice and fighting and straining and pushing against the thought that I hurt him is exhausting. It's better to look at the messages and think—yeah, maybe this is for the best. Trying to change is impossible. He'll go along with Vanessa's plan for the promo tour. He'll break up with me, and I'll go back to the life I was living before. It'll probably be harder to get work, now. I'll probably have to stay in this apartment under my dad's rule. It is what it is, right?

Another text buzzes. I check my phone from my spot in my bed. I haven't moved in about a day, since Audrey came.

It's Briggs. Let's talk.

It's almost a comfort, to see his name appear. I know Briggs. I know what to expect with him. Matt had on one of his podcasts, once, about how trauma rewires the brain—makes it feel safer to want what a person already knows, what they're already familiar with, no matter how much it hurts. I think he was hoping it'd help me.

About what?

Let's get lunch.

He probably wants to meet with me in public so that people can take photos of us together and the bad press he's been getting will lay off. Obviously, he didn't try to rape me if I'm with him. I don't know. If that's the story he wants, it's not a big deal for me to give it to him. I've always been good at giving people what they want.

I get out of bed and take a quick shower and throw on some clothes from one of the many piles on my bedroom floor. Shades on to hide the bags under my eyes, keys in my hand. I speed through the city, sunlight too bright. I screech to a stop near the restaurant and park, turning off the engine. A few people recognize me on the sidewalk, stopping to whisper and stare. Nothing I'm not used to. The restaurant has wood-paneled floors and walls and giant booths. It smells like grease and cigar smoke. It's the seedy type of place I usually only go to at three in the morning after a night of drinking and fucking. Haven't lived that kind of life in a while now. My days have been so filled with Mattie.

Briggs is already waiting at a table in the corner. He stands when he sees me. Claps a hand on my shoulder. I flinch, and his grin fades when he notices, but he doesn't say anything about it.

"Glad you came," he says, sitting back down again.

I sit opposite him without speaking. I'm tense. I usually don't give a fuck, being around Briggs. He treats me like shit all the time. There were moments when I didn't want him to hit me as hard as he did, or draw blood when he bit me, or tie me up and fuck me so hard that I would feel sick and my entire body would hurt for days. I told myself I liked the pain. A lot of people like pain, right? Yeah. I thought I was one of them. But I'm realizing now I didn't enjoy it so much. It felt better to pretend that I wanted someone like Briggs. Only difference between the last night I met with Briggs and all the other nights with him before was that I told him to stop and he didn't listen. Pretty big difference, I guess.

It's harder to breathe. I'm starting to leave my body again, and Matt isn't here to put a hand on my cheek and ask me if I'm still with him. Maybe I shouldn't have come here. Maybe I should leave.

"I'm surprised you agreed to meet up," Briggs says. "We left things off in a pretty shitty place."

"You claimed I attacked you."

"You fucking did," he says. He takes a breath. "But I'll admit it. I shouldn't have been so rough with you."

Is that how he's choosing to describe rape? Okay.

"I wanted to apologize in person," he says.

"And hopefully get a few photos of us together to show we're back to being friends?"

"You always were a smart one," he says, grin growing. "But this will help your image, too. People are still pissed at you for fucking me up." He raises a hand to the waitress. "What do you want? I'm buying."

We get beers. Neither of us are eating. I guess we both want to get out of here as fast as possible. Maybe that's just me. Briggs smirks over the rim of his glass as he drinks. His legs are long, so when he leans back in his seat, his knees bump into mine. He doesn't readjust.

"I was upset you thought I assaulted you."

"You *did* assault me."

"We've fucked like that plenty of times before. You never minded."

"I minded this time."

"Why?"

I shrug. I know the answer is Matt. I just don't want to say his name right now.

Briggs picks up on it anyway. "How's the boyfriend?" he asks.

"We're breaking up," I say.

He laughs. "Of course."

"Matt's supposed to post something on social tonight."

Briggs leans closer to me. "I'll have to keep an eye out, then."

I'm not attracted to Briggs. Not anymore. Was I ever? His

knees start to open mine. I don't want him to touch me. The thought makes me sick, and feeling his leg press against mine is pulling me out of my body again. I drink more beer. He takes the glass away from my mouth and out of my hand, forcing me to pay attention. That would've excited me, once. I would've considered him fun.

"Why don't we help the announcement along, then?"

I squint at him. "What?"

Briggs pulls back again, eyeing me. "We could make a show of it. Like we've done before."

I shrug. The fact that I didn't say "no" out loud is enough for him. He leans forward and presses his mouth to mine. He pushes his tongue against my lips. My body shuts down. I wonder, distantly, if this is technically assault also. He has to know I'm uncomfortable. That I don't want him touching me. I remember Matt. Even if we'd kissed a million times before, he always paused and asked me for permission. He was so aware of my constant need for consent that it upset me at first. Annoyed me, that he thought I was someone who had to be treated delicately. Who deserved to be shown so much care.

I pull away, unable to look at Briggs. "I'm going to go."

He wipes the corner of his mouth. "You used to be a lot more fun."

I slide my chair back, away from his knees. When I stand, I see that across the restaurant someone has their phone out, pointed at us. They're not embarrassed to be caught. They keep recording or taking pictures or whatever the hell it is they're doing. Probably going to make thousands on this. I can't even be mad at them. I chose to come here, right? I try to take my time as I leave, even though I'm shaking and my legs are weak.

Fuck. I'm tired. I'm tired of being caught in this cycle. Why would I even agree to meet Briggs like this? I knew what was going to happen: he would treat me like shit, push my boundaries, touch me without my consent. Around and around I go again.

RED ALERT: BREAKING NEWS

My dearest cherubs,

Feast your eyes on this latest visual entertainment:

[Video begins: The setting is a dark, grainy restaurant. Beneath the table, we see one man's leg rubbing another man's leg. The camera shakes and zooms in. The faces are blurry as one man kisses the other. One man gets up, looks at the camera. The image is blurry. Video ends.]

[Photos, side by side: Clearer images of Logan Gray sitting with Briggs Stevenson.]

I am so excited—no, *thrilled*—to return with more Logan Gray Is a Fucking Asshole™ content! I'm over the moon for this newest blessing, because honestly, where would I be in my life without reasons to shit on Logan Gray? It's like he writes these posts himself, and I'm ever-so-grateful that he continues to be the sort of trash fire human being that should probably off himself to stop this endless humiliation.

What? Too harsh?

Fine, then I'll revise: I think that he should *politely excuse himself from this earth and life*, for his own sake. But, thankfully for ours, he's still around so that we'll be able to witness and enjoy his consistent disgrace.

I'm looking forward to the vague apology for cheating on Matthew Cole that'll be released, so that I can begin the official countdown to the next Logan Gray incident.

Goodbye, my loves,

Angel

Twitter.com

Trending for You

HE CHEATED
#WeLoveMattieCole
#LoganGrayIsOverParty
#CancelLoganGrayPermanently

@parrotwars

I, for one, will be watching Write Anything to support Matthew Cole and the amazing cast and crew who put the movie together and to support the future of queer film. It's unfortunate that Logan Gray was ever attached to it.

💬 1.3K 🔁 11.7K 🤍 21.9K

@facinwashere

Is anyone really that shocked that he cheated????
He's treated people like shit for most of his adult life. UM HELLO, yes he's trash! He will always be trash!

💬 608 🔁 7K 🤍 10.2K

Video begins:

YouTube personality star Shaina Lively sits in front of bright yellow lights. Her eyes are puffy and red. She sniffs as she looks into the camera. She begins in her trademark Southern accent (which some, in the comments, have suggested is fake):

"Mattie Cole has had his heart broken by Logan Gray." She pauses. "I mean, I haven't actually seen him say that his heart was broken, but I'm assuming that it was, given those horrific photos that were leaked."

She blinks and wipes the corner of her eye, trying not to cry.

"I'm sorry, y'all. There's just something about this story that really does something to my heart. Matthew Cole deserves so much more than to be treated like crap by someone like Gray.

"It reminds me of the way I've ended up in cycles before, you know? I always find the same guys to run back to. The same ones who always treat me awfully in the end, like I'm not good enough for love. It's amazing how the same cycle just keeps appearing again and again until we're able to make a change. Like the same thing will keep happening until we start to heal. My exes even all *look* the same."

She laughs and wipes her face. "Ugh! It's not like I even know Mattie. We're not close friends. I don't know why I'm so emotional.

"Anyway, I didn't mean to come on here and talk about my personal life today. I just hope that Matthew Cole isn't trapped in a cycle like I was. I hope he can see that he is worth that starry-eyed, head-in-the-clouds romantic love where he's doted on by someone who wants him to be happy. I hope I figure out the same thing for myself, too."

Shaina smiles through the tears. "Well, that's all for now! Until next time."

Video ends.

MATTIE

I KNOCK ON Logan's apartment door. I don't know if he even wants me here. I've been in LA for three days now, going back and forth on whether I should just come over, and I finally gave in. My insecure fear has reached a crescendo. Isn't it possible that he never actually cared about me? Maybe I'm being a stalker now, and I just can't get the hint that he doesn't want me anymore. And even if those fears are wrong—even if he does love me, but he's struggling to show it   I'm still confused about the line between supporting him and caring for myself. I deserve more than this. I've spoken to him, multiple times, about how I deserve more.

The door opens. I jump back, startled. I'd stopped knocking for a while, only scrolling through my phone, thinking about calling Logan one more time. He stands in the doorway, hair in his eyes and bags so dark they look like bruises. I can see behind him that his apartment is a mess again. I meet his gaze. It's our first time seeing each other in over a month. His stare is shuttered, guarded, and...

I don't know if I can do this anymore. I don't know if I can continue to break down Logan's walls in an attempt to save him. I'm not even sure he wants the help to change—and maybe I should be focusing on saving myself.

"Why haven't you been answering me?" I ask him, voice low. "My calls, my texts..."

He shrugs. It's the typical Logan Gray shrug, like he can't be bothered to give a fuck. "Got bored."

And this. Not only are his walls back up, but he's on the offensive again—ready to hurt whoever he needs to if it means he'll feel safe. I want to cry. For him and for me. But there's anger, too. "Bored of me? Bored of the relationship?" I ask him. "Bored of what, Logan?"

He leans against the doorframe, watching me closely.

"You were with Briggs," I say. "Why?"

"He invited me to lunch."

"He hurt you." I take a breath. Maybe it isn't my place, to tell him where he can and can't go, who he can be with, even if it was someone who attacked him. Even if it feels like he met up with Briggs because he's still trapped by his trauma. "Why did you kiss him?"

"I can kiss whoever I want, can't I?"

"I fought for us," I tell him. "I want you to know that. I told Vanessa to fuck off, basically. I said that our relationship is real, and that I care about you, because it's true. I love you, Logan."

He stops looking at me. He stares hard at the ground. I want to touch his cheek, ask him to look at me, check and see if he's still here with me.

I clench my hand to my side. "But I can't do this. Not anymore. You refuse to work on yourself. You refuse to change. I can't force you to trust me or anyone else. I can't force you to stop harming others around you because you've been hurt yourself. I'm so sorry for what you've been through. You know that I am. But that doesn't mean I deserve to be treated this way."

And maybe that's been a part of the problem all along also. I've felt sorry for him. I've pitied him. That's wrong of me, too, to think of him as a victim who needs me. Logan doesn't look up from his feet. "I can't make you stop hurting me," I tell him. "But I can do what I need for myself."

I pause. It's painful to say these words.

He doesn't respond. He barely breathes.

"It's like you put your life and your world into acting so that you can live out other characters' stories without having to look at your own. Without having to face yourself and make the changes that you need to make."

Logan opens his mouth once, and then again, like he's trying to force himself to speak. I wait. It feels like a full minute passes of just us breathing and sharing the same space.

"I tried," he eventually says.

Is trying enough? "You tried, and then—what, you gave up?"

"It isn't as easy as you make it seem. To change. To become a different person."

My voice gets quiet. "You've been through a lot of shit, Logan. There's a lot you still need to heal. I thought I could be a part of that for you. Maybe that's on me. I'm sorry. I think a part of me did have a hero complex. I wanted to save you. But that isn't my place. I don't think I can do that for you. Me, or anyone else, but yourself."

"How?" His voice sounds so small.

"I don't know," I say. I'm also whispering. "Therapy, maybe." I'd suggested it to him before, but he'd laughed at the idea then. In his silence, I wonder if he's seriously considering it now. "Maybe—a place like rehab or something, that can give the support you need. Let you get out of the city and away from the industry and focus on yourself for a while."

He's quiet, but I know he has more to say. He clenches his jaw. His eyes are wet. "I'm sorry. I'm sorry I've hurt you so much. I care about you. I don't always know how to say it or show it, but I do."

I wish I could say it was okay. That we can begin again, and maybe this time, things will change. "I'm sorry, too," I tell him.

We stand there for a long while, silent—both of us afraid to move, because when we do, this will end. But there isn't anything else to say, so I force myself to focus on each step I take away from him instead of turning back to him again.

LOGAN

IT DOESN'T TAKE long to reach my dad's manor a few hours after Mattie leaves. He lives about thirty minutes away, up in the Hills. It's funny that I almost never see him. I don't run into him around town or on sets. He never visits me, and I never visit him. He has another life, separate from mine, where he hosts industry events and works on his action films. I never see him, but he still takes up so much space in my life.

His house is the basic white modern-style mansion clinging to the side of a cliff, an infinity pool in view as I make my way up the drive. I get to the gates and enter the passcode. The gates slowly slide open, and I speed onto the gravel.

When I ring the doorbell, a light blinks at me. My dad is on the other side of the camera, considering whether he wants to let me in. After what feels like a full minute, the door buzzes. I swing it open and let it shut behind me. I walk into the open living room space that's designed for parties and head to the balcony to look over the cityscape—the Hills and the skyline of the skyscrapers in the far distance.

There're footsteps behind me. My dad is tall, handsome—

dark hair and eyes, salt-and-pepper strands. He's wearing a casual white shirt and slacks. "You didn't say you were coming over," he tells me.

I look back out at the city. I'm not even sure I'm going to miss it. "I came to say goodbye."

"Going somewhere?"

I nod. "Yeah. I've decided to check into a facility."

"Rehab again?" He sounds disgusted.

"That's a part of it. It's supposed to focus on mental health." I swallow, then force myself to say, "Survivors of sexual abuse and assault, among other things."

I chance a look at him. He narrows his eyes. I've never spoken to him about this before. I've never discussed how he would leave me with execs and actors he needed money from when I was a kid. He had to know what would happen, right? He just didn't care.

"Survivor of sexual abuse and assault," he repeats. "That's dramatic, isn't it?"

I lean against the railing. "Pretty sure I figured out why you never talk to me about it. Why you want to downplay what happened." He blinks at me. Usually, I just take whatever he says silently. "You're too ashamed. Right? That has to be it. Who wouldn't be ashamed, knowing they abandoned their kid to be raped?"

"You weren't *raped*," he says.

"You weren't fucking there. You can't tell me what happened."

He turns away. He's in denial. I didn't even consider that possibility. Maybe he managed to convince himself that I wasn't going to be hurt when he left me behind. Maybe, somehow, he twisted shit around in his head so he could think my rape wasn't so bad.

"I did what I had to do for my family," he says, when he turns back to me. "For you. And because of—" He can't even finish the sentence. "Now, you're living in luxury, and you want to complain? Come here with these accusations?"

"I'm not accusing you of anything. Just letting you know that I'm leaving."

"You're acting like a piece of shit."

Maybe it's because of his own shame that he attacks me every time he sees me, to distract from how horrific he was to let people hurt me when he was supposed to protect me instead.

"I'm moving," I tell him. "I won't be in the apartment anymore."

He snorts. "You won't last a week. You'll spend all your fucking money on drugs. After this shit with Briggs Stevenson, do you think anyone's going to hire you? You'll come crawling back to me."

"No, I won't," I tell him. "I've decided I don't want anything else to do with you. I dropped off the car. Everything in the apartment is yours, technically. This is the last time we speak to each other."

He outright laughs now. "Who the fuck do you—"

"Don't call me anymore, telling me that I'm a piece of shit," I tell him. "I don't want any more contact."

"You're something else, you know that?"

"If you contact me again, I'm going to tell everyone how you used to drop me off at your friends' houses for *sleepovers* where I got raped."

He shuts his mouth. The frown grows grim. I feel a flinch of fear. He could always kill me. That'd take care of his problem. A part of me still wants to believe that he would never purposefully hurt me. That he loves me. Maybe he does, but it wouldn't matter in the end. He hasn't shown me the love I needed from him. Ever. Loving someone and treating them like shit is something I learned from him, I guess.

I want to believe that I deserve more. That I could one day be the kind of person who would welcome someone like Matt into my life. Where I don't fuck up the relationship out of fear, and go looking for people who will hurt me, again and again. I don't know how to change yet. But that's the next journey I get to look forward to.

"I'm leaving now," I tell him. "Goodbye."

I'm practically hyperventilating by the time I make it back outside, past the car and the gates and down the sloping pathway into the street. I pull out my phone. This was technically bought by my dad, too. Fuck. I'll really have to do an inventory and deep clean to get rid of everything bought by him. I get to the Uber app and type in the address. I keep looking over my shoulder with spikes of fear, terrified my dad will follow me down the road, screaming abusive shit at me again, but he never comes.

The car pulls up. The driver frowns at me from the front seat. He eyes me for a second, and I know he recognizes me, but maybe Uber drivers deal with celebrities all the time. "La Jolla?" he says. "Really?"

I get into the back, slamming the door shut. I didn't bring a duffel or anything. The clinic said to come empty-handed. "Yeah. Really."

Inside Hollywood Blog

Publicity for the film 'Write Anything' has begun, with its stars gracing the covers of various magazines and appearing at events leading up to the film's release. Matthew Cole has taken the brunt of the publicity with a promotional tour alongside castmates Julie Rodriguez, Keith Mackey, Scott Anders, and Monica Meyers. Most notably missing is lead actor Logan Gray. Inside sources say that Gray has checked into the Blue Skies Mental Wellness and Rehabilitation Clinic near San Diego.

Interviewers have remarked on how well Cole has been handling the stress of the promo tour. He says that he has had plenty of support from his castmates, especially Rodriguez, whom Cole says he is happy to call a friend. While many are disappointed Gray will not be in attendance for the promotional tour or the film's red-carpet premiere, it seems Cole will be just fine on his own.

—

Romance: Matthew Cole sat with our editor Kate Anderson for an interview about the film "Write Anything."

Kate Anderson (KA):   Thank you so much for joining me, Mattie.

Matthew Cole (MC):   Thanks for having me.

KA: I'm dying to ask you questions about "Write Anything," but first—how have you been?

MC: Well, there's no point in trying to beat around the bush. Everyone knows that Logan Gray and I broke up. Honestly? I'm heartbroken. I began to care for him and love him. I still do.

KA: It's rare to find people who're willing to admit they still have feelings for their exes.

MC: It's only the truth. I love him.

KA: Can I ask what happened?

MC: We turned out to not be what each other needed, I think.

KA: How do you feel about Logan now?

MC: I don't harbor any bad feelings toward him. I wish him happiness and peace. I really do. I'm grateful to him, in fact, because he helped me discover more about myself, too.

KA: I think that's why so many people love you, Mattie. You exude love and compassion. That must be helpful for acting in a romantic film like "Write Anything."

MC: You could say that. Acting as Riley Mason forced me to be more truthful with myself and my emotions. My own wants, instead of putting everyone else before me. I think there was a lot of growing I needed to do, too.

KA: It's amazing how much acting can change a person.

MC: Yes. I agree.

Happily Ever After: A Memoir

by Matthew Cole

Having worked in romance through films, stage productions, and eventually writing for so much of my life, I have learned one thing: audiences expect a holding-hands-into-the-sunset, sparkly fireworks, wedding-bells sort of happily ever after. A part of me resents this. I've come to think that real people with trauma might just begin to believe that love isn't meant for them. Their stories don't look like the romances we see on bookshelves and screens. Some would argue that a story that focuses on a person's pain isn't even a true romance.

Throughout my career, I eventually learned not to force a fake happiness into the roles I play. I once feared that audiences would turn away from the less-than-happy emotions. Romances that are forced to have a happily ever after make me even sadder, I think, because I can feel the lack of authenticity, the attempt at washing away the pain instead of facing it. True joy can't shine until we work through the darkness and look at the trauma—until we begin to heal. Isn't it more satisfying, then? To see a happily ever after that has been fought for in the end.

MATTIE

THE CABIN HASN'T changed much. The trees have grown even more untamed. The lake still shines, glimmering beneath the blue sky. The air feels like it's a blanket of peace. I stand on the shore and breathe.

Logan isn't here. I've questioned if I should come back at all. Every time I return, what am I hoping for? I know better now, I think, than to fall into old patterns. Logan still feels like an old pattern. Closure, maybe. I think I come back always hoping for some sort of closure—hoping he'll be at the cabin, waiting to tell me everything I've needed to hear.

I climb back into the car and start the drive to the hotel. My flight is in a couple of hours, back down to LAX. I've been living in Los Angeles for a few years now. I couldn't get used to the idea of living in the Hills, but I'm in a neighborhood close to where Logan was staying in West Hollywood before he left. I hadn't had a lot of space yet from everything that'd happened when I first bought the apartment, following the release of *Write Anything*.

Paola says that my career exploded partly because of how

well I'd handled the fallout. Vanessa Stone didn't hold a grudge from that meeting where I walked out. I ended up doing exactly what she wanted, posting about my breakup with Logan on social media. I continued to be offered auditions until, finally, I landed a film's number one lead role. Even better: I wasn't typecast as the sweet love interest. It was in a grittier film—a thriller where I was a detective, framed for the murder of my best friend, only for me to discover in the end that it really had been me all along, unable to remember I'd killed him in a fit of rage.

A lot of the blogs and comments on socials wondered if I could pull off a role like that. Sweet, cute, innocent Mattie? I wasn't sure myself, but I'd learned a lot from my time playing Riley Mason. I'd learned to let go of shame and access emotions I didn't even know I had. I had a lot more freedom to find a deeper part of me and discovered another layer of authenticity. It was amazing to watch myself back on-screen. Where the hell did I find that confidence? That scene where I smashed a glass against the wall, screaming so hard I lost my voice for two weeks straight—I mean, shit. I was powerful. I *am* powerful.

That role earned me my first Oscar. The dream. I've been living the dream.

Why, then, am I still so unhappy?

After the flight back, I get to my apartment. It's the sort that only has one neighbor living beneath me, an actress from France. I take the stairs instead of the elevator and unlock the front door, pushing it open. It smells like garlic. Phil looks up from where he's sitting at the counter.

"Hey."

"Hey." I toss my keys into a basket by the door and head over to kiss him. He puts a hand on my waist, pulling me closer. He's been growing his hair out since the *Good Dog* premiere—said he hoped it would expand his appeal.

"How was your break from LA? I thought you were going to be home hours ago."

I hesitate. I've never liked lying, even if it's by omission, especially after everything that happened with Logan and our publicity stunt. "It was fine. I mostly stayed in the hotel, and I took a long drive. Over by Logan Gray's family cabin, actually."

He frowns at me. "What? Why?"

Phillip and I started dating ten months ago, so he wouldn't know that I do this once a year on the anniversary of when Logan and I said we would return—flying out to San Francisco, staying in a hotel for a couple of days and enjoying a break from the city, driving up to the cabin. I lean against the counter. "It's an old promise we made to each other."

"It's been three years," he says.

"I know."

I've moved on. I'd like to think so, at least. My career has taken off and I've found a community of friends. Julie's been one of the best friends I've ever had in my life, and we meet with a group of artists and writers and actors once a week in a salon-type dinner party at her place in Los Feliz.

I'm in touch with my family all the time—my mom and Em, anyway. My dad and I have been trying to have more conversations. He had a cancer scare last year, and about three months after he had his biopsy, he got in touch to say that he wanted to work on our relationship. He said that he's willing to try to change his beliefs and learn to accept me. Being that close to death shook him to his core, and I've decided to give him another chance.

Life has been good, but Logan still pops up in my head every now and again. Maybe every year, the anniversary feels like a reminder. A chance to reflect on the promises I've made to myself.

Phillip is watching me carefully. It hits me that he's jealous. That isn't surprising. He's insecure about a lot, so something like this would only make that anxiety worse. Not that I'm judging. I've had my insecurities, too.

We've been trying. Phil and I have really been trying to work on this relationship. We've had several conversations at this point. In-depth, hours-long talks about whether our relationship is worth saving. I told him the truth: I just don't know if I love him. I feel comfortable and safe, but in the way that I might with a friend. I don't enjoy sex with him. I never have. Phil convinced me that since sex isn't the main part of a romantic relationship, we can grow closer first and let sex become something we both enjoy with more connection. But sex with Phillip still feels dry—slow, disconnected. My thoughts wander, and the few times I've managed to really get into it, it's always because I began to imagine being with other men I've known. Not Logan. Never Logan. That'd feel like a betrayal to both Phil and myself.

Phil argued that relationships are about dedication more than anything else. "Of course our relationship won't work if we give up at the first sign of trouble," he'd said.

I'm still not sure. Phil likes things to be done in a particular way. He loves to show perfect, smiling photos of us on Instagram, and he gets angry whenever he makes a mistake. I've imagined, over the years, reaching a place where I feel complete freedom. I'm not there yet, but I think I'm getting closer to becoming the sort of person who can laugh and sing and say what's really on my mind, without caring about what anyone else will think. I deserve to live fiercely with the kind of energy that feels like a celebration of life, without an ounce of shame for myself. Phillip, though—sometimes when he looks at me in the quiet moments, I feel judgment in his gaze, like he wants to box me in and turn me into someone he believes I should be. I don't feel free with Phillip. I'm not sure that I ever will.

Phil doesn't look at me. I can practically feel the jealousy rolling off him in waves. "Why are you still thinking about Logan?" he asks.

"I think," I say, hesitantly—I want to say the truth, but I also don't want to hurt him—"that I'm having a difficult time letting him go without knowing what happened. It's like he disappeared off the face of the earth."

I've tried searching for him on social media—got a few hits that he was seen in different cities, photos of him taken. But the search results have slowed down in the past couple of years. It's like everyone's forgotten about Logan and moved on.

"Isn't that better?" Phil asks. "He always treated you like crap, didn't he?"

"It's not like I'm trying to run back to him. I just want to know what happened. How he's doing. I cared about him. It's all right to care about him, isn't it?"

Phil sighs. A pot begins to overboil. He gets up and walks to the stove, stirring. "Would you do the same for me?"

Maybe this is what frustrates me about Phillip more than anything else. His constant need for validation, for me to say that I care about him. I want him to feel secure and safe and comfortable, too—everyone deserves that—but I can't reassure him when I know in my heart that this isn't going to work. I haven't been happy. He knows that, but he still asks these questions, waiting for the moment I'll change my mind.

I dated several men after Logan, but this is the first relationship since him. Phillip and I ending up together was positioned as the Hollywood ending I deserved. Everyone began to refer to us as the golden couple. From the outside, we look perfect and happy and in love.

But I'm tired of roles now. I'm tired of acting as someone else, giving up my own happiness and peace for the comfort of everyone around me. I'm being offered more roles than ever before, but...I don't even know if acting is my dream anymore. I accomplished what I set out to do: I became a major actor in Hollywood. Now what? That's ironic. I'd thought I changed this part of myself years ago, this part that likes to hide the truth. I didn't realize that I also needed to upend my entire life and start again, too.

I'm hurting Phillip by staying in this dance with him. I've tried to break up, and he always asks me to hang on, but I have enough agency that I can be firm. I know that this isn't what I want.

"We should break up, Phil."

He turns around, eyes wide, mid stir. He frowns and goes back to stirring again. "I thought we'd decided to keep giving this a try."

"Be honest," I tell him. "Do you want to stay with me because you love me, or because you're worried about what the world thinks of our relationship?"

Phil seems to consider, but I think we're both aware of the real answer. He nods. "I'll admit, the thought has crossed my mind. There wouldn't be a good response to either of us if we broke up."

"You don't make me happy," I tell him, "and I'm not making you happy, either."

He scratches his brow.

"I don't think I've been happy for a while, now, actually," I say.

"Since Logan, you mean?"

"No, I mean—I had this dream of making it in Hollywood, and now that I have..."

He frowns at me, confused. "Are you quitting acting?"

I've always loved acting. Maybe acting isn't the issue—just the industry, the spotlight. I never wanted the fame. "No. I don't think so. Maybe I just need to take a look at everything. At my life. At myself."

Phil turns off the stove. "I've loved you for some time, Matt. It wasn't only about the response we would receive. I really believed you could learn to fall in love with me."

"It isn't always that simple."

"Right. I know that now."

We're silent as he puts pasta on the plates. I take them to the table and we sit together. The quiet is more comfortable than it's been in a while. That's saying something.

"I can start planning to move out," Phil says.

I'm relieved he isn't fighting me this time. "It isn't a rush."

His voice has some anger. "I'd rather leave as quickly as possible."

I pick up my water. "Do you think you'll stay in LA, or go back to London?"

"Likely London. I haven't been receiving much work here anyway. Apparently I still need to work on my American accent a bit more."

"I still care about you as a friend. You know that, right?"

"Yeah. I care about you, too, Mattie."

I don't think he means it in the way that I do. We go back to eating in silence.

⟨⟩

Phillip leaves within a month. He was very serious about getting away from me quickly. I can't be upset at that. He deserves the space he needs. Being in the apartment alone after I was living with a partner for so many months is unexpectedly lonely, so I decide to fly down to Atlanta. Emma is still at Sarah Lawrence, finishing up her last year, so I get my mom to myself for a while.

I'd offered to buy her and my dad a new house, but my mom waved me off. "We're comfortable. This is where we've been for over thirty years. We don't need your fancy lifestyle, Mattie."

Thing is, I don't know if I need it, either. I have more money than I know what to do with. No one in the world needs millions of dollars, especially in a city like LA where so many people are suffering. I feel disgusting when I drive to my million-dollar apartment, past people who can't find a place to sleep in the streets. Maybe that's been a part of me needing to get out, to leave, to clear my head. I don't want to become one of those celebrities who lies to myself, thinking that I need a pair of shoes for hundreds of thousands of dollars, when that money could go to helping other human beings eat. I don't know. The culture, the politics of fame—everything about the city makes me desperate to escape these days.

When I talk to my mom about it, she isn't surprised. "You've always been down-to-earth. Don't let anyone or anything change who you are."

I have changed, though. I shake my head as I sit with her in the living room. "I think I need to start a new life."

"Yeah? Where're you thinking?"

I lean back into my seat. "I'm not sure yet."

"You'll figure it out," she says, patting my knee. "That's the exciting part."

LOGAN

MY APARTMENT DOOR slams shut behind me. My boots thump down the staircase, floor after floor, until I reach the bottom and push open the lobby's door, into the bright light. A guy on a bike whizzes by, and cars and taxis blare their horns. I hurry up the sidewalk, checking the time on my phone, then head down the steps to the subway.

I think I'm going to be late. I've been here for over a year, and I still haven't figured out the rhythm of Manhattan. The subways don't follow a schedule. Seems like they just come whenever they want to. I sit in an icy cold subway car, checking the time nervously again, before we slow at my stop. I run back up the stairs and into the coffee shop, Coffee Unlimited.

When I saw the name on the window, it reminded me of days of unlimited coffee on set, and...I don't know. There was a BARISTA WANTED sign in the window, and I was looking for a job, anyway. Just to have something to do. I have enough money to hold me over for rent for a while. I wasn't willing to get roommates with strangers after I had to share my bedroom for over a year at the wellness center. Maybe I shouldn't complain. We ended up being great friends. Tom moved out to Brooklyn a little after I came out here. We still meet up on the weekends.

I open the coffee shop door and the bell rings. Sarah is at the register already while Ashley is wiping down tables. "Hey, Logan," Sarah says with a wave. She owns the coffee shop even though she's only thirty-three or something ridiculously young to be a business owner in this city.

I give her a grin as I take over the register. "I thought I was going to be late."

"You always think you're going to be late," Ashley jokes as she walks past.

I pull on my apron. I've been working here for three months now. The thing I love the most about New York City is that people, really and truly, do not care. Sarah knew who I was the second I walked in the door and asked about the job opening. "Oh," she said, pointing at me and nodding. "You're that actor, right?"

Every now and then, someone will wander in and freak out and ask to take photos. Shit's gone viral a couple of times now. People think it's funny that the former actor Logan Gray posed in a photo while working the counter at an NYC coffee shop. It doesn't hurt that people's memories are short. I haven't been in the spotlight for a while now. Everyone, for the most part, has moved on.

Customers start to trickle in when Ashley flips the sign on the door. I make coffee with a smile. A real one. Maybe it's ridiculous, that working in a coffee shop would make me so happy. There were days when I didn't think I'd feel happiness again. There were multiple nights, when I arrived at the wellness clinic, that I considered suicide. But I was surrounded by a support system. I didn't trust anyone at first. I thought that they—people who worked there and my roommate and other patients—were all plotting against me. Looking for moments to take photos and share my shit on socials. Took me a while to realize no one there wanted to hurt me. Took me even longer to learn it was okay, it really was, to talk about everything that's happened.

I was in the clinic for a year and a half. There were days when I was screaming and fighting anyone who tried to talk me down. There were days when I sat in a circle that I'd started to not find cliché anymore and said that I would never know how to love. Days when I started to feel peace. Real peace.

After La Jolla, I spent time traveling. I wanted to get to know myself better. Figure out what I liked and didn't like, away from LA. I ended up in Florida for a bit and visited my mom. "You look happy," she said.

Yeah. I think I am happy. It's not like the depression and anxiety has disappeared. It's not like I can change the fact I was sexually abused and raped. But I'm feeling safer, I think, in my body. Enjoying that I'm still here.

Sarah leans against the counter beside me, bored. It's amazing to me that she figured out her own dream and made it happen. "How's the querying going?"

We've spoken a couple of times now about the fact that I'm writing. I don't want to act another day in my life again. I'm not even sure I ever enjoyed it. But while I was traveling, I tried out some new things. Scribbled out a couple of screenplays. Yeah, I don't know. I think something could be there.

"Heard back from an agent," I say. I feel an old instinct to shrug rising, but as my therapist, Amy, called me out on, my shrugging is a defense mechanism. "They're checking it out now."

"That's great," Ashley says, coming around the counter. "Congratulations!"

"Thanks."

Sarah pats my hand. We've flirted, on and off. I'm not sure it's a good idea, sleeping with my boss. I've been on a few dates since I got to NYC. I've made it clear that I want to get to know the person over coffee or dinner or something, instead of having sex with them right away like I might've done a few years ago. Another defense mechanism Amy helped me see more clearly, even though I'd started to recognize it myself, too.

My brain learned from an early age that sex is how I connect with others. I've been in a mixture of freeze and fawn response. I offer people my body, hoping that this will placate them and that they won't hurt me. I offered strangers and audiences my entire identity, letting them define me as an asshole and abuse me in punishment, thinking that this would equate to safety. Even if it hurt, it still felt safe, because that was all I'd known until Mattie. Everything new he offered—safety and love and real connection—felt scary and threatening and impossible because I hadn't experienced it before.

God. I can't believe I lived that way for most of my life, in a constant state of trauma response, but that was another biggie at the clinic. No point in shaming. We did what we had to do to survive. We figured out how to cope. "Good for you, Logan," Amy told me. "You learned how to live in a world that was harmful to you. Now, it's time to thank your younger self for helping you survive this long. Now, it's time to find another way to exist."

I'm lost in thought when the door opens again with a jingle. I look up, smile on my face, ready to take the next order. My mouth freezes, half-open.

Sarah whispers beside me. "Who is that? He looks really familiar."

He hasn't even seen me yet. He's still staring up at the menu above the counter. He has his shades on, but it's a pretty shitty disguise. Still, this is New York. Most people really don't give a fuck about who you are.

He looks like he made up his mind. He steps forward, glances at me. "Caramel cappuccino, please." He looks at me again when I don't move or say anything, then stiffens.

"Hey, Mattie."

Sarah snaps her fingers. "Matthew Cole," she whispers.

Matt slips off his shades. "Logan?"

I raise my hands. "In the flesh."

"What—what the hell?" He stares at me so hard that I'm not sure he believes what he's seeing.

He looks good. He's built out a little more. Must be for the last role he had in *Fish Mate* as that detective. I tried to distance myself from him. Not to look him up or follow him along in the news. It still hurt, no matter how much healing I'd done, the way things ended between us. But I was excited for him. I really was. A fucking Oscar?

"It's good to see you."

"What're you doing here?" he says. "How long have you been in New York?"

"A few months," I say. He looks shocked and amazed and maybe a little angry.

Sarah makes an *oh* sound, and I know another piece of information has clicked into place for her: this is a reunion between two ex-boyfriends. "Logan, why don't you take your break early?" she says.

I look at Mattie. "Do you want to get a coffee with me? Catch up?"

He bites his lip. I feel a twinge of warmth. It's the little things you don't even realize you miss. "I've got—shit, I've got a meeting downtown."

"Okay. That's okay."

"A stage production."

"Yeah?"

He hesitates. "You know what? I'll—yeah, I'll let them know I'm running late."

"You don't have to do that, Matt."

"I'm a little scared you'll disappear again if I don't talk to you now."

That's fair. That used to be the sort of thing I would do. I wouldn't answer his calls or texts. I left LA without any warning. I didn't tell anyone where I went except for my father. I threw away my phone once I arrived at the center.

"I won't disappear," I tell him. "I promise. I still need this job."

Sarah snorts.

"My shift ends at four."

"My meeting's done at five."

"I'll wait at the park across the street," I say. "Or I could come down and meet you."

"I'll—uh, I'll come back here. The park you said?"

I point through the window. "Yeah. Right across the street."

From the worry in his eyes, I can tell he still doesn't trust me. But that's been a part of the healing process, too. Learning about responsibility and accountability. Having the courage to own up to mistakes and apologize and make change. I owe Mattie an apology for everything that went down. Yeah, I had my trauma. But that didn't mean I should have hurt him the way I did, over and over again.

"All right," he says. "I'll meet you then."

315

Anxiety builds throughout the day. A few years ago, I would've pushed it all away. I would've tried to numb the emotions. Alcohol, drugs, sex—anything to not feel. Instead, now, I ask Sarah for a break. I sit in the back room. Eyes closed, I breathe. I let anxiety ripple through me. "Honor your emotions," Amy always said.

Acknowledging the anxiety helps. I remember it's a sensation that will pass. That the anxiety isn't my body. It isn't me. It eventually fades the deeper I breathe. I take one last breath and open my eyes. Sarah looks up at me from the register when I swing open the back room's door. "Better?" she asks.

"Yeah. Better."

When my shift is over, I stick around an extra hour at a table in the back. I pull my laptop out of my bag and start writing. I wouldn't say that screenwriting is my new dream. It isn't my only goal in life. But it's something to focus on. Something that lets me use my creativity. I usually write in the evenings. I read other screenplays, since I still have a hard time watching TV and films. I take walks on the days I have off from the coffee shop. I sit in the park and just—I don't know. Breathe. Watch the world turn. It's been good. Life has been good.

Five o'clock comes around, so I pack my laptop into my bag and head across the street to the park. Nervousness buzzes through me. It's been a few years since the last time I had a real conversation with Mattie. I wonder how he's changed. I sure as hell know I'm a different person.

I don't have any expectations. I only have one goal. Apologize. Acknowledge that I fucked up. Let him know, maybe, that I'm doing a lot better now. And I want to thank him. I really do. Everything in my life changed because of him. Even if we weren't good for each other, he was the catalyst for me realizing I was trapped in a cycle—for helping me see there were other ways to live.

I wait on the bench by the park's entrance and watch people walk by, some with their dogs on leashes. Someone rides their bike. A kid runs past with a laugh, looking back at their parent. Mattie walks up to me, shoes crunching on the gravel. He used to wear yellow sneakers, but he's in a pair of scuffed brown boots now. They go a little more with the style of the movie that got him the Oscar.

"You look good, Matt," I say when he sits down beside me.

He watches me closely, his brown eyes soft with . . . suspicion? Skepticism? Surprise, maybe, that I'm really here.

"You do, too," he finally says. "Logan—God, what happened to you?"

I take a deep breath. "A lot. The story's kind of long."

"I don't mind. I've got the time."

I tell him everything. That I broke off contact with my father and went to La Jolla and checked myself into the clinic and started intensive therapy with one on one and group sessions, was introduced to meditation and learned about trauma.

"There's a lot of scientific shit that goes into it," I say, crossing one leg over the other. "A lot of neuroscience and studies about rewiring the brain and . . . I don't know, I spent months reading about it nonstop. There were a lot of days before the clinic where I was afraid it was impossible for me to change, but while I was there, I felt like I'd been given a second shot at life."

Mattie's near tears. Some things don't change.

"I'm really happy for you," he tells me. "I was scared you had hurt yourself, or . . . I don't know."

"Yeah." I don't need to tell him how close I was to doing just that when I first got to La Jolla. "I was at the clinic for about a year and a half before I began to travel." I went across the states for a couple of months, then to Europe. I didn't even do anything, really, except walk around small villages and towns, getting used to feeling safe in my body. Figuring out what felt good, what little pleasures I enjoyed. After I visited my mom in Florida, I decided to try New York. "Got a job in the coffee shop by chance. I liked the name. Coffee Unlimited. Reminded me of the days of unlimited coffee on set."

He laughs. "Jesus, that's the same reason I came in."

"No shit, really?"

"That's an incredible story," he says. "It was brave of you. I mean, going to the clinic and everything…It's admirable."

"I don't know. Being the sort of person I want to be isn't that brave. It's just about accountability." Speaking of which. "I'm glad we ran into each other. I've been thinking for a while now that I should try to reach out to you. I told myself it'd probably be impossible to get in touch, with you being a Hollywood star and everything, but I think I was just using that as an excuse. I was afraid to."

"Why were you afraid?"

"Because I knew what I'd have to do. I want to apologize. The way I treated you was wrong."

He shuts his mouth, jaw set. He nods, looking away. I can see it in his eyes. I really hurt him. "Yeah. It was."

I swallow. This is the hard part. "If you want to tell me… express, I mean, how I hurt you…" I stop speaking because I'm not sure how to finish—but Mattie seems to get the point. He's silent for a while, nodding to himself and staring anywhere but at me before he speaks again.

"Hurting me like that, over and over again—treating me like crap and pushing me away when I was trying to be there for you...Shit, Logan, especially with everything that happened in the end and you wouldn't even speak to me—I had to chase you down..."

I nod. I know now that it was a trauma response. I was frozen, shut down, didn't know *how* to speak to him, let alone what to say—but that doesn't mean I didn't hurt him. "Yeah. I understand. I fucked up."

"For a while, it was hard to trust the guys I dated wouldn't push me away like that."

Guys he dated. I feel a flinch of regret, but that's not his shit to deal with. "I'm sorry. Fuck. I'm sorry I did that to you."

"But, you know—I understand. You'd been through so much."

"Being traumatized isn't an excuse to cause trauma, too," I say. I sound like one of the leaders for the group sessions. I want to roll my eyes at myself, but it's true. "I shouldn't have pushed you away because I was afraid."

Matt's quiet, thoughtful. His voice is soft. "I forgive you."

I'm not expecting the rise of emotion that wells in my eyes. I hadn't realized how badly I wanted to hear those words from him. He didn't have to forgive me for anything. "Thank you."

I'd been ashamed, for a while, realizing how much harm I've caused, but that was another thing I had to learn: there isn't any point in being ashamed for my mistakes. Shame isn't the same as guilt. Guilt—yeah, I should have that for the shit I've done. I should try to right the wrongs. Shame, though, is more about how much I hated myself. I hated myself so much, and I didn't even know it.

"I hope you're not beating yourself up over everything," Matt says. "Be compassionate to yourself, you know?"

He'd told me that, once. He probably doesn't even remember, but those words stuck with me. "Yeah. I do have compassion for myself. No, really," I say, when he gives me a skeptical look. "I was stuck in the trauma. I wasn't able to heal until I found a way out."

"Are you healed?"

He always knew how to pick up on the little shit. I smirk. "Healing. I'm learning who I am outside of LA, away from my father, out of the spotlight." And I think I like this person. Might even start to love him.

Matt's eyes are hooded. "It's incredible that I even ran into you."

"You mentioned you're doing a play?"

"I thought acting in a smaller production might be a good chance to get away from the attention for a while. Lie low and take inventory of what I really want." He swallows, then looks away. "I—uh—actually just broke up with my boyfriend. Phillip Desmond."

"Phil, huh?" I don't bother pretending to be surprised. I've seen them splashed across enough tabloid and magazine covers for the past few months.

"Yeah. We worked out okay at first, but the relationship wasn't what I wanted, and...I don't know. It was scary to step away from the life I'd spent so much time building, but I understand what you mean. I wanted to get to know myself more, too."

We sit in an easy silence for a while. I remember how uncomfortable I was when we shared the same space. When he showed me genuine love. My brain just didn't know what to do with that yet. I think of Quinn and Riley's romance. A story like that never would've been meant for someone like me. It's like Mattie and I tried to have the expected romance, the fun rom-com shit—but with my trauma, I hit a wall I couldn't pass through. I needed to heal before I could even think about letting myself accept the kind of love Matt was offering. But, I don't know—maybe my healing was a part of our romance, too.

"I'm happy for you, Logan," Matt says. "I really am." He meets my eye. There's a flinch of fear in his gaze. Fear, maybe, that I'll just push him away again. I can't blame him. But I've learned a lot. Enough to know when the anxiety is rising. Enough to know when to say I need a second—to explain what's going on in my head.

"Thank you. I'm happy for you, too."

The fear eases. "You know that trip to the cabin?" he says.

"Yeah."

"We said we'd go back once a year on the same day."

I remember that.

He seems embarrassed. "Actually, I—uh, I've been going back every year since."

My smile grows. "Really?"

"I don't know why. The nostalgia, maybe. The closure. I needed closure from you, so running into you at the coffee shop…It was everything I needed. Thanks for meeting with me, Logan."

I'm not sure how to express the gratitude flowering inside of me. "You don't have to thank me. I should be the one thanking you."

We go back to sitting in silence. I think our time here is done. There's an old part of me that wants to stay, to keep talking to Matt, but—well, I don't think I'm *not* worth his time. But I know I hurt him. I can't expect him to want to stay here with me in a park, speaking to me for hours. I'm lucky that he gave me a chance to apologize at all. "Should probably get back home."

I'm not sure if I'm imagining the disappointment. He nods. "Sure."

We stand from the park bench. "I'm headed to Queens," I tell him. "You?"

"I'm staying downtown."

We walk toward the train together in silence. Regret grows with every step. This is probably going to be the last time I speak to him again. I'll see him in the tabloids and think about how I'd missed out on the best person in my life. And—shit, even though I know it has to be, I wish this wasn't goodbye.

But Amy always said I have needs, too—wants and desires, just as much as any other person. It's all right to express them. Matt was usually the one chasing after me, and now, the idea of chasing after him instead feels new and fucking terrifying. My heart hammers at the thought, imagining that he'll reject me—and wouldn't I deserve it? A part of me feels like I shouldn't even ask, not when I'm the one who has hurt him. Is it fucked up of me, to want to pull him back in?

But I've done the work. And in the quiet space between the tangled thoughts and my hammering heart, there's a breath.

"Matt," I say, before I can change my mind. My voice cracks with nerves. He looks at me, surprised. "Would you— I don't know, want to get a coffee sometime?"

He stops walking. "Coffee?" he repeats.

I'm not breathing. I know that, but I still can't force myself to take a slow inhale like I've been practicing. I brace myself for the rejection. "Yeah," I say, words starting to come out faster now. "I've missed you, to be honest, and I'd like to spend time with you again, but—yeah, God, I understand if you don't want to."

He watches me, his mouth open in a small O, not saying a word.

I look away. "Sorry. I shouldn't have asked."

"No," he says quickly. "I mean—shit, I mean yes. I want to." He rubs the back of his neck. "I just moved here for the next few months and don't know anyone and it'd be nice to catch up and...I'm rambling."

I meet his eye. Relief spreads through me, but even then my shoulders tense, waiting for Matt to laugh in my face. "Are you sure?"

"Yeah," he says, nodding. "I mean—it doesn't have to be as..."

"Right. It doesn't have to be a date."

"No. But I'd like to keep talking."

"Same," I say. All the fear of the moment begins to fade. I hesitate. "I have to tell you, though, that I'm still working on myself."

"I know."

"I might have to communicate a lot, you know? It could get weird sometimes. But I have to say when I'm feeling anxious and scared and when I need to pull back."

"I'd like you to do that. As long as you don't start to push me away." He seems to have a hard time looking at me.

"I won't. I might have a hard time unraveling my emotions. There're—well, there are still a lot of emotions to unpack."

He frowns. "Really?"

"Yeah. I was in love with you. It isn't easy to forget those feelings."

"You were in love with me?" he says, like he doesn't believe me.

"Yeah. Yes. I loved you, Matt." I still might. I'm not sure. I think about him all the time—him and the way he treated me with so much love and compassion, the days we had together on and off set, lying in bed together. I loved him then, and seeing him in front of me now, familiar emotions settle in my chest again.

"You never told me that," Matt says. "I told you that I loved you, but you never said the words back."

Fuck. Another way I hurt him, and I didn't even realize it. I remember him saying that he loved me, and in those moments thinking that I didn't believe him. I was unable to say that I loved him, too. I was so afraid then.

"I'm sorry," I say. "I should have. Because I did. I loved you."

Matt looks upset. He clenches his jaw, eyes wet. He's allowed to be angry at me. I can't help that.

I wait for him to speak.

"I'm not even sure I really knew you," he eventually says. "Maybe you didn't know me, either. We only knew the versions we shared with the world. Our personas, our roles. I began to love you when I started to see the truth you hid from everyone else. I don't know." He meets my eye. "I'd like to get to know you. The real you, Logan."

In that moment, I think he might be saying something else. Maybe that he wants to fall in love with me again. "Yeah," I tell him. "Me, too."

MATTIE

THOUGH MOST OF my time is taken with the play over the next few weeks, and a significant amount is spent on myself—resting, reading, listening to podcasts, *breathing*—I want to spend time with Logan also. I don't want to jump right back into what we had before. That isn't my intention at all. I even tell myself, at first, that maybe we should meet only as friends. But just as Logan had to admit he has emotions to unpack, I realize that closure was the end of one story with Logan, and that now, a new story is beginning—and I think that might be okay, too.

A few coffee meetups and friendly lunch dates turn into dinners and long walks on the weekends. We're firm in keeping this platonic for now—at least, that's what we tell ourselves. Slow, steady, nice and easy—Logan, taking the time he needs to make sure he feels safe. Me, making sure I'm focusing on myself. It'd be too easy to fall back into old patterns. I think that's what scares both of us.

That's what scares me, anyway, when Logan invites me over to his apartment. He must understand what my silence on the phone means. He's been so intentional, communicating and reaching out more than he ever had before.

"I've been practicing recipes," he says, "and I wanted to try to cook for someone." He pauses. "Well, not for someone. For you, specifically."

I remember when we were both unable to make much more than spaghetti at his family's cabin. That's another issue that I struggle with: the constant nostalgia. The happy memories. We weren't always so bad together, were we?

"I would love that."

I get lost on the train a few times—it's still taking me a while to get used to the rush of NYC. It's almost laughable that I thought LA was fast-paced. I get turned around before I find his apartment. The complex looks a lot more ordinary and run-down than I was expecting, but maybe after a few years in LA, I've become more of a snob than I thought. I press his apartment number on a keypad, and he buzzes me in. Before I've walked up to the second floor, Logan already has the door open, waiting against the threshold.

"Hey," he says, ducking his head. I feel his waves of discomfort. It reminds me of when he would open himself up to me, only to push me away by the end of the night. He clenches his jaw, takes a breath, and meets my eye with a shy smile.

I feel guilty, that I want to kiss him. I feel like I should have his permission to want something like that. I bite my lip. "Hey."

He steps aside and lets me into his apartment. It's *him*, so much more than the stark loft in LA. It looks like he might have found some of his worn furniture with faded paint on the street, and the abstract paintings with splashes of color seem random, but they show sparks of his personality. The living room is cramped, the white kitchen even smaller. Logan's already started cooking.

"Do you need any help?"

"No, no," he says, waving me away. He's already cleared a spot on his sofa for me. "Sit down. Relax. Do you want to watch something?" He searches for his TV's remote. "I barely turn this thing on. I don't know where—"

"Logan. Logan," I say. He stops his frantic, nervous search, embarrassed. "It's okay. I'm fine. I'd love to talk to you while you cook, if that's okay?" He hesitates. "Unless you need to focus..."

"No," he says. "I mean—yes, yeah, I'd love that."

I want to laugh. We're like awkward teenagers, more than we ever were when we first started to fall in love. He asks how things have been going with the play, and I describe the long days and the fear that there is no *cut* or additional takes.

"Is it weird for you, hearing about acting?" I ask.

Logan looks up from chopping. He's surrounded by vegetables, oil in a pan already sizzling and what smells like ginger burning. "A little, yeah," he says. "But that doesn't mean I don't want to hear about it from you."

He's so nervous about making a mistake with me again, I can tell he is—and that isn't a fair pressure to have on him, to think that he'll never make a mistake again. Of course he will. He's human. And maybe it also isn't fair of either of us to act like he's the only one who messed up. Even though it's been two months since he apologized, I can't stop thinking that maybe I have a few apologies of my own to make. I've been scared to bring this up, scared to delve back into our past when we're trying something new...but Logan has been so courageous. Maybe he deserves the same from me, too.

"You know, Logan," I say. He looks up, surprised, some

wavy strands falling into his eyes. "I've been meaning to apologize to you."

He looks genuinely confused, head tilting. "Apologize? For what?"

I take a deep breath. "I've been thinking, and—I know I made mistakes, too. When we were together, I mean."

He frowns, still confused, but he doesn't say anything else as he listens.

"I remember telling you, once, that I would always be with you, because I accepted you." I swallow. "That was a promise I never should've made."

The pain in his eyes, for that flinch of a second, is more than enough for me to turn my gaze to the ground. But I take a breath.

"I did believe it at the time," I tell him, "but I don't think that's a promise I can or should ever make. Saying that means I'll always be there for you and for your needs. It ignores my own. Ignores that my needs might change and ignores the possibility that you can't or won't meet them." I look up at him again.

His intense gaze is more than familiar. He doesn't speak, waiting for me to continue.

"I don't know where things will go for us now." That's something we've said a few times—acknowledged we don't know what our relationship is, the awkward gray space between platonic friendship and romance, the tentative uncertainty overflowing with memories, both good and bad. "But that's something I should make clear from the start. I can't promise that I'll be by your side forever."

The silence stretches. The ginger is really burning now. Logan curses and spins to the stove, turning it off with a click.

"How do you feel about that?" I ask him, nervous that it

might've been too serious of a conversation for us and where we are right now.

"I'm grateful," he says, moving the pan to another burner. "I'm thankful that you can be so honest with me. And," he adds, "my anxiety is taking over a little, and I'm terrified that I'll let myself love you, only for you to leave me because I can't meet your needs."

I nod. "I'm anxious, too. But I think that's where the work for a relationship comes in. Speaking about our needs, hoping they align—working to meet each other where and when we can. It might take a lot of work."

He doesn't look at me, but I believe him when he says, "I think I'm ready. I had to do work on myself before I could be. But I think I'm ready now."

I think that he's ready, too, just from what he's shown me, and that I might be ready also, from the calm that I feel with him. But I'm still afraid to ask the question now, to say the words. Slow and steady has been working for us. Maybe it'll take another month before I ask him, officially, if he would like to be my boyfriend again.

Logan brings over plates of vegetables in red curry and jasmine rice. He might've used too much ginger, but it's delicious and bright. "I'm impressed."

He blushes. "Thank you."

I take a sip of water. He was able to become the person he is now on his own—with tools and support and community, yes, but mostly on his own, of his own volition, because he wanted to change. "I have another apology to make," I tell him.

Logan looks genuinely surprised now, like he's wondering what else I could have possibly done.

"I had such a hero complex with you," I say, stirring my

vegetables around. "I thought it was my responsibility to save you. I should've known that you could save yourself."

There's a long pause before he reaches across the table, taking my hand so that I look up at him. "I saved myself," he says, "but I didn't even know that change was possible before you. I never would've tried without you, Mattie."

I squeeze his hand. He lets go, and we eat in a comfortable silence.

LOGAN

IT'S ONLY BEEN a few days since Matt came over for my first attempt at vegetables in red curry (way too much ginger, I'll cut back next time), but I already want to meet with him again. Our conversation, his apologies—me telling him that I think I might be ready...I've appreciated the slow pace. I've needed it. But I know what I want now. I need to know if Mattie feels the same.

I invite him over to Central Park on a Saturday afternoon. His play's production is in two weeks, so I'm mindful of how much time I'm taking up in his schedule. It's okay if you're too busy, I texted. But he promised it was all right. I'll set my boundaries and say no if I can't

Touché. He really has been focusing on taking care of his needs. It reminds me of the glimmers of power I'd seen from him years back. Mattie's so powerful now. It's amazing to see.

Matt grins as he sees me, waving and walking down the path. I stand from the bench where I was waiting. An awkward pause, where it feels like we could hug or kiss, but instead we just smile and start walking.

"So, why the park?" he asks me.

I meet his eye. "Remember when you said you wanted to go running through a field naked?"

He bursts out laughing. "I can't believe you remember that."

"Here's your chance."

Matt shakes his head, still smiling. "Maybe another time, Logan." A moment of walking and peaceful silence. "I'm glad you invited me out," he says. "I needed to escape my apartment."

And I just wanted to see him. "Good."

He nudges me with his arm. "You okay?"

I don't like seeing the worry in his eyes—the worry that I won't communicate, maybe. I take a breath. "Yes. I'm okay. I'm just—nervous, I guess."

"Nervous? Why?"

We pause and face each other. It's a quiet path, no one else around, breeze rustling through the trees. I swallow and force myself to say the words. "I've been thinking a lot, recently," I say. "I—"

He's waiting, hope fluttering across his expression.

"I really want to try again."

Matt pauses. I'm not sure what he's thinking. "Yeah?"

"Yeah. Yes. If that's something you want, too."

"It is," he says. I don't think either of us mean to step closer to each other. It's more like gravity has us leaning in. "I've been waiting to ask you the same thing." His voice lowers. "I wanted to make sure we weren't moving too quickly."

"I know. I've appreciated that." I'm whispering, too. He's biting his lip, maybe too afraid to ask for what I'm pretty sure we both want. He'd always been the one to ask for consent for every little touch. I can do the same, too. "Is it all right if I kiss you?"

A small smile—he nods.

We meet in the middle. It's been years since I kissed Matt. The kiss feels so familiar, so nostalgic, so much like home that I might start to cry. The kiss feels like all the comfort he'd shown me, the love when I needed it most, the joy I'd allowed myself to feel with him, the peace I learned I deserve. And it reminds me, too, of how much I fucked up and lost it all.

I pull back. I would've hated that I'm crying, once. Matt touches my hand with a finger. "You okay?" he asks, but when I look up, I see his eyes are wet, too.

I nod. "Yeah." I take his hand, and we both slide our arms around each other, holding our bodies close. We hug like that for maybe a minute, maybe ten. Just holding each other and breathing.

He pulls away first, kissing my cheek. "I don't know how slow or fast you want to go with—with the physical..."

I'm not sure either. This would be my first time having sex in a few years. I'd had random hookups at the facility, at first, before Amy convinced me that sex with strangers was a part of my trauma response. The break from sex was necessary for me to heal. I'm nervous, ending my celibacy. I don't know how I'll react. This is uncharted territory. But maybe it's okay, to figure it out together.

"Do you want to come over?" I ask him.

His eyes are hooded. "Are you sure?"

I squeeze his hand. "Yeah."

We hold hands and sit quietly on the subway. We have a couple of double glances—people who might recognize Mattie, people who might remember me—and I worry that a photo will be snapped, Matt pulled into a firestorm again. But he doesn't seem to care. He rubs a thumb over my knuckles. That would've scared the shit out of me once, but I intertwine our fingers now.

When we get to my apartment, Matt hovers uncomfortably by the bedroom door as I pick up clumps of dirty clothes and toss them into the hamper. I've never returned to the states of mess I had when I was trapped in my depression—but I've also discovered that I'm just a messy guy, and that's fine.

I turn to Mattie and take a deep breath. I don't know what to do. I don't know what might trigger a trauma response. But I trust I know how to help myself when I am triggered. That if I say I need to pause and breathe, Matt will listen to me. He's safe. I can trust that.

"What would you like to do?" he asks uncertainly.

My voice shakes. "Maybe—maybe just kiss a little?"

He steps forward, gaze on my face. This is familiar, too. This take-charge attitude that I always loved. He's waiting for me, I realize, so I lean down to kiss him. It starts as slow and tender as we'd kissed in the park, before the energy shifts. Longing, maybe? Desperation. We're pressing against each other. I guide Mattie to the bed and we tip over, Mattie on top. Our hands roam and grab, tugging at each other's clothes. It's always been easy to let go, let my body take over, just focus on making the other person I'm with feel good—

We could have sex. I could keep going, the way things are, without thinking about it. Mattie could ask for consent, and I could nod and insist that this is what I want, and after we have sex we could cuddle, and I could say that I'm all right even when I feel anxiety stringing through me.

"Hey," he whispers, staring down at me. "You okay?"

I don't know. I take a shuddering breath. I've had more

time to practice being in my body—figuring out what feels good. Feels safe. But now, I'm realizing I'm not in my body. I don't know if this feels good. I don't know, honestly, if this is consent.

Mattie sits back, watching me closely. "Do you want to stop?"

I would've asked to keep going, once. "Yeah. I do."

He's nodding. "Okay." He hesitates. "Should I leave?"

I take a deep breath. Having sex with Mattie right now wouldn't feel good. But lying here with him—kissing him, touching him, holding him. That's what I want, more than anything.

"No," I tell him. "Please. Stay. If that's what you want also, anyway."

His smile is hopeful. "Yeah. I'd love that."

We lie down together, quiet, Mattie resting against my chest, listening to my heart beat.

Happily Ever After: A Memoir

by Matthew Cole

Maybe one reason I'd always struggled with the idea of a happily ever after is the suggestion that one person can make you happy for the rest of your life. I've realized, as I've grown older, that this isn't true. There is no guarantee that one person will make us happy for the rest of our lives. Instead, there's something else more powerful, even deeper: the realization of love we have for ourselves—and the joy in sharing this love with someone else, and experiencing the love they have for themselves, too. Instead of depending on each other for happiness, we find our happiness individually, and then share that happiness with each other.

This is what I've experienced with Logan, for these past several decades. I've experienced growing to know myself and love myself to levels deeper than I ever have, and so has he; and as we have both grown, we have also celebrated life with each other. It's true that my life could possibly take me on a path different from where Logan is now, and Logan's life could possibly take him on a path different from where I am now, and we would not be together anymore, and we would, technically, not have had a happily ever after. It's also true that I would still carry Logan with me, wherever I go and whatever I experience next, because I have changed so much, and learned so much, and grown so much alongside him, and because of him.

We moved to Georgia to start our family. Logan writes for film full-time now, while I've gladly retired from acting. Every year, on our anniversary, we go to the cabin in the mountains—not his father's, no; though that cabin had been so important in our relationship, we could never return together, even after Jameson Gray passed away. The cabin symbolized too much pain for Logan, so we started our new tradition instead.

This is where I can say that I found my happily ever after. Logan is beside me now, as I write the ending pages of this memoir. He's reading over my shoulder, laughing—a sound that feels freer the longer I've known him. I'm glad, now, that we had time away from each other, to grow on our own. I'm grateful that, when we sat down to discuss our relationship and our futures, we agreed to share our happiness together.

ACKNOWLEDGMENTS

Stars in Your Eyes took a lot of risks as my first adult romance novel, and I'm so grateful to everyone who championed the story from beginning to end:

Thank you to Beth Phelan, Marietta Zacker, Nancy Gallt, Erin Casey Westin, and the rest of the Gallt & Zacker team who continue to support my writing career, wherever it'll take me next!

Leah Hultenschmidt, whose enthusiasm and love for *Stars* first convinced and then proved to me that I couldn't have hoped for a better home for this book. Thank you, from the bottom of my heart, for truly understanding the themes and characters, for the incredible edits, and for advocating for my story.

Thank you to the entire team at Forever and Grand Central Publishing: Sabrina Flemming, Daniela Medina, Mari Okuda, Deborah Friedman, Jeff Stiefel, Estelle Hallick, Dana Cuadrado, Joelle Dieu, and anyone who has helped to put this book into the world and the hands of readers.

Thank you to early readers for your insight and knowledge: Rhiannon Moller-Trotter, Jared Pascoe, and Erin Tillman.

And, finally, thank you to the readers, librarians, and booksellers who have supported my books and my work so that my dream as a writer can live on. So much love to you all!

ABOUT THE AUTHOR

Kacen Callender is a bestselling and award-winning author of multiple novels for children, teens, and adults, including the National Book Award–winning *King and the Dragonflies* and the bestselling novel *Felix Ever After*.